tHE WRONG BAD GUY...

"Are you sure you saw someone here, Ms. Cosi?" asked Quinn.

"*Heard* someone. Upstairs." I pointed to the short flight of carpeted wooden stairs tucked beside a large closet next to the kitchen. All three of us stilled and listened. The creek of floorboards was unmistakable. Someone was up there walking around.

"Stand back, Ms. Cosi," whispered Quinn.

His hand dipped into the leather holster strapped beneath his shoulder. I swallowed a gasp when he pulled the weapon free. He pointed the barrel, which looked to me like a small cannon, at the floor and moved to the base of the staircase.

Langley followed, his gun—just as big—drawn, too.

"Is that necessary?" I whispered.

"I hope not," he said softly.

Quinn and Langley climbed the stairs, and there was a hideous few seconds of absolute silence. Then a muted voice of surprise—male. The intruder was male.

"POLICE. Hands on your head. NOW."

"MOVE."

Langley appeared at the top of the staircase. He moved down, the intruder behind him, hands behind his back. They'd cuffed him, I'd realized. *Good.* Another few steps and Langley would be out of the way, and I'd finally get a look at this nervy bastard's face.

Oh, no, I thought.

"Matt?"

"Clare?"

"You know this guy?" asked Quinn.

On What Grounds

CLEO COYLE

BERKLEY PRIME CRIME, NEW YORK

THE BERKLEY PUBLISHING GROUP
Published by the Penguin Group
Penguin Group (USA) Inc.
375 Hudson Street, New York, New York 10014, USA

USA / Canada / UK / Ireland / Australia / New Zealand / India / South Africa / China

Penguin Books Ltd., Registered Offices: 80 Strand, London WC2R 0RL, England
For more information about the Penguin Group, visit penguin.com.

ON WHAT GROUNDS

A Berkley Prime Crime Book / published by arrangement with the author

Berkley Prime Crime Books are published by The Berkley Publishing Group.
BERKLEY® PRIME CRIME and the PRIME CRIME logo are trademarks of
Penguin Group (USA) Inc.
A COFFEEHOUSE MYSTERY is a registered trademark of Penguin Group (USA) Inc.

For information, address: The Berkley Publishing Group,
a division of Penguin Group (USA) Inc.,
375 Hudson Street, New York, New York 10014.

ISBN: 978-0-425-19213-9

PUBLISHING HISTORY
Berkley Prime Crime mass-market edition / September 2003

PRINTED IN THE UNITED STATES OF AMERICA

27   26   25   24   23   22   21   20

Cover illustration by Cathy Gendron.
Cover design and logo by Rita Frangie.
Interior text design by Kristin del Rosario.

This is a work of fiction. Names, characters, places, and incidents either are the product
of the author's imagination or are used fictitiously, and any resemblance to actual persons,
living or dead, business establishments, events, or locales is entirely coincidental.
The publisher does not have any control over and does not assume any responsibility for
author or third-party websites or their content.

PUBLISHER'S NOTE: The recipes contained in this book are to be followed exactly as
written. The publisher is not responsible for your specific health or allergy needs that may
require medical supervision. The publisher is not responsible for any adverse reactions
to the recipes contained in this book.

ALWAYS LEARNING   **PEARSON**

Acknowledgments

The author wishes to convey sincerest thanks to her excellent editor, Martha Bushko, and her exemplary agent, John Talbot, for having faith in this brew.

Visit Cleo Coyle's virtual Village Blend
at www.CoffeehouseMystery.com

"I have measured out my life with coffee spoons."

—T. S. ELIOT,
The Love Song of J. Alfred Prufrock

PROLOGUE

~~~~~~~~~~~~~~~~~~~~~~~~~~~~~~~

SHE was a dancer. Young, slender, pretty, but not particularly beautiful. And not special.

From the corner of Hudson Street, the stalker watched
her prancing about behind the tall French doors, sweeping, mopping, wiping—the gleaming wood floor, the
marble-topped tables, and the silver espresso machine.

The hour was late. The place was closed, but the
coffeehouse lights beyond the tall clear windows shone
with a disturbing intensity, harsh beacons that burned
through the thin layer of fog rolling in off the cold, dismal
river just a few blocks away.

With tentative movements, the stalker followed those
beacons, descending the curb into the empty street. Wisps
of pale mist flowed in waves across the gray cobblestones,
sweeping the stalker along in its ethereal current like
some passenger on a ferryboat bound for the underworld.

Reaching the other side, the stalker moved onto the
wide, clean sidewalk. From above, a faux gaslamp buzzed

and sputtered. How appropriate, thought the stalker, and how typical. The vile little streetlight had the façade of class, but inside it was fake—the forced flickering of a cheap electric light, an inferior imitation of the real thing—

Just like Anabelle.

Nothing special.

The four-story red brick townhouse that held the coffeehouse was no different, the stalker decided. Just one of many in this historic area. Common. Ordinary.

Below the arched front window, an antique wrought-iron bench sat bolted to the sidewalk. Seeing it, the stalker sank to its cold, hard surface.

Breathing became difficult. No longer unconscious but an intentional thing. Purposeful, planned, and premeditated—

IN THEN OUT.

OUT THEN IN.

Deliberate counts. Deliberate breaths. Wave after wave until finally the stalker rose and once again made an approach.

The Village Blend's door loomed large. Beveled glass in an oak wood frame. Pulsing music leaked through. The intense aroma of roasting coffee.

The stalker's knuckles rapped: One knock. Two.

Inside, Anabelle spun. A dancer's turn. The long, blond ponytail swung around the slender neck. Blue eyes widened in the oval face. The pert nose wrinkled; delicate eyebrows drew together, forcing unflattering folds into the high smooth forehead.

When she aged, that's what she'd look like, thought the stalker. Shriveled and wrinkled and used up—

It was only a matter of years.

Surprise registered on Anabelle's face as she stared at the figure beyond the glass. Slight suspicion was evident, but not alarm, and not panic.

Good, *thought the stalker.* Very good.

It took a week for Anabelle to cross the wood-plank floor. A day for her to click-clock the dead bolt. Finally, the framed beveled glass cracked, and the stalker stiffened, swallowing down the upsurge of bile.

THIS GIRL HAS IT COMING.

SHE'S BROUGHT IT ON HERSELF.

For days these thoughts had been repeated and repeated on breath after breath, in wave after wave. An unrelenting force, they became the current that carried away any last surge of sentiment, of creeping conscience, of warning whisper that one day there might be regret.

"Hello?" said Anabelle, warily. "I didn't expect to see you."

THIS GIRL HAS IT COMING.

SHE'S BROUGHT IT ON HERSELF.

"Do you want to come in?"

The stalker nodded, forced a smile. Then Anabelle cracked the door wider, the music pulsed louder, and the stalker strode in, vowing—at least for this one brief moment—never to look back.

One

❦❦❦❦❦❦❦❦❦❦❦❦❦❦❦❦❦

THE perfect cup of coffee is a mystifying thing.

To many of my customers, the entire process seems like some sort of alchemy they dare not try at home.

If the beans are Robusta rather than Arabica, the roasting time too long or short, the filtering water too hot or cold, the grinds too finely or coarsely milled, the brew allowed to sit too long—any of it can harm the end product. Vigilance is what gets you that perfect cup—vigilance and stubbornness in protecting the quality.

As the 1902 coffee almanac put it, "When coffee is bad it is the wickedest thing in town; when good, the most glorious."

Of course, seeking that perfect cup of coffee is not without risks. For instance, after you've found it, and then gotten yourself *addicted* to drinking it, you've made yourself vulnerable. Because, on those rare mornings when you are *prevented* from getting it—well, to put it as indelicately as my ex-husband might—

You're screwed.

I was in that very position the morning I'd found Anabelle's body.

Trapped behind the wheel of my ten-year-old Honda, I'd been in traffic for, oh, about three months, and my one little espresso at 6 A.M. had worn off hours ago. With the freeway rest stops offering their standard range of brews—from weak as warm dishwater to bitterly burnt— I began to practice a sort of Zen caffeine visualization exercise.

All the way across Jersey, through the Lincoln Tunnel, and into the streets of midtown Manhattan, I imagined the Village Blend cup floating in front of my windshield, the earthy liquid inside, mellow and warm, yet rich and satisfying, tendrils of pearl-colored steam curling into the clouds—

"Son of a *gun*!"

A taxi swerved into my lane, cutting me off to pick up a fare. I slammed the brake pedal and my bumper stopped so close to the cab's passenger door I thought the per-mile rates printed there would end up tattooed to my forehead.

I honked. The beturban cab driver cursed. And the Brooks Brothers suit climbed into his hired yellow box on wheels. With a door slam, we were off again. Half a block—and a stand still.

"Great. Just great."

In a jarring instant, the real world had snatched away my perfect cup. Seconds later I knew how Shakleton felt trying to sail through icebergs. Four-ninety-five at least had been *moving*. This parking lot purporting to be the route between midtown and the West Village was driving me to homicide.

To top it off, a feeling of desperation hung in the chilly Thursday air. The early-morning clouds were black, and commuters were rushing toward their tall office buildings and storefront shops before the heavy September skies opened up on them.

Thank goodness I'm almost there.

Last night was literally my last night at my Jersey house. After only a few weeks on the market, the suburban three-bedroom ranch with front lawn and back garden had sold to a young married couple from the Upper West Side whose moving van was pulling up as I was pulling out. I'd donated most of my functional (albeit style-free) Ikea furniture to Goodwill, along with the very last of my eighties shoulder-pads. Now the bulk of my things was either in storage or had been moved to the city already.

This morning, I'd packed my remaining items, grabbed my cat, Java, and didn't look back. The feline now sat aloofly in her pink PetLove cat carrier, licking her coffee-bean-colored paw, utterly indifferent to the desperately stressed state of her owner.

"Well, at least *one* of us is having a good trip."

When I finally neared the Village Blend coffeehouse—and the duplex apartment above it—I saw only one space available, just off Hudson. With a few Hosannas, I slid into it—*Finally some vehicular luck!* (Okay, so it was near a hydrant. But it wasn't that close, really, and I wasn't going to be long. After unpacking my car, I intended to move it to the nearby garage, where I had rented a monthly space.)

Grabbing Java's carrier, I headed for the consciously *non*commercial front of the red brick coffeehouse, ready to check in with Anabelle, who'd be serving the morning crush—and definitely more than ready to savor a cup of the Village Blend's heavenly house blend before beginning my unloading. As I neared the twelve-foot-tall arched front windows, however, I saw the lights inside were on, but the place was empty.

Empty.

No customers.

Not one.

Inconceivable, I thought.

As bad as the previous manager had been (in six months he'd actually eroded the customer base by almost fifty percent), the Blend had always seen *plenty* of morning business.

I tried the door. *Locked.* And the CLOSED sign was in the window!

What the hell is going on? It was almost nine—and the Blend was supposed to take its bakery delivery at five-thirty and be open to customers by six!

That meant we'd already lost the rush-hour regulars: the Satay & Satay Ad people, the Assets Bank office workers, the Berk and Lee Publishing people, and the NYU crowd. If I didn't get the place open soon, we'd even lose the neighborhood regulars, who often grabbed a mid-morning cup before heading up- or downtown on business.

And Anabelle Hart had been *so* trustworthy since I'd come back to managing the Blend a month ago!

"Don't worry, Clare, I'll take care of everything."

Those were her last words to me after she'd volunteered to both close the coffeehouse last night and open it again this morning. With no one else available to cover for me, it was the only way I could complete my move from Jersey. I'd even promised her a nice bonus in her next paycheck.

Anabelle was one of my best workers, too. Once I corrected the bad training she'd received in making her espressos too fast (yes, too fast—but I'll get to that later!), she became my top employee. Not so much for her barista skills, although those were vital to the Blend's reputation, but because I could trust her.

One thing you learn in this business: Character can't be taught. You're reliable or you're not. You do what you say you're going to, or you don't. Anabelle had character. She never bugged out on a shift or made an excuse to leave early. She was there when I needed her, didn't neglect or abuse the customers, and deftly handled any abuse flung at her or the staff. This was, after all, retail. Abuse was a given. It was also New York City, land of the chronically dissatisfied.

Short of a Wonder Woman cape, you had to possess a special kind of character to resist bouncing back double-fold what came at you, to magically dissipate all hostility into the atmosphere.

Most of my part-timers were naïve college students, barely beyond adolescence—meaning hostility was handled with the most juvenile of boomerang reactions. This was why I needed assistant managers with the aforementioned special character traits.

Anabelle was the same age as my college student part-timers, but she displayed a much more advanced maturity level. An incident just the week before proved it—

An emaciated advertising executive in an Anne Klein suit and a near-permanent expression of displeasure on her thin, pallid face, ordered a Caffé Cannella (Italian for cinnamon coffee). We were very busy, and Maxwell, one of our part-time baristas, presented it quickly then turned to continue making the other coffee drinks.

"Hey, you!" the woman called to Max.

"What?"

"You've *ruined* my drink with too much cinnamon!"

"Lady, it's the way we *always* make it."

"You're an *idiot*."

"Who are you calling an idiot, you stupid bi—"

"Ma'am! Let me fix the problem," Anabelle said, gliding in with the grace of a gull to retrieve the offending drink. I had been going over schedules in the corner and watched the entire save with admiration.

In two seconds flat, Anabelle had inserted herself between the angry young barista and the overwrought businesswoman, soothing ruffled feathers with apologies, chatting about not liking too much cinnamon herself, and getting a new drink made *tout de suite*. She even placed the cinnamon shaker next to the cup to allow the woman to sprinkle as much or as little as she preferred.

"Remember, garbage flows downhill," I'd told Anabelle during the first week I'd reclaimed my position as manager of the Blend, "and a percentage of the population in this town comes out of its offices, shops, hospitals, and homes looking for the first excuse to dump a portion of it directly on our heads."

"Don't worry, Clare," she'd answered. "If there's anything I've had plenty of experience with, it's handling garbage."

I never asked why and how she'd gained that experience. I just knew she was my saving angel, someone I'd come to rely on during my first month getting the Blend back on its feet. In fact, I had *just* promoted her from barista to assistant manager.

After fishing through my shoulder bag for the key, I unlocked the shop's glass front door and cursed like that cabbie who'd almost killed me on Ninth Avenue.

There was no sign that Anabelle—or anyone else—was even getting ready to open up. Not even the scent of brewing coffee. And the sound system was silent. Not one classical note in the air—

I sighed with the sort of profound disappointment you usually reserve for your child.

"Oh, Aaaa-na-belle," I singsonged, much the same way I used to scold my daughter. "You're blow-ing your bo-nus."

I set Java's carrier down, strode across the gleaming, freshly waxed wood-plank floor (which, under the previous manager, Moffat Flaste, had been allowed to deteriorate into a scuffed and grimy mess). I stepped past the refrigerated display of cold beverages (Pellegrino, Evian, and imported ginger-, lemon-, and orange-flavored Italian sodas) that I'd made "Madame," the Blend's owner, buy when I'd first managed the Blend for her ten years before (and which had added ten percent to the annual gross sales). I walked the length of the blueberry-colored marble coffee bar, then stopped, appalled, at the pastry display.

The shelves of the six-foot-long glass case should have been jammed with warm croissants, muffins, bagels, doughy cinnamon rolls, and fresh-baked streudels. The afternoon delivery would have a different mix of goods— biscotti, tarts, cookies, European-style pastries, and miniature bundt cakes. But never, *ever,* was it supposed to be *empty,* as it was now!

I moved from the main room into the back foyer, which amounted to a square of wood floor with the supply pantry on the left, the service staircase to the right, and the back door dead in front of me. The door was unchained, yet still bolted, and the area was dark.

I stepped in something slippery and flailed a bit, nearly tripping over a large object. Flipping on the light, I saw that one of the stainless steel under-counter garbage cans had been moved to the top of the service staircase that led to the basement.

No reason for this! I thought instantly.

Why would Anabelle have moved the heavy can when she could easily have pulled out the plastic bag lining it and taken it to the shop's outside Dumpster?

The can's lid was nowhere in sight and black coffee grounds were flowing over the top, across the wood floor, and down the top few steps.

"Anabelle, I'm going to kill you!" I cried, frowning at the mess. Then I glanced down the stairway and gasped.

It looked like someone had beaten me to it.

Two

᭡᭡᭡᭡᭡᭡᭡᭡᭡᭡᭡᭡᭡᭡᭡᭡᭡᭡᭡᭡᭡᭡᭡

I ran down to the basement, almost slipping on the messy coffee grounds spilled all over the steps. Anabelle's body was crumpled at the bottom on the cold concrete floor. Her delicate features were pale, almost milk-white. Her head was cocked at a terrible angle and her long blond ponytail stretched perpendicular to it like the yellow plume of a fragile bird.

Her twenty-year-old face appeared lifeless—but if she truly *were* lifeless, her limbs would be rigid. They weren't. Rigor mortis certainly hadn't set in. I knelt next to her and checked for vital signs, trying not to move the body in case of spinal injury. First I placed my ear to the girl's nose and mouth. Thank God, she was breathing! Shallow but evident. Next I put two fingers to the girl's neck. The skin was cold, slightly clammy. The pulse feeble as butterfly wings.

"Anabelle? Anabelle?"

Her clothes appeared to be the same ones she'd worn last evening when she'd reported to work. Blue jeans and a white midriff T-shirt with DANCE 10 printed across the chest.

I ran back upstairs and made a frantic call to 911. Next I rang Anabelle's roommate, Esther Best, an NYU English major from Long Island, and a weekend barista at the Blend. She lived with Anabelle in a tiny rented apartment about ten blocks away.

"Esther, it's Clare Cosi. Anabelle—" I said.

"Well, she's not here," Esther cut in. "She never came home last night, although *that's* not unusual. She might be with The Dick. You might try her cell. Unless she's got a new one already—boyfriend, I mean, not cell phone."

"Esther, *listen.* She's had an accident. Come down to the Blend *now.*" I went back downstairs to sit with Anabelle until the ambulance arrived.

The next fifteen minutes passed more like fifteen hours. Mostly, I spent it fretting, and praying, and staring at Anabelle's limp slender form, thinking of my Joy. My daughter's features weren't as perfectly chiseled as Anabelle's; they were more common, like mine. Yet my Joy had more of an impish energy than Anabelle, a sense of carefree innocence that Anabelle, though she was only a year older than my daughter, seemed to lack.

I had admired Anabelle's maturity as a worker, but seeing her like this made me admit to myself that there was something brittle and a little desperate about Anabelle Hart. Something fragile and sad, too.

This can't be the end of her life, I prayed. *No one should die so young . . . for so careless a reason.*

Finally, the sound of sirens echoed off the Federal-style townhouses and boutique shop windows of Hudson. After a moment of silence, thick-soled paramedic shoes began clumping around the first floor.

"Down here! Hurry!" I called, then saw them round

the corner and almost slip just as I had on the coffee grounds.

"Watch out!"

Two men, both young Hispanics in white shirts and slacks, cursed loudly then continued down. I stepped away, and they began to work. They checked Anabelle's heart with a stethoscope, her pupils with a small flashlight, and attempted to wake her by calling her name. They tried smelling salts. Nothing worked.

Finally, they fastened a brace around her head and neck, moved her to a flat board, and strapped her down. Anabelle seemed more like a corpse than a person now. Her limbs were limp, her face ashen.

I *hated* not being able to help, *hated* being forced to watch impotently as strangers took her away.

Tears blurred my vision, made my nose run. *This can't be happening* echoed through my mind so many times I was no longer sure whether I was thinking it, saying it, or screaming it.

At the top of the stairs, the paramedics placed the board on a folding stretcher, then pushed the thing swiftly across the main room.

About then, Esther Best burst into the Blend's entrance. She stopped dead at the pallid, rag-doll body of her roommate.

"Ohmygod, what happened!" she cried with uncharacteristic emotion. Even Esther's brown eyes, which were usually narrowed in some sort of jaded, hypercritical observation behind her black-framed glasses, now stared in wide-open shock.

In front of me, the two paramedics were pushing tables out of the way. I followed closely behind, so focused on the stretcher, its wheels thundering across the wood-plank floor, that I didn't even hear the male voice calling until I tried following Anabelle out the shop's front door—

Like a steel curtain, an impenetrable blue wall slid closed before me. Navy shirts, gun belts, nickel-silver badges. I collided right into it.

The officers stood shoulder to shoulder. Both looked to be in their mid-twenties. One tall and lean, the other shorter and broader through the chest and shoulders. The tall one with the light hair and gray eyes whose name tag read LANGLEY spoke first. He was holding a notebook.

"Woah, there, ma'am! Sorry, but we need to ask you some questions."

"Where are they taking her?" I asked, bouncing backward. Instantly, I tried to move around them, but they bobbed and weaved right along with me: Left, right, left, right, left—

The whole thing looked like a pathetic one-on-two basketball game. And with my small stature, there were definitely no NBA offers in my future.

"Calm down, ma'am. They're taking her to St. Vincent's," said the other cop. He was the shorter one. Dark eyes and hair. His name tag read DEMETRIOS.

I strained once more to look around the uniformed young men. On the street, a large crowd of onlookers had gathered—students with backpacks and older residents, many of them Blend regulars. Esther was speaking with one of the paramedics. All eyes watched as the other paramedic shut the two back doors simultaneously. The single loud thud struck me with a terrible premonition of finality.

"Yeah," said Langley. "They'll do what they can for her. And her roommate says she'll go to the hospital. We got some basic information about the victim from the roommate, but right now we need to hear what happened from you."

After the ambulance drove away—much too slowly, as far as I was concerned—Letitia Vale, one of the Blend's regulars, poked her head of wrapped gray braids inside the front door.

"Clare? Are you all right? What happened?"

Letitia was the third-chair viola player with the Metropolitan Symphony. A tea drinker. (Tea was not the Blend's specialty, but we did have a standard selection. Earl Grey, jasmine, camomile—the teas one would expect.) Letitia said what she mostly enjoyed about the Blend was its atmosphere and its anisette biscotti.

When I had first managed the Blend almost ten years ago, Letitia had been a loyal customer. She'd even pulled together a little chamber ensemble to play at the Blend's annual holiday parties.

"Oh, Letitia, Anabelle had an accident . . ." My voice choked to a stop.

"Heaven and earth! Is there anything I can do?" asked Letitia.

"I'm sorry, ma'am," the cop named Demetrios told Letitia as he moved his body to block hers in yet another bob-and-weave game, "but we need to close the store now."

"Oh! Oh, of course. Clare, I'll come back later." She waved reassuringly.

I nodded, no longer trusting my voice.

"Okay, ma'am," said Langley, opening his notebook. "It's Clare, right? Why don't we start with your full name and address."

I stared at him. Suddenly I had trouble focusing.

"Ma'am?" Langley prompted.

"What?" I asked.

He gazed into my face for a long moment.

"Okay, ma'am, I need you to take it easy, okay? I need you to take some deep breaths and sit down." He motioned to the empty chair at one of the store's twenty Italian marble-topped tables. "Can you tell us how you found the body—"

"Body?" My stomach turned, saliva filled my mouth. "I'm not . . . feeling so well."

Demetrios shot Langley a look.

"Uh, sorry, ma'am," he said quickly. "I didn't mean the body. I meant, uh, the girl."

"Sit down, okay?" advised Demetrios. "You don't look so good."

I tried, but couldn't. It only made me feel worse. All I could think of was what Grandma Cosi used to say to women who'd just suffered a loss or shocking news and came to her kitchen for a reading of coffee grounds. *Do something familiar so you don't faint.* I looked up. Saw Demetrios's name tag.

"That's a Greek name, isn't it?" I asked.

"Yeah."

"Let me make you some coffee."

"What? No, ma'am, that's not necessary—"

But I was already moving behind the counter, grabbing the tall, long-handled brass *ibrik,* measuring the water, and placing it on an electric burner.

The cops, mumbling between themselves, seemed unhappy with my activity, but it was helping me feel less numb and more normal. I'd prepared Greek-style coffee (aka Turkish coffee) many times. I'd learned how from my world-traveling ex-husband, who'd enjoyed the strong taste—even more powerful than espresso.

As I made the coffee, the cops stood at the counter and watched. After a minute or so, they began to ask me some questions.

(What time had I arrived this morning? Was the shop open or locked? How long had the girl worked for the store?)

As long as I kept busy making the coffee, I found I could answer pretty well.

(Close to nine. Locked. Six months, but I had known her only one.)

I'd explained how I'd just moved in above the store.

How I'd managed the place ten years ago but had left to live and work in New Jersey.

They wanted to know why I'd decided to come back after so long.

"A lot of reasons," I told them absently.

And over the next few minutes, as I continued to prepare the Greek coffee, I silently reminded myself of a few of them—starting with that early-morning phone call four weeks ago from Madame . . .

THREE

∽∽∽∽∽∽∽∽∽∽∽∽∽∽∽∽∽∽∽∽

"I'VE done away with Flaste," Madame had announced that morning without preamble. "He's an utter moron."

Flaste? Flaste? I tried to recall with a yawn. *Who was Flaste again? And how would Madame have "done away" with him?*

The picture of a rotund, effeminate man finally came to mind. A surreal montage ensued: I saw Madame's wrinkled hands pushing the fat man off the Village Blend's four-story roof; her bejeweled fingers stirring arsenic into his morning latte; her determined knuckle clenching a revolver's cold, metal trigger.

Wiping the sleep from my eyes, I rolled over. The phone's death-black cord coiled across my starched white pillow. Blood-red digits glowed next to the bed. I made out a five, a zero, and a two.

5:02 A.M.

Good lord.

Half-opened miniblinds revealed the striated sky—a

dark cobalt dome lightening to streaks of pale blue. Silver stars flickered a losing battle, their waning light a pallid display in the face of the brilliant noise just below the horizon.

I knew how those poor, pathetic stars felt. At thirty-nine and counting, I was forty years younger than Madame Dreyfus Allegro Dubois, yet I always felt comparatively little and weak in the presence of her burning energy.

Madame's dawn phone call may have seemed odd, but ever since her husband had passed away six months before, her vigilance with the Blend had grown keener, almost obsessive. She'd begun ringing me about everything that had gone wrong or been mishandled—in the greatest of detail, and at the oddest hours.

"Do you know what that conniving boob did?" Madame asked. "*Do* you?"

At last, a moment where I was expected to respond. "Uh. No," I said.

"He had the gall to actually *sell* the plaque—the Village Blend plaque!—to a roving antiques agent!"

I grimaced. A part of me felt sorry for the poor bastard who'd become the latest in a long string of hired—and fired—Blend managers. Lord, if Flaste had sold that plaque, he *was* an utter moron.

From the day it opened in 1895, the Village Blend's only signage has been that brass plaque, engraved with simple black lettering: FRESH ROASTED COFFEE SERVED DAILY. "And that is the way it *should* be," Madame had always insisted. No lights, no awning, no vulgar oversized neon sign. Just the old plaque. Subtle. Gracious. Like a gentlewoman. Elegant, sophisticated, never calling attention to herself, simply drawing people closer with her regal air and fetching bouquet.

Situated on a quiet corner of Hudson Street, in the first two floors of a four-story red brick townhouse, the Blend had been sending her rich, earthy aroma of freshly brewed coffee into the winding lanes of Greenwich Village for over one hundred years. The historic streets surrounding the place had once felt the footsteps of Thomas Paine, Mark Twain, e.e. cummings, Willa Cather, Theodore Dreiser, Edward Albee, Jackson Pollock, and countless musicians, poets, painters, and politicians who'd influenced American and world culture.

Within a few blocks sat the Commerce Street home where Washington Irving wrote *Sleepy Hollow*; the historic church of St. Luke in the Field, whose founding vestryman, Clement Moore, composed *'Twas the Night Before Christmas*; and the off-Broadway Cherry Lane Theater, which was started in the 1920s by a group that included poet Edna St. Vincent Millay and decades later employed a young usher by the name of Barbra Streisand.

In more recent years, film, theater, and television stars had patronized the Blend, along with novelists, reporters, musicians, and fashion designers. Fortune holders as well as fortune hunters and most every famous resident of the Village had at one time or another stopped by for a famous Blend cup.

The coffeehouse had been a part of the area's history—through good times and bad. And the sign wasn't just a sign. It was practically a holy relic. Every manager of the Blend soon understood that *correctly* displaying the thing was less a matter of nostalgia than job security.

"I not only fired him, I made certain he was visited at one A.M. by two of New York's Finest."

Madame never did suffer fools gladly.

If anyone knew this fact, I did. For almost ten years, between the ages of twenty and thirty, I'd worked as the manager of Madame's beloved Blend. (She maintains I was the "absolute best.") Consequently, I got to know my former employer as well as my own mother (that is, *if* I had known my mother—she had left me and my father before my seventh birthday, but that's another story). Anyway, even after I'd quit the Blend, we'd remained close.

"I'm curious," I said after an enormous yawn. "What did Flaste get for the sign?"

"You know, that's rather interesting. He sold it for nine hundred and seventy dollars, which was lucky for him, according to the officers who arrested him."

"Doesn't *sound* lucky."

"It was thirty dollars under a thousand, you see."

"Not yet."

"Well, my dear, theft of one thousand dollars is a Class E felony. So the officers were forced to book him only on a petit larceny charge, a mere misdemeanor. Consequently, Moffat 'walked'—as the policemen put it—after an appearance in night court."

"Not exactly a case for an Alan Derschowitz defense," I said.

"Nevertheless, I made my point."

"Your point?"

"I may be old, but I'm not stupid."

I laughed. "What about the plaque?"

"Oh, those polite boys from the Sixth Precinct who explained the charges, they retrieved it for me. I was so happy to have it back where it belonged that I told them to come by anytime for a free cup of Kona. The *real* thing, Clare. *You* know what I mean."

Indeed, I did.

Coffee and crime may not *seem* the likeliest of pairs, but you'd be surprised how often they went together. Take the great Kona scandal of 1996. A cabal of coffee producers, one of whom Madame had known rather well, had been caught rebagging cheaper Central American blends and transshipping them through Hawaii marked as that exceptional bean, Kona—ironically mellow for something grown in volcanic lava. As far as anyone knows, at least at this writing, Madame's friend is still in federal prison.

"Now, the reason I called," continued Madame. "You must come to see me, Clare. *This morning*."

A long silence followed in which I heard opera music on the other end of the line. The mellifluous tenor was singing an exceptionally gorgeous piece from Puccini's *Turnadot.* "*Nessun dorma!*" Translation from the Italian: "Nobody shall sleep!"

Appropriate, I thought, because Madame wasn't just playing opera. She was trying to make a point. Besides being one of my favorite pieces—full of all the tragic yearning and beautiful heartbreak that exemplified Italian opera—it was orchestrating what Madame had promised would one day come: my *wake-up* call.

No, I can't come, the coward in me wanted to say. *I have a deadline.* Which was, in fact, true. For the past twenty days I'd been writing a two-part article for *Wholesale Beverage* magazine on the quality of Latin American coffee harvests. The piece was due next week.

But I had to admit, if only to myself, that I was grateful for the call and the invitation to get out of the house—because I was ready to tear my hair out. The subject of the article wasn't the problem, the *isolation* was.

Working at home had been fine while I was raising Joy. But since my lively daughter had moved out the month before, I found the small house in the sleepy suburbs of New Jersey to be less than stimulating. Lately I'd begun staring at the lengthening grass in the front yard and thinking about Madame's furious words the day I had quit my job managing the Blend.

"I *do* understand why you feel the need to leave," Madame had said after much wailing and breast beating. "But the suburbs! I swear, Clare, one day you will wake up to find the suburbs have far too much in common with the cemetery."

"The cemetery!" (I had been outraged, hurt, and angry at Madame for her lack of support, given my personal circumstances at the time.)

"Yes," Madame had countered. "Both have well-tended lawns, far too much silence, and far too little traffic in the full range of the human condition."

"It's safe! And restful!"

"Safety and rest *I'll* enjoy when I'm dead. I'm warning you, Clare, you're making a mistake, and one day you will admit it."

I had ignored Madame, of course, and moved ninety minutes west of the city, determined to prove the woman wrong. And for the most part, Madame *had* been wrong—

Raising Joy had been a joy, and the income I'd made from a combination of jobs (providing paid help at a day-care center, baking part-time for a local caterer, and writing the "In the Kitchen With Clare" column for a small local paper) had helped make the difference between the monthly bills and my ex-husband's inconsistent child support payments.

Then just last year, after a rather soul-searching thirty-ninth birthday, I had actually pushed myself to pitch articles to food-and-beverage trade magazines like *Wholesale Beverage, Cupping,* and *In Stock,* and miracle of miracles, they'd actually bought a few.

But now that Joy had packed up and moved to Manhattan to attend culinary school . . . well, things were different. Unlike many teenagers, my daughter had centered her social life around the house and a close group of girl-friends. Half a dozen teenagers hanging around wasn't unusual. And I often joined their Video-Movie-Rental parties and "Martha Stewart Survivor nights," in which the group of girls would cut out cooking projects from Martha Stewart's *Living* magazine, then randomly pick them out of a brown paper bag and have to complete the dish in ninety minutes—even if it meant racing to the store for missing ingredients.

(With a game like that, it was no surprise to me when Joy and all four of her friends ended up enrolled in culinary schools or restaurant management programs after their high school graduation.)

These days, however, my evenings had been spent eating Snackwell cookies (what's the point of baking for one?), watching Lifetime movies, and blowing catnip-laced soap bubbles for Java (whose fur happened to match the color of a medium-roast Arabica bean).

The truth was a bitter residue building up at the bottom of my underused life: fulfillment (except when it came to my daughter) remained elusive. Madame's call was a welcome excuse for me to take the express bus to the Port Authority terminal on Forty-second Street. And, after my morning espresso and a bracing shower, that's precisely what I did.

MADAME lived near Washington Square in an expansive suite of rooms capping one of those old buildings on Fifth Avenue that had a concrete moat and a doorman who dressed like a refugee from a Gilbert and Sullivan operetta. Pierre Dubois, her late second husband, insisted she move in with him there in the early 1980s. He'd said he vastly preferred it to Madame's more modest West Village duplex above the Blend, which was the site of their original steamy encounters.

Much like Madame herself, the venerable Fifth Avenue address bridged two worlds. Nearby was New School University. A mecca for writers, artists, and philosophers, it had once served as a "University in Exile" for intelligentsia fleeing Nazi Germany during the 1930s. Also nearby was the *Forbes* Magazine Building, which housed a lavish collection once owned by millionaire Malcolm

Forbes—everything from ship models to Fabergé eggs made for Russian czars. It served as another sort of mecca: a capitalist's.

Pierre had definitely leaned toward the Forbes end of that particular spectrum. His vast Fifth Avenue penthouse apartment firmly reflected this—as well as his affinity for all things "Old World." *Really* old—like eighteenth century.

Brocade drapes, heavy gilt-edged furniture, and overwrought statuary made me feel as though I'd entered a Gallic museum. Then again, Madame's late spouse always had harbored a love for Napoleon, whom the short-statured Pierre had even slightly resembled.

My trips here always had me contemplating Madame's contradictions. While I understood she had fallen in love with an Old World man, I also knew that the New World was still a very important part of her. Why else would there be such a note of tremendous pride in her voice when she told her tales of sobering up Jackson Pollack, William de Kooning, and other abstract expressionists at the Blend with more than one pot of hot black French roast? Or allowing the occasional struggling poet (such as the young Jean-Louis—"Jack"—Kerouac) or evicted playwright to sleep on one of the second-floor couches?

Upon my arrival, Madame emerged from her bedroom suite still wearing mourning black, yet elegant and regal as ever. The unadorned dress was impeccably tailored. Her only jewelry was Pierre's diamond and platinum wedding band. Her hair, once a rich dark brown, had long ago turned gray and was now rinsed a beautiful silver and blunt-cut above her shoulders. Today she wore it in a French twist, a sleek and simple black pearl comb holding it in place.

This elegant façade had deceived many over the years into assuming Madame was nothing more than an elite socialite.

But I knew the truth.

There was unbreakable marble in that woman's satin glove, and I'd seen it unveiled on every sort of person in this city: from corrupt health inspectors, shady garbage collectors, and chauvinist vendors to bratty debutantes, self-important executives, and narcissistic ex-hippies.

The key to Madame's contradictions was quite simple, really. Although her family had been very wealthy back in prewar Paris, they'd lost everything to the Nazi invasion and were forced to flee to struggling relatives in America with nothing but the clothes on their backs.

Little Blanche Dreyfus may have been raised a pampered, cultured Old World girl, but her harrowing trip to America, during which both her mother and sister had died of pneumonia, made her grateful for its shelter, and every day since her arrival in the New World, she had risen from her bed determined to make a contribution to its greatest city.

So you see, no matter what her affectations, her core beliefs were no different from any other destitute immigrant's. Few people recognized this, but I had, because of my own immigrant grandmother, who'd pretty much raised me from the age of seven. Grandma Cosi had the same sense of honor, of spirit, that same combination of gratefulness, determination, and frayed-lace pride. I suppose that's why Madame liked me so much. I guess she knew how deeply I understood her.

"What did Flaste do with the cash, by the way? I mean, after he'd sold the Blend's plaque?" I asked without preamble.

(Madame and I had always shared the ability to resume conversations within hours, days, or even weeks of when we'd started them.)

"He immediately spent it," Madame said as we settled into the French antiques showroom that served as the Dubois salon. "The bill confirmed the entire transaction amount was used to purchase a pair of cuff links apparently worn by Jerry Lewis during the opening night party for *Cinderfella.*"

"You're joking."

"Clare, you know I *never* joke when it comes to swindlers."

"Yes," I said, "but still, he sounds more like a movie buff than a criminal."

"Mad for *celebrity.* Like most of the Western world. I'm sure he wanted to show them off at those theater parties he was always attending."

"Well, if it's a piece of fame he wanted to own, it's a wonder he didn't keep the plaque itself, given its noteworthy place in cultural history—"

"Oh, yes," Madame said with sublime gravity. "An O. Henry short story, an Andy Warhol print, and a Bob Dylan song . . . at last count."

"Of course I can also see where Flaste wouldn't want it," I said. "I mean, it's not as if he could wear a ten-pound brass plaque to a cocktail party. Even as a conversation piece, it would be cumbersome."

"A swindler, I say. With a revolting lack of respect for the Blend's heritage. And a pig besides."

"You mean *prig,* don't you?" I asked.

"*Pig,* my dear. In the six months since I hired him, he's gained fifteen pounds alone from eating half the shop's morning pastry selection. The profits have never been lower."

"How in the world did you end up hiring him?"

"Well, you know, he's just the latest in a long string of disappointments. Eduardo Lebreux actually recommended him. *Highly* recommended him, if you can believe that. Flaste had worked for Eddy. And Eddy had worked for Pierre so . . ." Madame shook her head and sighed.

"I see," I said.

"What can I say? I took a gamble and lost. And I've grown tired of gambling. I want you to manage it again."

My breath stopped for at least ten seconds. "You know I can't."

"I know no such thing. Come now, Clare, aren't you yet weary of the wilderness?"

"It's *New Jersey,* Madame. Not Nepal."

"And your dear daughter. She's in the city now. Wouldn't you rather be closer to her?"

I hated it when Madame hit a bull's-eye. I shifted on the velvet cushions. Still, there were issues. Big ones. First of all there was the long commute, and barring that, the astronomical rents of Manhattan. I was almost forty years old, and I wasn't about to regress to my college years by cohabitating with a roommate, for heaven's sake.

Then there was the issue of my future, and my continued struggle to build a career out of a string of freelance magazine assignments. Despite my unhappiness with the isolation of writing, it was going pretty well. Just this month I'd actually sold a short piece on the trends in U.S. coffee consumption to *The New York Times Magazine.*

(Almost fifty percent of the population drinks it, averaging about three cups a day, with the market trending toward higher-quality varieties.)

But all those reasons aside, there was still one *unavoidable* reason why I did not wish to return to the Blend. It sat like a big blue tiger in the center of the room and neither I nor Madame wanted to acknowledge it.

With a sigh, Madame snapped opened a twenty-four-carat cigarette case, encrusted with gemstones and filigreed with her initials. Pierre had bought it for her years ago on the Ponte Vecchio, the "old bridge" of Florence, renowned for its gold trade. She pulled out an unfiltered cylinder of tobacco and lit it. This was something I rarely saw Madame do unless she was overly anxious.

"Do you recall the first cup of coffee you ever made me?" she asked.

"Of course. An espresso."

"On an old gas range, using a five-dollar stovetop machine."

I smiled. My Grandmother Cosi, an immigrant who had settled in Western Pennsylvania (where waves of Italians had come to work in the steel mills), had run an Italian grocery with her husband for most of her life. She'd brought the little three-cup silver pot with her from Italy and given it to me the day I'd left for New York.

I knew the two-part octagonal-shaped pot looked far too old-fashioned, even suspiciously simple to most appliance-happy Americans, who firmly believed that the more they spent on their espresso maker, the happier it would make them.

I had seen this same little unassuming stovetop pot on every old Italian's stove in my childhood neighborhood. For me, it would always be the most satisfying way to make the boldly potent beverage that condensed into a lovely demitasse cup the truest essence of coffee, extracting from the beans the finest concentration of aromas.

Stovetop espresso pots usually come in three-, six-, and nine-cup models. Using one is quite simple. First you unscrew the bottom of the pot and fill the base with water, up to the small steam spout. Then grind whole beans. (The Blend uses one heaping tablespoon of grounds for every 3 ounces of water.)

The term *espresso* refers to the *method* of brewing and not to the bean so a quality bean will give you a good cup, and the Village Blend suggests a dark roast like French or Italian.

Grind them into fine particles, but be careful not to overgrind! Beans ground too fine, into a powder, will make the brew bitter.

Once the proper amount is ground, place the grinds in

the little basket provided with the machine, tamp it down tightly. The basket will sit above the water as you screw on the top part of the pot.

Next place the pot over low heat. In a few minutes, the water will boil. Steam will rapidly force the water up through the grounds and into the empty pot, filling it almost instantly.

The stovetop method also leaves more grounds in the cup than the steam method. Grounds are essential for "readings." Not that I'm ruled by superstitions, but I certainly don't ignore them. Besides, when I was a child, my grandmother taught me how to read coffee grounds, and I've always enjoyed the parlor game.

"I've had Roman baristas use thousand-dollar machines who couldn't make a cup that good," Madame told me that morning with a lilt of motherly pride.

I was shocked by the light blush that came to my cheeks. It had been so long since anyone had expressed pride in me, I couldn't even recall the last time. (The inevitable result of middle age and motherhood—let's face it, everyone expects *you* to do the expressing.)

"Oh, come on," I said, brushing it off. "The fact is, you were relieved when you met me. You were terrified I would turn out to be some harlot with a tube top and tattoos. You liked *me,* so you decided to like my coffee."

"I never pretend to like coffee, my dear, and you very well know that. It's either good or it's garbage. And yours was *very* good."

"And you know very well it was my grandmother who taught me how to perfect it," I said.

"Yes. She taught you. And then *I* taught you."

"Yes, of course. I know. I owe you a lot, Madame—"

"You owe me nothing. But you do owe yourself, Clare. We woman all owe ourselves. And we forget to pay."

I shifted, cleared my throat. "You think I'm not being true to myself?"

"Yes, that's right. You know where you belong. You know what will make you happy, but you ignore it."

I took a deep breath. "I have to."

"You're just hiding. Hiding from *him*."

There it is, I thought, bracing herself. *The big blue tiger.*

"It's cowardly," continued Madame. "And it makes no sense when it's not what you want out of life." Madame blew out a puff of smoke then raised an eyebrow. "I noticed what you said at the end of your *Times* article: 'When we drink coffee, we drink its history, which is also our own history.'"

I squirmed. I had not attributed that line to Madame. Under the pressure of impressing my editor, I had decided to simply convey the sentiment as part of my own coffee I.Q. But the truth was, much of my knowledge had come from my years of running the Village Blend under Madame's tutelage.

"I'm sorry," I said softly. "I should have attributed the words to you—"

"Don't be stupid. I'm not scolding you. I'm *reminding* you." Madame rose, walked to an end table, and picked up the week-old *Times Magazine*. She waved it proudly at me, returned to her seat, then placed her reading glasses on the end of her nose.

"And I quote," she began, " 'If we are a civilization of coffee drinkers, then the coffee we buy, brew, and drink should be as great as our civilized heritage. For though coffee may seem a small thing, it is a ritual that reflects the daily standards we set for ourselves throughout our lives. Whether the highest or the lowest, it is the standard we pass on to our children. And if we fail to pass on the highest standards, even in the smallest things, then how can we, as a civilization, hope to progress? Perhaps T. S. Eliot was right: Some of us do measure out our lives with coffee spoons. All the more reason to pay attention to the quality of the bean.' "

Madame smiled. "That wasn't me. That was *you*, my dear."

"I learned it from you."

"Have you? Prove it then." She stubbed out the half-smoked cigarette and reached for a small bell. "I've drawn up an offer, Clare. I want you to read it and then accept it."

The tinkling bell brought Madame's personal maid with a silver tray. On it was an official-looking contract next to a small egg timer, a thermal carafe of steaming water, and a French press that I knew from the aroma contained perfectly ground Jamaica Blue Mountain.

I nearly swooned.

This full-bodied yet mellow and delightfully aromatic bean grown on the 7,000-foot-high Jamaica Blue Mountains has a limited harvest: a mere 800 bags annually compared to the 15,000 bags of the lesser Jamaican varieties (High Mountain and Prime Jamaica Washed). While importers and roasters have used Blue "blends" to cut the price along with the quality, true Blue has sold for as high as $35.00 a pound and more. I hadn't tasted a drop in ten years. Not since I'd left the Blend.

In silence, Madame placed the contract in my hands, then she poured the steaming water over the grounds in the press, replaced the lid, turned over the egg timer, and gave me a look that said—

Five minutes.

In the time it took to steep the coffee, Madame expected me to read the contract and agree to it.

With a deep breath, I read the terms. If I signed on for five years, I would receive:

1. A piece of equity in the business to the tune of fifteen percent ownership right away with five percent more added for every fiscal year that came up with a ten percent or greater profit.

2. The keys to the furnished duplex apartment on top of the shop. (One cannot exaggerate the invaluable opportunity to live in a rent-free two-bedroom with a fireplace, balcony, and garden courtyard in the heart of the most in-demand neighborhood in Manhattan.)

And finally:

3. The assurance by Madame that the Blend's unnervingly charismatic coffee buyer would be consulting with me no more than one week a month.

"You can't control him with a contract. You know that. He's still a pirate," I found it necessary to point out when the timer ran down.

"He's his father's son," answered Madame as she pushed the French press's plunger, squeezing the grounds to the bottom of the glass pot with a bit more force than necessary. She looked up into my eyes. "What else can I say?"

"It's all right," I said as Madame poured the coffee into the simple cream-colored French-café-style cups that sat on the silver tray. "We've been down this road a few times before."

"Yes, my dear. It was a bumpy ride . . . for both of us."

There was a long pause, as there always was right before the painful subject of Madame's son was dropped. Matteo Allegro, now in his early forties, was not only the Blend's coffee importer and Madame's only child by her late first husband, Antonio Allegro—Matt Allegro also happened to be my ex-husband and the father of my pride named Joy.

I took a cup from Madame's elegant tray, added a splash of cream, then sipped the freshly made Jamaica Blue Mountain. The sensual, sweet, full-bodied aroma of the coffee flowed over me as I considered Matt, along with Madame's very tempting offer.

"So, my dear, what is your answer?"

I looked up and for the first time noticed that my ex-mother-in-law's eyes were not quite the color I remembered. They seemed more gray now than blue since her second husband had died. And the elusive lines about her mouth and eyes—the ones that used to appear and disappear depending on her expression—now seemed to be permanently with her, like cruel, unejectable tenants.

A dark thought occurred to me. Married couples sometimes died within a year of one another. The first would expire from a major disease, but then the second would go soon after—usually for some minor reason (like a cold that suddenly developed into pneumonia). Doctors diagnosed it clinically—a depressed immune system during a traumatic time. But it was still death due to grief. To loss.

Madame did seem a bit frail today. Quite a change from when she'd first trained me to run the Blend. The woman's stamina a decade ago had little to do with the caffeine in her pots. Pride had driven her, a sense of wanting the Blend to live up to the thousand stories about its own history, its colorful customers, its high standards, and its commitment to serving the community.

After her first husband had died, Madame had run the Blend by herself for years, right up to the day before her wedding to Pierre, one of the city's foremost importers of French perfume, wine, and coffee. Right up to the day before her life had suddenly changed into a whirlwind of travels and uptown dinner parties, of entertaining Pierre's clients, adopting and raising Pierre's teenage children, and running a European villa every August.

The coffeehouse had moved, like the days of her youth, onto a back burner. But it never moved off the stove. Even though Pierre's fortune was immense,

Madame had refused to sell the Village Blend. For all these years, she had hung on, as if it were a thread to something so vital, so precious, that she'd fight to her last breath before letting it go.

"I need you, Clare," Madame said at last, her tone dropping to an octave I rarely heard.

She's choosing me, I realized in that moment. *I'm the one she wants to carry it on.*

I suddenly wondered what the Dubois children would think about this decision of their stepmother's. I'd met most of them over the years. And none seemed to understand the importance of the Blend—not to the community as an institution nor to their stepmother as a symbol of her convictions.

Of course, their attitudes weren't surprising to me. Raised in wealth, educated in elite schools, constantly surrounded by art and culture, the Dubois children believed themselves above the difficult daily toil of managing a small business. They were all grown now, of course. Some resided in Europe, others on the West Coast and New York, all in the upper reaches of society, and consequently out of touch with the way most of the world lived.

Matteo Allegro had next to nothing in common with them. I could say that for my ex. But he was apparently not Madame's choice for guardianship of her beloved coffeehouse, either.

While Matt worked *around* coffee, his passion came not from serving the beans but from traveling the world in pursuit of them (among other things—usually women). The man was a hard worker, but he couldn't hack a marriage commitment, let alone the stationary lifestyle that running a daily business would require. And his own mother apparently knew it, too—just as she knew that *business* was never the point.

The Blend wasn't about buying and selling. It was

about tradition. About legacy. About love. And that, more than anything, was why I agreed to sign her contract.

"I'll do it, Madame," I promised, finally meeting the woman's gaze.

"Thank you, my dear. Thank you."

Four
༄༅༄༅༄༅༄༅༄༅༄༅༄༅༄༅༄

MAKING Greek coffee was a simple, straightforward process, really—

Three ounces of water and one very heaping teaspoon of dark roast coffee per serving. (I used half Italian roast, and half Maracaibo—a lovely Venezualan coffee, named for the country's major port; rich in flavor, with delicate wine overtones.)

Water and finely ground beans both go into the *ibrik* together. The water is then brought to a boil over medium heat.

The *ibrik* has no lid. It's tall and tapered toward the top to keep the mixture from boiling over and has a lip to allow the coffee to be poured without grounds following.

The two police officers watched me work. As I reached for the sugar, I noticed the squeaky-clean state of the area behind the counter. If Anabelle had fallen down the staircase the evening before, I realized, then she must have fallen *after* she'd already cleaned and restocked the service area. The espresso machine was gleaming, and the cupboards were filled with cups, napkins, and wooden stirrers.

So why is there such a mess in the pantry, above the stairs? Why was the garbage can hauled over there and coffee grounds spilled so negligently?

I kept the mixture swirling over the heat, and the scent of strong coffee began to rise from the *ibrik* and fill the shop.

The custom for serving Greek or Turkish coffee at unhappy occasions, such as funerals (or assistant managers being carted away in ambulances), was to leave out the sugar. But I refused, adding one heaping teaspoon per cup with a kind of conjuring hope that it was *not* a tragic occasion and Anabelle would be all right.

"Pardon me, but are you open?"

A handsome thirtyish man with salon-styled floppy hair and a cashmere crew-neck poked his head into the open front door.

"No," said Officer Langley. "The place is closed."

"Check back later in the day," said the other cop.

"But I *only* want a double espresso to go," said the man, his finely creased khakis stepping quickly inside. "How much trouble is *that*?"

"Come back later," said Demetrios.

"I'll just wait at a table—" said the man, snapping open his *Times* and heading for a chair.

I wasn't surprised by this customer's behavior. There was a certain part of the Manhattan population that just didn't hear the word *no*. Not as if it applied to *them*, anyway. Rules existed, sure—for everyone else.

"I'm speaking English, right?" Demetrios tossed to Langley.

The man didn't get more than two steps from a chair. Demetrios stiff-armed him all the way out to the curb, then returned to the shop, closing and locking the door behind him.

The moment the ebony mixture in the *ibrik* began to boil, I poured half the contents into three tall, thin glasses, shaped cylindrically to keep any stray grounds far away from the lips. I returned the remaining bit of coffee to the heat, stirring to create a foam that I spooned onto each glass. Silver holders with filagreed loops for handles served as ornate cradles for the hot glasses, which I placed on a tray and carried to one of the Blend's marble-topped tables.

Demetrios looked at me with astonishment.

"You even got the face on there," he said, taking a seat.

I nodded, sitting next to him. "Yes, but I cheated and used a spoon. I'm not feeling steady enough to pour it right from the pot."

"*What* face?" asked Langley, taking the third chair.

"The foam," I said. (On a better day I could actually drop that last bit of foamy coffee right from the *ibrik* without transferring anything but the finest trace of grounds.)

"Yeah," said Demetrios, "they call it 'the face' because you lose face if you serve the coffee without it." He sipped and sighed. Then he said something in Greek.

I gave him a feeble smile. "What does that mean?"

"What? You make Greek coffee this good and you're not Greek?"

I shook my head.

Demetrios laughed. "I said, 'It's like my mama used to make.' "

"Holy Mother, not mine," said Langley after taking a sip. "Wow, that's strong."

"But good?" I asked.

"Yeah," said Langley, sipping again. "But it needs Irish whiskey and lots of straight cream."

"Drink it like a man, Langley. It'll put hair on your chest," said Demetrios, then he winked at me.

Usually, I hate winkers—winkers and trigger-finger clickers. But it wasn't *that* kind of a wink, you know? Not a bad used-car salesman sort of "I'm joking—don't ya get it" sort of wink. It was more of a "Buck up, kid, we're here for you" kind of wink, which made me feel a little less like I needed to throw up, but not much.

"That's what they told us Greek kids," Demetrios continued. "And believe me, Langley *needs* some chest hair."

"Get Plato here," said Langley. "He forgets that Greek kids don't get hair just on their chest. They get it everywhere else, too. Especially places you definitely don't want hair."

A loud knock sounded from the front door. A tall man stood beyond the pane. He wore brown pants, a white shirt, and a red and gold striped tie in a loose knot. A beige, worn trenchcoat in need of a good cleaning hung off his broad shoulders. His dark blond hair was cut pragmatically short, and his fortyish face sported shadowy stubble along the jaw and dark smudges under his eyes.

I liked him on sight and, for a moment, felt badly about the place being closed. Unlike the previous customer, if any man looked in true need of a double espresso, it was this haggard, exhausted guy. But we were closed for a good reason, so I shook my head and gestured with a wave of my hand that he should shoo.

"Oh, shit." The curse came from Langley, who suddenly shot up, raced to the door, unlocked it, and held it open as if this morose-looking trenchcoated man were the Prince of Wales.

"Am I open now?" I asked Demetrios with hope. My mind began to race. One phone call and I could have Tucker (my afternoon barista) take over the store and then I could run over to St. Vincent's and sit with Anabelle.

"No. You're still closed," said Demetrios. "Langley's

letting in Lieutenant Quinn. From the Sixth's detective squad."

"A detective? What does he detect?"

"Homicides."

Suddenly I wasn't feeling so well again.

FIVE

~~~~~~

"OKAY, lady, what's your name?"

Lieutenant Quinn had a voice like boiled coffee. Wrung out and bitter.

I stared, trying to make sense of a homicide detective showing up in my coffeehouse, when I noticed the beige stain on the lapel of his trenchcoat. Probably Robusta bean crap from one of those Sixth Avenue bodegas. *Milk, no sugar* was my guess.

Why in heaven's name did these cops drink swill when just a few blocks away for a single buck more they could drink silk? Wasn't a single buck worth a rich, warm, satisfying experience?

"Lady?" prompted the detective. "Are you with me?"

I squinted up at him. Hadn't I answered him already? I wasn't sure for a moment. My brain still seemed to be processing the idea of a *homicide* detective showing up after Anabelle's accident.

Accident . . . I found myself considering . . . *or homicide?*

Had someone actually broken into Madame's coffeehouse under my management and assaulted Anabelle? With this thought, I must have looked ill or gone pale or something because the detective turned, his square-jawed profile addressing Officer Langley. "Does she need medical attention or not?"

The words sounded almost accusatory. Langley's response was a shrug.

"What's that supposed to mean?" asked the detective. "Articulate your response, Officer."

Demetrios, who'd jumped to his feet the moment the detective had come on the scene, now broke in. "We were just—"

"Was I speaking to you, Demetrios?" the detective asked.

Demetrios's jaw clenched and his body stiffened. He seemed to be struggling with a retort, but clearly thought better of it and instead looked away.

The detective turned his gaze back on Langley, folded his arms, and waited.

Langley shrugged again. "I don't think she needs medical attention, okay, Lieutenant? She's not in clinical shock. She's functioning. Demetrios and I just thought she needed to putter around so she could calm herself down."

" 'Putter around'?" repeated the detective. " 'Putter around' a potential crime scene?"

"Yes, that's right," I said, speaking up at last—it was either that or let them continue talking about me in the third person, which I found beyond condescending. "Officer Langley is correct, that is exactly what I was doing."

Lieutenant Quinn eyeballed me. I eyeballed him right back.

He now stood directly in front of my seated form—although "standing" didn't exactly describe what he was doing. It was more like *looming.* Or at the very least, *towering.* He was at least six-three and looked down at me with midnight blue eyes that were bloodshot but still sharp enough to cut the breath from my lungs.

Slowly, his dark blond brows rose.

"Well, Mrs.—"

"Ms."

A barely perceptible sigh came next, and then: "What *is* your last name, anyway?" he asked. "Officers Langley and Demetrios here somehow failed to get it."

"It's Cosi—Clare Cosi." I stood, hands on hips, slightly indignant, trying to regain a bit of my lost control. I was in charge of the place, after all.

But the gesture didn't help matters much. Even with the comfortable, low-heeled boots I'd pulled on this morning before my favorite pair of straight-legged blue jeans, I barely made five feet three—a good twelve inches below the detective, which he seemed to take note of with mild amusement.

"Spell it, please." Lieutenant Quinn brought out his notebook and began to scribble, asking me the same general information I'd already given to Langley and Demetrios—except my last name, of course, which was really just a simple oversight in my opinion.

"Okay, Ms. Cosi," said the detective. "Now show me where you found the body."

"Girl," I said.

"What?" Quinn mumbled. He was looking around the room, taking more notes.

"She's not a 'body,' " I said. "She's a girl. She's alive. And breathing."

"Just a figure of speech," Quinn tossed back.

"Anabelle Hart is *not* a figure of speech. She's a pretty young woman. *Alive and breathing.* Not a *body*—so frankly, I don't see *why* you need to be here. Nobody is *dead*!"

The detective's pen stilled on his rectangular note-book. He looked at me. Then he glanced at Langley and Demetrios. I couldn't see their faces, but I knew my own face was hot. It was probably flushed bright red by now, and I could feel my lungs laboring with each breath.

"New York City Homicide detectives don't just inves-tigate shootings, stabbings, and stranglings," Quinn said, so calmly and slowly I got the feeling he thought I was about one step from Bellevue's psych ward. "We also in-vestigate any suspicious death or accident that appears will result in death. No need to get emotional, Ms. Cosi."

There is nothing that makes me *more* emotional than a man telling me *not* to get emotional. My ex did that, too. As I recall, he'd said it the very day I had to tell him our marriage was over. If only everything else would have been over that day, too, including and especially the emo-tion. But it hadn't. It took well over a year before I stopped wearing his ring.

I suddenly noticed the gold band on the detective's left hand. Automatically, I glanced at the pockets of his trenchcoat. Sure enough one held that telltale sign—tiny smudges of chocolate, made by little searching fingers. *Daddy, what did you bring me?*

Matteo had played that same game with Joy when she'd been very young. Coming back from whatever continent he'd been exploring that month, he always had something special for her, some trinket, exotic toy, or candy. As she grew older, childish gifts gave way to audiotapes of for-eign pop bands or interesting native recipes; and as she grew into a young woman and began to understand just how long Daddy was sometimes gone—without so much as a hotel postcard—the gifts became downright lavish: hand-tooled leather backpacks and jackets, filigreed rings, and necklaces of pearl, platinum, jade, and ivory.

I resented the gifts at first, saw them as cheap, pacifying bribes from a man too busy to be a father. But then I realized how much they meant to Joy. And how much her father meant. And I said nothing after that.

"We have amazing miniature pastries in the afternoon," I told the detective. "Tiny chocolate éclairs and mini canollis. Children love them."

Lieutenant Quinn's brow furrowed. Now he really was looking at me as if I'd gone over the edge.

"Your right pocket," I said, quickly realizing the pastry comment probably sounded like the looniest nonsequitur on record.

"My *what*?"

"Right pocket. Of your trenchcoat."

Langley, Demetrios, and Quinn all turned their gazes to Quinn's trenchcoat pocket.

"It's got chocolate smudges," I pointed out. "Part of a little hand print. You have a small child at home, don't you? A little one who checks Daddy's pocket for a treat when he comes home?"

Langley smiled. Demetrios let out an amused grunt. And the detective's face reddened slightly. He sent a warning look to the two young officers, then turned his sharp blue eyes back on me.

"Ms. Cosi, I'm asking the questions here—"

"If you have a child, then you must understand how I feel about Anabelle. I didn't know her long, but she's my employee, and only one year older than my daughter—"

"Which is?"

"Twenty." It was Langley who answered this time, consulting his own notebook. "The victim was—uh, sorry"—he glanced guiltily at me—"*is* twenty. Dance student. We interviewed the girl's roommate before she went to the hospital."

Quinn squinted at me. "So *you* have a nineteen-year-old daughter?"

I nodded, and he gave me a skeptical once-over. The entire assessment probably took a few seconds at the most. To me, however, it felt as though time had stopped for a day or so.

He started at the tips of my black boots, ran quickly up my straight-legged blue jeans, slowing on the curve of my hip like a sports car on a sharp turn. The scrutiny continued up my black turtleneck sweater. He lingered much longer than necessary on my C-cups, which, I admit, have been a generous advantage for a woman with a petite frame, but under the circumstances I wasn't at all comfortable with any attention given to that particular determination. Finally, his gaze took in my heart-shaped face and shoulder-length, Italian-roast brown hair.

His cobalt eyes narrowed on my green ones. "And you're *how* old?"

"Thirty-nine." God, it pained me to say that out loud.

The detective glanced away, flipping back a few pages in his notebook. "You don't look it," he said softly as he jotted it down.

"Thank you," I said, just as softly.

Then the detective turned to Langley and Demetrios. "Okay, show me."

The two officers led the detective across the coffeehouse's rectangular-shaped main floor. There were fifteen coral-colored marble-topped tables here, many of them circa 1919, stretching along a row of white French doors, which drenched the room in sunlight and, in warmer months, were thrown open for sidewalk seating. As we walked, the detective seemed to be surveying these floor-to-ceiling doors, I assumed, for any sign of forced entry. There was none.

At the back end of the main room was an exposed brick wall with a fireplace and a circular staircase of wrought iron that led to the second-floor seating area, which was also used for private parties. The circular staircase was just for customers. The staff used the service staircase, which was where we were headed.

The officers and detective moved along the short hallway to the back door, which was located on the landing just above the flight of service stairs that led to the basement. I watched the detective make silent observations and jot down notes. He frowned at the mess of black, slippery grounds overflowing from the heavy stainless steel waste can.

"That shouldn't be there," I said. "The can, I mean."

"Where did it come from?" asked the detective.

"We keep three cans in the work area, behind the marble counter—one under the sink, one under the coffee urns, and one next to the dishwasher. This one was under the sink, the closest to this back area."

"I see."

"It makes no sense, though," I said. "Anabelle knows better than to drag this heavy can over here. Our policy is to remove the plastic lining and take it to the Dumpster."

"And where is the Dumpster?"

"Out this back door, down four concrete steps and to the right. It's a private alley. We've used the same garbage pickup company for the last twenty years."

"Paserelli and Sons?"

"Yes."

The detective nodded as he examined the back door, hands behind his back. It was heavy steel with no window. "They've got the contract for most of Hudson. This the way you found the door?"

"Yes," I told him. "Bolted but unchained."

"You normally keep it chained?"

"Yes, especially at night."

"And Anabelle Hart was your closer last night?"

"Yes."

"Alone?"

"Yes."

"And what time do you close?"

"On weeknights like last evening, at midnight. On Fridays, Saturdays, and Sundays, it depends on the customers."

"Because those are date nights?" the detective asked.

"Yes, we get lots of restaurant and nightclub overflow. You know, a couple hits it off and needs a place to continue to get to know each other after the dinner or the clubbing."

"Very romantic," said Langley absently.

Demetrios laughed. "Geez, Langley, I didn't know you were such a Romeo."

"That's right, Plato. You do the thinking. I'll do the romancing."

"In my day," remarked the detective walking carefully down the steps, "we didn't hit coffeehouses after getting steamy on the dance floor, we just hit the sheets."

"Your day was before AIDS," I called down to him.

"Just barely," he shouted back, examining the area at the bottom of the stairs where Anabelle had been found. "You have any other doors in the basement?"

"Only one. The sidewalk trap door. But we only use it for bulk deliveries. It should be bolted."

"It's secure," the detective called up. "Okay. Nothing down here." The detective came back up the stairs. "What's that big machine down there?"

"A coffee roaster. We roast our own beans here."

Quinn nodded. "Smells good."

"That's the idea," I told him. "The pleasure of fine coffee drinking is more than fifty percent aroma."

"Un-hunh."

Quinn stared at me with the blank blink of the unconverted. Typical of a Robusta-bean caffeine swiller, but I wasn't discouraged. I'd convert him yet.

Quinn continued up the back staircase.

The second floor of the Blend was also rectangular in

shape with a bank of windows running the length of one side. As on the first floor, the back wall had exposed brick and a fireplace. At the far end of the room, a door led to my small manager's office. The wooden floor was buffered with a number of area rugs. Like the first floor, there were marble-topped tables, but most of the second floor was replete with overstuffed furniture.

The intentionally mismatched mix of French flea market sofas, loveseats, armchairs, and reading lamps was arranged in the cozy conversational nooks. It looked like a bohemian living room—and for practical purposes, it was. With so many Village residents jammed into tiny studio or one-bedroom apartments, the Blend's second floor became an extension of their own living spaces. It also served as a private meeting space for various neighborhood groups.

"Nice place you've got here, Ms. Cosi," said the detective as he inspected the closed and locked windows.

We'd already checked my small manager's office and nothing had been disturbed. Not the wall safe nor the sealed glass case to the side of it, which displayed the priceless book of secret Blend recipes that had been handed down through the Allegro family for over one hundred years.

"Thank you. You should let me make you some coffee."

"Not necessary."

"Really, it's no trouble. I promise it'll be a thousand times better than your usual Sixth Avenue bodega's milk, no sugar."

The detective stopped and stared at me with an expression somewhere between stunned and annoyed.

"Your left lapel," I said.

He glanced down, saw the coffee stain, and frowned.

"How about a fresh cup?" I asked, a tiny smile edging up the corner of my mouth. "As I said, we roast our blends right here, in the basement."

He stepped up to me, emphasizing his height in that towering way again. "Another time," he said flatly.

"On the house," I offered, craning my neck backward. *God*, I thought, *if his wife is as short as me, she must need neck traction every night.*

"No sign of forced entry here," he said to the young officers. "Let's go." He led us back into the service staircase, pausing at the second door on the landing. "Where does this go?"

"My duplex. It's one flight up. There's an entrance to the private stairway here. There's also a separate entrance on an outside stairway leading up from the back garden."

"Do you keep this door locked?"

"Of course."

The detective reached into his pocket, put a latex glove on his right hand, and tried the door. It didn't budge. He examined the frame. "Locked. Okay, let's go back down."

We descended the service stairs and returned to the main room.

"I'm going to check the back alley," Quinn said and went out the front door and toward the back. I watched his lanky form disappear around the corner and turned to the young officers.

"Quinn's a pretty serious detective, isn't he?"

Langley laughed. Demetrios grunted.

"What's so funny?" I asked.

"If you only knew," said Demetrios.

"Knew what?"

"It's like this," said Langley. "Quinn's the guy who put a Proverbs saying up in the Sixth's detective squad room. He wrote it out in that real ornate kind of writing—it's like his hobby—what's it called? You know—"

"Calligraphy," said Demetrios.

"I don't understand," I said.

"You would if you read the saying," said Langley.

"Well, what does it say exactly?" I asked.

Langley glanced at Demetrios, whose black eyes glanced down and then back up with the sort of deadly serious look reserved for city morgues.

" 'If a man is burdened with the blood of another, let him be a fugitive until death. Let no one help him.' "

Six

~~~~~~

THE front door opened again; Quinn was back.

"See anything?" I asked.

"No sign of attempted forced entry or anything else out of the ordinary in the alley—just this."

Quinn's long legs reached me in a few strides across the wood-plank floor. With a latex-gloved hand, he held out a torn piece of thick paper printed with heavy black ink.

"JFK," I read aloud.

Langley took a look. "It's one of those airport luggage tags."

"Not a smudge or footprint on it," said Quinn. "Clean. And in your alley. So it was very recently dropped, I'd say. Could it be yours, Ms. Cosi?"

"No. And I can't think of anyone on my staff who's come back from a trip in the last few weeks."

"Could be nothing," Quinn said to me as he placed it in a small plastic bag and set it carefully on one of the marble-topped tables. "But listen, I have something to ask you. Officer Langley informed me that the shop's front door was open when he arrived. Was it open when *you* arrived?"

"No," I said. "It was locked. I mentioned that already, didn't I? I had to use my key."

The detective glanced at Langley and Demetrios standing behind me, but I couldn't read his expression. "Thank you, I just needed to confirm that. It's very important. And was there anything missing from the shop? Anything valuable?"

A robbery. The thought slapped me as obvious. I'd been so flustered by the morning's events, I hadn't considered the most obvious explanation. *A robbery? My God, a robbery.* I raced to the register, my hand digging into my jeans pocket for the thick ring of keys. I separated out the short one and was about to slap it into the register lock to open the drawer when one word boomed across the shop—

"FREEZE!"

The perfectly measured burr of a dispassionate detective had suddenly changed into the explosive boom of a take-no-shit street cop.

Suffice it to say, I froze.

"What's wrong?" I asked as Quinn came barreling up behind me.

"You were about to disturb evidence."

"Evidence?"

"Within a crime scene, Ms. Cosi, *everything* is evidence."

"Oh. Right." I suppose it seemed elemental to him, but this was my place, my world, and I couldn't just automatically start thinking of it as a crime scene.

Besides, Demetrios and Langley had already let me make Greek coffee back here, hadn't they? I glanced over at them, and they suddenly seemed more than a little uncomfortable with this whole area of conversation. I decided I wouldn't mention it if they wouldn't.

The detective examined the register, again with hands behind his back. "Looks untouched," he said. "Can you open it?"

"Yes, of course. Why do you think I was racing over here and fumbling with my—"

"Open it."

I slipped the small key into the register lock and turned it. I pressed the NO SALE button and the drawer, full of twenties, tens, fives, and ones, slid open. "Looks like a typical evening's take."

"Where do you keep the store's cash?"

"Safe. Upstairs office."

"Let's go take another look."

But the contents of the safe hadn't been disturbed. Neither had anything in the office. We returned to the first floor.

"Anything else that could be missing?" pressed the detective. *"Really* look."

I quickly surveyed the room, which displayed an eclectic array of coffee antiques gathered over the last century: from a cast-iron, two-wheeled grinding mill (used in the late 1800s, when the Blend was primarily a wholesale shop) to copper English coffeepots, and Turkish side-handled *ibriks* made of brass.

Behind the coffee bar hung a row of colorful demitasse cups collected from a variety of European cafés and a three-foot-tall bullet-shaped La Victoria Aruino espresso machine. Imported from Italy in the 1920s, and strewn with dials and valves, the machine was for show only and had since been supplanted by a much more efficient, low-slung espresso maker.

Antique tin signs from the early twenties advertising various coffee brands were all accounted for on the walls.

And the shelf above the fireplace still held the Russian samovar and French lacquered coffee urn Madame had placed there years ago. Nothing seemed to be disturbed or missing.

Then I remembered. The plaque! I rushed to the front window.

"No. It's there."

"What?"

"The famous Village Blend plaque. It's over one hundred years old, probably the most valuable antique in the store. It had been stolen by the previous manager. I believe your precinct took care of the arrest."

"Moffat Flaste," said Demetrios. "I remember. It was us, Ms. Cosi. We were the ones who booked him."

"You? And Officer Langley?"

"Yeah."

"You never stopped by for your Kona, did you? At least I haven't seen you here before."

The officers shrugged.

"Well, you be sure to. You don't want to insult Madame. She never speaks idly about free coffee, especially when it comes to Kona—"

"Excuse me." The detective looked a tad exasperated. "That's the sign in the window, right? It's there, right?"

"Yes."

"What about Anabelle's possessions? Was her purse on her when you found her?"

"No. She usually keeps it in the office upstairs, hanging on the coat rack. I didn't see it up there. Or her jacket, for that matter—"

"Okay," said Quinn, "we might have a lead here. Missing purse and jacket—"

"But if she was getting ready to close up," I broke in, "she may have moved it down here."

I stepped behind the blue marble counter again, remembering not to touch anything—I passed the used *ib-*

rik pot and amended my thoughts, resolving not to touch anything *more* anyway. Anabelle's jean jacket and small leather handbag were on an empty spot of shelf behind the counter.

"Here," I said, pointing. "Here they are."

The detective came around the counter, put on his latex gloves again, and removed the jacket and small red leather purse. He opened the purse and pulled out the contents. A brush with strands of blond hair, clear lip gloss, a compact, a red leather wallet, and her keys.

"Keys," he said tonelessly, resolutely, as if it were the final punctuation to a sentence.

"Are these Anabelle Hart's keys to this shop?" asked Quinn.

I glanced at the thick ring of keys. I recognized the PETE'S PAINT AND HARDWARE logo on several of them. We used that shop to make all our duplicate keys—everything from the doors to the supply closets. Seeing the little silver ballet dancer charm dangling from the ring made me absolutely sure. "Yes, these are Anabelle's keys all right."

Langley and Demetrios glanced at each other and nodded.

"That's it, then," said the detective, putting Anabelle's things back in her purse and placing it carefully on her jean jacket on the counter.

"What's it?" I asked. "I don't understand."

"Locked shop. No forced entry. No sign of foul play. Keys weren't stolen to relock the door. They're right here. The hospital will examine the girl for sexual assault or any other sign of attack, but it looks like a tragic accident," said the detective. "End of story. I'm sorry."

"No. Wait. That can't be it—"

"Don't take it too hard," said Quinn. "I'm sure the store has insurance, right?"

"For Anabelle's hospitalization, of course."

"And for the lawsuit."

"Lawsuit?"

"Sure. Employees usually sue in these cases. Unsafe workplace."

"This is *not* an unsafe workplace!"

The detective put his hands on my shoulders. He spoke quietly. "It was for Anabelle."

I suddenly felt ill again. But this time I wasn't losing control. The warmth of Quinn's hands seemed to help; they were large and strong and steadying.

"It wasn't an accident," I told him. "Even though every piece of evidence may say it is, I know this coffee-house better than the back of my hand. It doesn't add up to an accident."

"How do you know?"

"I just do. In my gut."

"There are things our guts know and then there are things we can prove. The proof is what makes cases, Ms. Cosi. Isn't that right, Langley?" The detective glanced back at the young officer.

Langley nodded. "I'm sorry, Ms. Cosi," he said gently. "But the lieutenant's right."

I broke away and began to pace. "Listen to me: If Anabelle dragged the garbage can from under the counter, then why isn't there a garbage trail along the floor? And why did I have to turn on the light in the back area when I arrived? If Anabelle's fall had been an accident, surely the light would have stayed on. Who turned it off?"

"You're talking about circumstantial evidence, Ms. Cosi," said Quinn, rubbing the bridge of his nose with his thumb and forefinger. "There could be other explanations. Maybe the girl was in a hurry and didn't turn on the light, then she lost her balance and spilled the can before she misstepped and fell down the stairs."

"But Anabelle is a dance student, Lieutenant. She has exceptional balance. She's so light on her feet. If only you could have seen her move around the shop. She's so beautiful and graceful. She doesn't walk, she glides, floats."

I knew I was rationalizing, trying to find a logical justification for the feeling in my gut. I knew that Quinn had a point, that he'd seen a hundred crime scenes to my one. But my guts were never wrong. Well, hardly ever anyway, and it had taken thirty-nine years for me to learn to trust them, so that's what I was going to do.

"No, no, no!" I shook my head violently. "Something *wrong* happened here. It wasn't just an accident."

"Ms. Cosi, you have to have grounds for theories of foul play—other than the ones on your floor."

"But what if Anabelle wakes up and tells us what those grounds are?" I asked. "What if it turns out that someone tried to harm her? Don't you need to collect evidence to prove her charges?"

Quinn nodded. "We've got a Crime Scene Unit coming down. Demetrios, check in with dispatch on an ETA."

"Sure. They should have been here by now."

"It's been a busy night."

"That Ivanoff shooting?" asked Langley.

"Yeah," said the detective.

"You on that, too?" asked Demetrios.

"Jackson and I have been working it since past midnight. Drury's on leave. Sanchez has the flu, and Turelli and Katz are working a fresh stabbing. So I'm doubling up on this one." The detective checked his watch. "Guess I've been up about twenty-eight hours now."

"No offense, Detective," said Langley, "but you look it."

"Let me make you that coffee," I said. "I can make it upstairs, in my apartment, and bring it down so I won't disturb anything more."

Quinn pulled out a chair and sat down. When he did, his face fell completely and his entire body seemed to finally give in to exhaustion. "Yeah," he said after a long exhale. "Guess I could use it while I wait for the CSU to get here. Thanks."

"Of course," I said. "I'll be right back."

"Ms. Cosi?" Quinn called.

"Yes?"

"I'll need a list of employee names and addresses—anyone who's worked here since Anabelle started."

"Of course, of course!"

"Look, don't get your hopes up," he warned as I picked up Java's carrier and headed for the back stairs. (She'd managed to cat nap through this morning's entire *Dragnet* scenario.)

"What do you mean?" I asked.

"I mean I'll pursue this on a limited basis, but chances are it was simply an accident, so prepare yourself. If the medical evidence supports that conclusion, the girl will have a case against the store—and you'd better prepare the owner. If she dies, the family may end up owning this place."

I didn't respond. What was there to say? Quinn was in no shape to be argued with. I simply gritted my teeth and headed for my duplex apartment above the Blend, quietly determined to find out what had really happened here last night—with or without the help of Homicide Detective Lieutenant Quinn.

Seven

~~~~~~

"**O**KAY, Java, I'm breaking you out."

On hold with St. Vincent's, I swung open the cage door of the PetLove carrier. A pink nose and white whiskers emerged, then four coffee bean–colored paws. Java excitedly sniffed every inch of the intricately patterned area rug that covered a large square of the parquet floor.

A nurse came on the line. Anabelle had been admitted to the intensive care unit, but the nurse couldn't tell me anything more. I sighed, hung up, and said a short prayer as Java's soft brown fur rubbed against my leg. I bent to stroke her. She stretched, arching her back, then continued to sniff out the place.

"So what do you think of your new home?"

The *mrrrrow* sounded like an approval to me, but then Java always did have good taste. Madame had lived here long before real estate values in the West Village had pushed the price tag on a duplex like this one into the million-dollar range.

The gorgeous apartment was one of the big reasons I'd agreed to manage the Blend again. That and being closer to Joy. At the thought of her, I automatically dialed her cell. It rang four times and then: "You've reached Joy. I'm probably sautéing something right now, so leave a message!"

"Hi, Cookie, it's me—" I tried hard to keep my voice from shaking. "Something's happened this morning at the Blend . . . and . . . oh, you know, I just wanted to see you tonight. If you're free, come on over for dinner. Otherwise, maybe you can stop by for a cup of java—"

"*Mrrrow.*"

"Not you, Java," I said as I hung up, immediately feeling guilty. Joy was busy with culinary school in Soho and a new Manhattan social life. The last thing she needed was Mommy butting in. But after seeing Anabelle lying motionless on that cold basement floor, I knew I wouldn't sleep tonight until I saw my daughter again.

Sighing, I took in the room. "It *is* something, isn't it, Java?"

Madame had decorated the place with her romantic setting on high. The main room—with its carved rosewood and silk sofa and chairs; its Persian prayer rug in muted shades of blue, green, and coral; its cream-marble fireplace, and its French doors opening to a narrow wrought-iron balcony of flower boxes—felt more like something you'd find in a Montmartre courtyard than a Federal-style walk-up.

The walls were muted peach, the draperies ivory silk, and from the fleur-de-lys molding in the center of the ceiling hung a charming bronze pulley chandelier holding six peach-tinted globes of faceted crystal. A lyre-back antique chair stood against one wall, and in a nod to the Colonial, the cozy dining room, adjacent to the living area, had a Chippendale table with four claw-footed chairs and a mahogany and satinwood English sideboard.

The upstairs had a bedroom even more worthy of sighs, along with a large luxurious marble bath and a spacious dressing room.

"Now remember, Java, no using the Persian to sharpen your claws."

"Mrrrow!"

Tail held high, she turned her back, seemingly offended—but then she always did like to pour on the guilt. Just her way of controlling her hapless owner.

I wasn't really worried about the rug. I kept Java's claws pretty well trimmed as a rule, and I'd already brought over her favorite catnip-laced scratching post, which stood at the edge of the Persian to lure her away like a kitty beacon.

With lures on my mind, I headed for the kitchen to prepare the pot of coffee for Lieutenant Quinn. There were several methods to choose from. I narrowed them down to percolator, electric drip, or Melitta.

If the man was used to that awful bodega coffee, then I didn't want to choose a method too foreign. It might turn him off. My eye caught sight of the French press on an open shelf, and I inhaled, almost painfully. Unbidden, an image came to mind of serving Quinn's lanky form fresh-pressed Kona first thing in the morning.

"Geez, Clare, get a grip."

Quinn was an appealing man, but he was also married, with children. And I was an absolute philistine for thinking of such a thing when Anabelle was lying in a hospital bed.

"That's what I get for living like a nun in suburban couple-land for a decade," I mumbled to Java, disgusted with myself. "First intriguing man near my age who gives me a compliment and I'm spinning French press bedroom scenarios. Bean choice, Clare, *focus* on the java—"

"Mrrrow?"

"No, no, not you."

"Mrrrow!"

Java didn't give a fig about bean choice, I realized, she just wanted to be fed. I opened a box of Cat Chow, and she crunched happily as I continued my work.

"Light, medium, or dark roast?" I wondered aloud, surveying the array of tightly sealed ceramic containers on my cupboard shelf. Properly storing coffee was serious business in my house—integral to maintaining any coffee's freshness and flavor.

Whenever I walk into a kitchen and see beans stored in a clear glass jar on the countertop, I shudder. Exposure to light will affect the beans' freshness and the coffee will lose its flavor.

I shudder twice as violently when I see storage directions on some of those inferior grocery store coffee brands. They actually tell you to "Store your coffee in the refrigerator," implying you should simply take the bag you just bought at the grocery, open it, and put it in the fridge to be retrieved daily. Big mistake!

When the storage bag or container is removed from a refrigerator or freezer for *daily* use, it exposes the coffee to moisture in the air. The container then goes back in the freezer or fridge, and the moisture condenses and *ruins* the coffee.

A refrigerator or freezer should be used for *long-term* storage only. A vacuum-sealed bag, for example, can be placed in the fridge or freezer and opened only when ready to be used. But once the bag is opened, the beans should be transferred to a proper container, and not returned to the fridge or freezer.

My customers always ask me the best storage method. I'll tell you what I tell them—

When it comes to storing coffee, just remember these four basic points:

1. Do keep your beans *away* from excessive air, moisture, heat, and light.

2. Do not freeze or refrigerate your daily supply of coffee!

3. Do store your coffee in an air-tight container and keep it in a dark and cool location.

4. *Do* buy freshly roasted coffee often and buy only what you will use in the next one or two weeks since the fresh smell and taste of coffee begin to decline almost immediately after roasting.

So, anyway, there I was, surveying my tightly sealed ceramic coffee containers (color-coded by blend) and thinking about Quinn. How would I impress him, surprise him, yet not turn him off with an experience that was too exotic?

"That's easy," I murmured, reaching for the Village Blend's House Blend, a complex mixture of imported Central and South American beans roasted dark yet with a mellow, nutty finish and rich, earthy overtones. It didn't have the caffeine of a lighter roast but neither would it have the awful acidity of that stale crap Quinn was used to downing daily. Our house blend made fresh was a beautifully smooth cup.

"Perfect." If I could hook Quinn on that, then he'd be back for more. And if he came back for more, then no matter what the official ruling was on Anabelle's fall, he might be willing to help me get to the bottom of what *really* happened.

I ground the beans fresh, filled the water reservoir of the electric drip coffee maker, dumped the fresh-smelling roast into the gold filter basket, and hit the START button.

While the coffee brewed, I prepared a tray with sugar, fresh cream, and six cups, making the assumption that the people in this "Crime Scene Unit" that Quinn was waiting for might want some, too.

I was just reaching for the vacuum thermos to transport the coffee when I heard something—

A *thud*. Right above my head.

Next came a *thump*.

Then the upstairs floorboards began to creak.

I froze, cocked an ear, listened as hard as I could.

Clomp, clomp, clomp . . .

No doubt about it. Someone with heavy feet was walking around upstairs, from the master bedroom to the bath.

How the person had gotten into my duplex I didn't know, and at the moment, I didn't care. All I knew was that heavy feet were walking around and then—"Ohmygod!"—it hit me.

If Annabelle had been the victim of foul play, then the perpetrator could be some psycho who'd stuck around for more victims.

The sound of the shower turning on full blast was enough to send me out the door. I pushed the protesting Java back into her carrier and flew down the service staircase, returning to the first floor of the coffeehouse.

"I need your help."

Quinn was sitting where I'd left him, chatting with Langley and Demetrios. One look at my face and they stopped their conversation cold.

"There's an intruder in my apartment—"

Quinn got to his feet, the drooping lids of his tired blue eyes lifting fast.

"Are you sure it's an intruder?" he asked.

"Yes. I don't have any roommates or guests. My daughter doesn't even have a key yet."

"Okay," said Quinn, removing his trenchcoat and tweedy brown jacket and throwing them over the back of a chair. The discarded layers revealed a dark brown leather holster strapped over a white dress shirt. Quinn unsnapped the small leather strip holding the gun in place under his left arm, then he turned to Demetrios.

"Watch the back alley."

"Sure, Lieutenant." Demetrios headed out the front entrance and toward the back of the building.

"That's the only other exit, right?" asked Quinn. "You mentioned an outside set of stairs, leading up to your place—you can only get to them through the back alley, right?"

"Yes, that's right."

"Okay. Langley, follow me."

Technically, Quinn hadn't told *me* to follow, too. But he hadn't told me to stay put, either, so I set Java's carrier on a table and quietly followed the two men up the back stairs.

"Stay behind us," Quinn warned when he saw me.

They entered the place carefully, checking the living room, small dining area, and kitchen.

Quinn eyed the only other way into or out of the duplex—it was the door off the kitchen, which led to an outside staircase. That second door was solidly bolted and chained. Obviously no one had broken in through there.

"Are you sure you saw someone in here, Ms. Cosi?" asked Quinn.

"*Heard* someone. Upstairs." I pointed to the short flight of carpeted wooden stairs tucked beside a large closet next to the kitchen.

All three of us stilled and listened.

The creek of floorboards was unmistakable. Someone was walking around.

"Stand back," Quinn whispered to me.

His hand dipped into the leather holster strapped beneath his shoulder and he pulled his weapon free—

(I'd really only seen guns on NYPD Blue and in the occasional noir movie on the Turner Classic Movie channel. This real-life one seemed awfully darned big, and I found myself consciously swallowing a spontaneous gasp.)

He pointed the barrel, which looked to me like a small cannon, at the floor and moved to the base of the staircase.

Langley followed, his gun—just as big—drawn, too.

"Is that necessary?" I whispered.

"I hope not," Quinn said softly, then he moved his foot like Java, carefully, slowly, testing the first step. It gave off a soft creak. He glanced back at Langley and motioned for him to stay.

I held my breath watching Quinn move to the top of the staircase, never guessing a guy so big could move so stealthily. I wondered for a moment why Langley was staying behind, and then I realized Quinn was concerned the intruder might get by him. In that case, he obviously wanted someone at the base of the stairs to prevent the escape. Having someone substantially bigger than me—not to mention armed—was clearly preferred.

Quinn turned the corner and there was a hideous few seconds of absolute silence. Then came a muted voice of surprise—followed by the detective's: "*Police. Hands on your head. Now.*"

Langley ran up the stairs.

More muted voices.

Quinn talked to Langley. Then Langley said something to Quinn.

There was a scuffling movement, an *oof*, a string of curse words.

Loud voices.

Silence again.

"*Move.*"

Langley appeared at the top of the staircase. He moved down, the intruder behind him, hands behind his back. They'd cuffed him, I realized. *Good.* Another few steps and Langley would be out of the way, and I'd finally get a look at this nervy bastard's face.

I watched parts of him revealed. The bare feet, the pair of worn buttonfly jeans, an expanse of tanned, sculpted chest—

Oh, God, I thought. I know that chest—and the chiseled chin. The Roman nose. The short black Ceasar cut.

"Matt," I choked out. "Is that you?"

"Clare?"

Oh, darnit.

"Ms. Cosi, You know this guy?" Quinn asked, bringing up the rear of this morning's little arrest-the-perp train.

"*Yes,* she *knows* me!" Matt stated. "In the biblical sense!"

"*Was I talking to you—*"

"I know him, Lieutenant," I quickly broke in. "But I have no idea why he's here."

"Who is he?" Quinn asked once more.

"My ex-husband."

EIGHT

~~~~~~~~~~~~~~~~~~~~~~~~~~~~~~

THIS can't be happening. This can't be happening.

I knew very well that chanting to myself wasn't going to make the ludicrous tableau in front of me disappear. But at the time I was desperate enough to try anything. "Detective—"

"Clare, what the *hell* is going on? Tell me this isn't about those missed child support payments. I *thought* we'd agreed! As long as I cover Joy's tuition—"

"Matteo," I began, "don't get upset—"

"Upset? *Upset?* Clare, you've got me in handcuffs here!"

"Calm down! It's not *me* who's got you in handcuffs—and *you're* the one who—" I stopped, hearing that embarrassing ex-wife tone in my voice. I closed my eyes, flashing on every domestic disturbance dispute I'd ever seen on those reality cop shows.

"Detective," I tried again, with excessive calm. "There's obviously been a mistake."

Matt turned to Quinn. "You heard her." He rattled his chain-linked wrists. "So get these damned things off me. *Now.*"

For a good ten seconds, Quinn didn't move a corpuscle. Officer Langley, on the other hand, shifted uneasily. He turned to me. "Ms. Cosi, you say this man is your ex—"

"Husband, yes," I affirmed.

The young officer glanced at Quinn and scratched his head, clearly unsure whether this was yet another of the detective's tests. Then Langley moved toward Matt's wrists. Quinn's arm blocked the way.

"Detective?" asked Langley.

"I have a few questions first."

"Jesus H.—" said Matt.

"First of all, Mr. Cosi—" Quinn began.

"It's Allegro," snapped Matt.

"Cosi's my maiden name," I explained.

"Yes, she took it back—in record time," Matt announced, as he usually did, with the tone of *The Wounded*—an indefensible stance in my opinion, considering his behavior during our marriage.

"Mr. *Allegro*," Quinn tried again. "I need you to calm down."

"Don't patronize me—"

"I need you to calm down," Quinn repeated.

"Jesus."

Quinn glanced at Langley. "Let's find him a seat."

Langley grasped Matt's ample bicep and paused when Matt tensed. Visiting high-altitude coffee plantations had been Matteo's occupation for years. The remote regions had fed his passion for hiking, biking, rock-climbing, and cliff diving—all of which had honed a formidable physique.

I wasn't surprised it had taken two men to cuff my ex-husband. And Langley didn't appear overjoyed about wrestling him any further. But the moment's resistance on Matt's part was only an automatic reflex. A second later he exhaled, snapped out a "Fine, let's go," and allowed Langley to lead him into the living room.

Quinn followed, signaling through the back windows to Demetrios that everything was under control. Next he pulled the lyre-backed chair away from the wall and plopped it down in front of the fireplace, right in the center of the Persian prayer rug.

My breath caught a moment. If memory served, Madame once told me that lyre-backed chair was one of only thirty-two in existence. It was originally fashioned for the nearby Saint Luke in the Fields, founded in 1822, when Greenwich Village was still a rural hamlet.

Saint Luke's, which still had the tidy, cozy feel of a rural parish, was one of the oldest churches in Manhattan. In 1953, Madame had attended poet Dylan Thomas's funeral there, and in 1981, when the original chapel had been gutted by fire, the church held an auction of basement relics to raise money for the restoration. The Village Blend had provided the coffee and pastries free of charge and also purchased this finely made chair.

Langley led Matt to the chair and I cringed, dreading what another wrestling match would do to the delicate piece.

"Wait!" I cried. "Don't move!"

The three men froze as I raced into the kitchen, brought back a sturdy Pottery Barn knockoff of a French café cane-backed turn-of-the-century Thonet.

I placed the Thonet down, returned the lyre-back to its place by the wall, and finally announced, "Go ahead, Detective . . . with your interrogation . . . or whatever."

Matt let out a snort at the confused expressions on the other men's faces. "She used to be sane," Matt told them. "Back when I first met her. Before my mother got hold of her."

I glared and he tilted his head, leering at me in that

awful, confident way that seemed to say, "You never cease to amuse me, Clare." Then he sat on the Thonet—its seat adorned by a Bordeaux velvet chair cushion—and coolly leaned back.

"Well, Detective. I'm seated. I'm relatively calm. But unless you want to charge me with something, I'm not about to answer any questions."

"All right," said Quinn. "Then I take it you don't want to explain *this*?"

The detective's hand disappeared into his shirt pocket and reappeared with a small vial positioned between his thumb and forefinger. Three-quarters of the vial was filled with white powder.

"Here we go—" said Matt wearily.

"Where did you find that!" I blurted to Quinn, knowing full well I didn't want to know the answer.

"The right front pocket of your ex-husband's jeans."

I closed my eyes, shook my head. Didn't want to hear it. Didn't want to see it. Didn't want to go through it. Not again.

"Take it easy, Clare," said Matt. "It's not what you think—"

"Matt, I can't believe you'd take us down this road again—"

"I didn't."

"I can book you right now for possession," said Quinn.

"Possession of what, Detective? Just what do you think you've got there?"

"Cocaine!" Langley blurted. "Right, Detective?"

"Wrong," said Matt.

"I see," said Quinn. "And from you ex-wife's reaction, you're going to tell me you weren't an addict?"

"Christ. It's *caffeine*."

"Excuse me?" said Quinn.

"Caffeine. Pure caffeine."

I laughed. It was a little hysterical, I admit, but I knew

Matt was telling the truth. He'd said something to me last year about finding a way to get over jet lag without subjecting himself to the heinous vagaries of airport coffee. This must have been the solution.

"Rub a little on your gums, Detective, and you'll see," said Matt. "Coke numbs the gums. This doesn't."

Quinn shook the vial, contemplating the powder. "Caffeine?"

"Isn't caffeine *brown*?" Langley asked.

"Coffee's brown," I told him. "Because of the roasting process the green beans are put through. But if that white powder is caffeine, it's the by-product of the chemical process for decaffeinating coffee beans. It's what supplies the caffeine in soft drinks."

"And *if* it's caffeine, this amount is legal?" Quinn asked.

"Well," said Matt, "you're holding about ten grams. A cup of joe has anywhere from one hundred to two hundred milligrams of caffeine. So I *guess* if you want to book me for possessing the equivalent of one hundred cups of coffee, you can try."

"I don't know," said Quinn without a moment's hesitation. "I *guess* I can believe you. Or maybe I can have it tested. That might take a while. Maybe even a day or two. Now where do you think I'd have you waiting during that time?"

"Fine," said Matteo at last. "Ask your damned questions. What do you want to know?"

I couldn't believe it. I hadn't seen anyone trump Matteo Allegro in years. Quinn had managed it inside of five minutes.

Quinn glanced at Langley. "Take the cuffs off."

"*Thank* you," said Matt, standing up so Langley could release him.

"What are you doing here? Your ex-wife says you don't live here."

"I travel most of the year," said Matt, rubbing his wrists and sitting back down on the cane-backed Thonet. "But my mother owns this building, and around a month ago, when I was in Rio, she sent me a contract giving me the right to use this duplex when I'm in New York—"

"She what?!" It wasn't that I couldn't believe my own ears. I just didn't want to.

"Ms. Cosi," said Quinn. "I have to ask you to—"

"She made *no mention* of that to *me*!" I blurted.

"Why should she?" asked Matt. "You live in New Jersey, don't you?"

"Not anymore. Last month I signed a contract with her, too," I said. "I'm managing the Blend for a salary, a share of equity, and the right to live in this duplex!"

"Oh, Jesus." Matt sighed. "Not again."

Madame had perpetrated numerous schemes to get Matt and me back together. This was obviously her latest.

"Matt, don't tell me you're earning equity, too?"

"Yes," said Matt. "Apparently she eventually wants us to co-own this place."

"Excuse me, Ms. Cosi," said Quinn, "but if you don't allow me to continue with my questions, I'll have to ask Officer Langley to escort you out of the room."

"Okay, okay. I'll sit. I'll listen."

But for a minute or two after taking a seat on one of the carved rosewood chairs, I did little more than silently stew. How could Madame have tricked me like this? *How?!*

In the meantime, Quinn was asking Matt a series of specific questions about his whereabouts the night before. I watched him take careful notes about the name of the airline he'd been traveling on and his flight number, and it occurred to me, with slow alarm, that Quinn was trying to determine whether Matt had anything to do with Anabelle's fall.

"Did anyone witness your arrival here?" asked Quinn.

"Sure. The taxi driver."

"Did you get his name or license?"

Matt smirked at Quinn for five long seconds. "What do you think?"

"And no one else saw you arrive?"

"It was five-fifteen in the morning. I was exhausted from a six-hour Jeep ride out of the Peruvian Andes, a fourteen-hour connecting flight from Lima to Dallas to JFK, and a two-and-a half-hour tango with U.S. customs. I collected my luggage, fell in a cab, and collapsed into bed the first chance I got. That's it."

"Did you notice anyone entering or leaving the premises when you arrived?" asked Quinn.

"No."

"Notice anything out of the ordinary? Anything at all?"

"No."

"Think about it, Mr. Allegro. What did you see when you exited the cab?"

Matt began to shift in his chair. He crossed a leg over his knee, rubbed his forehead, turned toward me. "Clare, did something happen last night at the coffeehouse?"

"Don't talk to her right now," said Quinn. "Just answer my question."

Matt inhaled and closed his eyes. "The lights to the coffeehouse were on. I remember thinking it was early for that, but then I checked my watch and realized the bakery delivery was due between five-thirty and six."

"And did you see anyone inside, through the windows?"

"No."

"You didn't enter the coffeehouse at all?"

"No. I was exhausted. I came in through the alley, went up the back garden stairs to the duplex, and that's it."

"Do you know Anabelle Hart?"

Matt looked taken aback. I leaned forward.

"Anabelle Hart?" asked Matt. "What's *she* got to do with—"

"Just tell me," said Quinn.

"Of course I know her. She's one of our baristas downstairs."

"And?"

"And what? That's it."

Quinn seemed unsatisfied with Matt's answer. Or the way he answered. He stared for a few silent moments. "You don't have any sort of special relationship with her?"

"Christ. She's my daughter's age."

"Meaning?"

"Meaning she's a *child*. She works downstairs. She works well. She has a boyfriend. That's all I know. Why? What's she been telling you?"

"No reason to have been angry with her?"

"What's this about? *Clare*?"

I was about to answer when Quinn spoke up—

"Miss Hart's had an accident. A fall down the service staircase."

Matt's eyes met mine. "Clare? Is she all right?"

I shook my head. "It's not good. She's in intensive care."

"Aw, no—"

"Mr. Allegro, you have a key to the duplex, correct?" asked Quinn, continuing to scribble in his rectangular notebook.

"That's obvious."

"And a key to the coffeehouse downstairs?"

"Yes, of course. I'm the Blend's coffee buyer and the owner's son."

"We may have more questions for you, Mr. Allegro," said Quinn. "Do you have any plans to leave the city in the next week?"

"No. I'll be here for at least two."

"And you'll be living here—"

"No!" I blurted. "He's *not* living here."

Matt's eyebrow rose. "We'll see," he mouthed. Then he rose and dug into his back pocket. "Here's my card. Cell phone number's on there."

"Fine," said Quinn. He held up the vial of white powder. "I'm going to have this tested."

"Christ," said Matt. "Why? I don't plan on participating in any Olympic events in the next forty-eight hours, and that's about the *only* institution I can think of that considers caffeine a prohibited substance."

Matt was right. One of our customers, a former Olympic fencer and coffee lover, had nearly tested positive for more than 12 micrograms of caffeine per milliliter of urine. He'd drunk something like three cups of coffee before his event. Consuming just two more would have gotten him banned from the Games.

"I'm testing it purely for Ms. Cosi's sake," said Quinn. "I think she has a right to know whether or not her ex-husband is telling her the truth about kicking his addiction."

Matt's eyes found mine. "I am."

A moment later Langley was pulling open the door to the back staircase and heading out. Quinn was about to follow when Matt called, "Detective—"

"Yeah?"

"I'm really sorry to hear about Anabelle. If there's anything more I can do, let me know. I mean that."

Quinn paused to study Matt's face, then he nodded and, after a brief unreadable glance at me, the detective turned and left.

Nine

On the other side of the door, two pairs of heavy-soled shoes clomped down the back steps with the conviction of people who knew exactly where they were going and why.

On *our* side of the door, it was another climate entirely.

Matt and I didn't move.

We didn't speak.

We didn't breathe.

An arctic freeze had settled in to the extent that *if* we'd breathed, condensation clouds surely would have appeared.

The silence was so deafening the ringing phone felt like a World War II air-raid siren. I jumped and Matt shuddered. When it rang a second time, Matt moved toward the side table, where the cordless receiver sat nestled in its recharging unit.

But it was *my* apartment, I thought, and therefore *my*

phone, so I moved, too. My hand grasped the receiver a millisecond before his.

What I hadn't figured on was the collision.

In recent years, Matt may have shown signs of aging in the slight wrinkles around the edges of his eyes and the gray strands threading through his black hair. But his athletic body seemed to have aged very little—and our unexpected contact, unfortunately, proved it.

Receiver in hand, I glanced off his tanned torso, nearly taking a fall. But his arms were quick, wrapping around my waist in an automatic save that crushed my pillowy C-cups into the slab of granite he called a chest.

The phone rang again. I pushed the ON-OFF button then put it to my ear.

"Hello?"

"Hello—" I managed while attempting to wriggle free of the warm, naked flesh of my ex-husband's chest. Much to my annoyance, Matt's muscular arms held firm.

"Mom, what's up? Your message sounded weird."

"Everything's okay, honey—"

I met Matt's eyes. "It's Joy," I whispered, trying to ignore the fresh, clean smell of recently showered male skin.

"Who's there?" my daughter asked at once.

"Your father."

"He's back! Oh, boy! Put him on, I want to say *Hi!*"

"Uh—yeah, okay—"

Reluctantly I offered up the cordless receiver. I felt one of Matt's arms move off my waist to reach for it. The other arm, he kept firmly around me. I could back off now, I reasoned, but if I did that, I'd be too far away to hear Joy's end of the conversation, and I wanted to eavesdrop.

"Hi, muffin," said Matt.

"Hi, Daddy!"

Dawn broke in Matt's face. A grin from coast to coast.

"When did you get in?"

"The wee hours."

"Whatcha doin' at Mom's?"

One of Matt's dark eyebrows arched suggestively as he stared down at me. "Getting into trouble."

"Like—as usual!"

"Yeah, like that."

"Mom invited me for dinner," Joy said, "so I'll be coming by tonight. Tell her, okay?"

"Okay," said Matt.

"And you come, too, Daddy. Okay?"

"Wouldn't miss it."

Damn. I thought. This was *not* a good idea—

"And, Daddy, tell Mom I'm bringing a surprise, okay?"

"Sure. She'll like that. I have a surprise for you, too."

"Cool!" cried Joy. "But I'm late. Gotta get to my saucier class!"

"Bye, honey."

"Bye, Daddy, see you tonight."

He clicked off the phone, and I exhaled. After the morning's events, I was glad, at least, to have finally heard Joy's voice.

"She's coming for dinner tonight." His free arm returned to its earlier position, locking around my waist.

"I heard."

"Then you know I'm invited, too."

"Yes, but do you think that's a good idea—"

"Of course," said Matt, obviously ignoring my conflicted tone. "And she's bringing a surprise—"

"Matt, I don't think it's a good idea—"

"Wonder what she's making?"

"—for her to see you and I here together—"

"She wrote me that she's having a hell of a time with the French sauces. Maybe it's a new dessert. She loves baking."

"I'm telling you, Matt, it's *not* a good idea. Don't you remember that time when she was thirteen and we spent the night together—and she thought—"

"You know what, Clare?"

"What?"

"I never kissed you hello."

I felt his muscles moving, his lower body trying to establish a more significant press between us.

"We *don't* kiss hello," I told him, beginning to squirm again. "Not anymore."

"But I'd like to."

His hand lifted off my waist and landed light as a sparrow on the back of my neck. His thumb and fingers began to move there, slowly, tenderly, breaking up the knots of stress I wasn't even aware had formed there.

I could let him kiss me. I knew that.

And I would enjoy it. I knew that, too.

Matt's kisses were like a late-afternoon cup of full-city roast. Warm, earthy, relaxing yet stimulating, too. And he meant them to be. Like a full-city roast, they had enough potency to wake up parts of me I didn't want woken.

Make your decision now, I told myself. *Because in another minute your body's going to make it for you—*

"No, Matt," I said. "Don't."

It was the frosty tone. A thermostat level he knew well. Applying palm to chest, I pushed. Hard.

He broke off immediately and stepped back. "Too bad," he said, his brown eyes registering hurt, rejection. *The Wounded.*

God, he had nerve. The very idea made my blood pressure begin to rise again.

"Stale," he said a few seconds later. His look had changed. His eyes were squinting in distaste.

"More *soured* than stale," I said, contemplating our relationship. After all, I thought, the chemistry was still there between us, so "stale" really wasn't the right word. The problems between us were more—

"Coffee doesn't sour, Clare."

"Coffee?"

"Yes, of course." Matt sniffed the air and lifted his chin toward the kitchen. "You've got stale coffee in there—"

"Oh my god, Lieutenant Quinn's coffee!"

I rushed into the kitchen and the acrid scent assaulted me at once. The coffee had been sitting on the burner for nearly forty-five minutes. What a waste! After ten minutes, fifteen to eighteen at the very most, there was no point in trying to pass off any cup of coffee as good, let alone great.

I poured the bitter brew down the drain and shut off the electric drip coffee maker. Then I took the jug of filtered water from the fridge and poured it into a kettle. The electric drip machine would take ten minutes to cool off so the Melitta method would have to do.

I pulled out the Melitta cone, cleaned my gold-plated mesh filter and placed it inside, plopped it over the mouth of the thermal carafe, and began scooping whole beans into the grinder.

"You're not staying here, you know," I called into the living room.

Matt sauntered over, crossed bare arms over bare chest, and leaned against the archway.

"It's my place, too, Clare," he said. "By contract."

"I just sold my house, Matt, and *I'm* not about to leave."

"So don't."

"And I'm not about to shack up with you—"

"Shack up?" Matt laughed. "What are you doing? Watching old Doris Day movies on the Classic Movie channel again?"

"Move into a hotel."

"I only need to use the place, at the *most*, ten days or so out of every month. Some months you won't even see me. I won't get in your way."

"You *will* get in my way, and you know it."

"Do you know what a ten-day hotel bill comes to in Manhattan?"

"I don't care."

"Well, you should if you want me to continue taking care of Joy's tuition and living expenses."

"If money's a problem, why don't you ask your mother."

Matt sighed. "You don't know?"

"Know what?"

"She's got no money, Clare."

"What are you talking about? Pierre's penthouse alone is worth—"

"Stop right there because you've nailed it. The penthouse, the villa, the stocks, the holdings, all of the money, all of it was *Pierre's*, and all of it is now controlled by his children."

"No. It can't be. Madame was his wife for two decades—"

"She was his *second* wife. Pierre's late *first* wife was the one who had inherited the importing business from her father. Pierre married into most of his fortune, and it was *her* will that stipulated nothing could be left to any future wife. Everything he owned was left to their children."

I sat down, stared a moment. The kettle's whistle brought me back (water for the Melitta method should be heated just to boiling). I got up and poured the steaming water over the freshly ground coffee beans, piled inside the gold filter like brown earth on a miner's treasure.

The trick with a Melitta is to pour slowly and stir, allowing the water to seep smoothly through the layers of grinds and into the carafe without channeling up. And of course, one must use a cone-shaped filter. Flat-bottom filters of any sort should be outlawed in my opinion, as they require more beans per fluid ounce of water to get the same strength of brew. Flat bottoms dissipate. Cones concentrate, saving beans and consequently costs, something I could see this family was going to have to remain vigilant about.

I never expected Madame to pay my way. But I did make an assumption—that she might leave Joy a healthy inheritance, enough so I'd never have to worry about my daughter's financial future for the rest of my life. In one short conversation with my ex-husband, I could see that assumption had been a terrible mistake.

"So, if she's broke," I said softly, "why doesn't she sell the coffeehouse?"

"You know why," said Matt.

And I did. Madame's bills were clearly being paid by whatever final arrangement Pierre had made with his children. Other than that, her main concern seemed to be her legacy at the Blend—*and* being able to leave something of worth to Matt and to Joy, and apparently, to me.

"So how is Anabelle doing, do you think?" asked Matt softly, changing the subject. He walked in and sat down, inhaled the aroma of the coffee slowly brewing on the table.

"I called St. Vincent's, but they couldn't or wouldn't tell me. Her roommate, Esther Best, went with her to the hospital, but Anabelle was unconscious and she didn't look good."

Matt exhaled. "Do you want me to go over?"

"No. I'd like to do that myself if you don't mind looking after the Blend. Tucker is our afternoon barista. I'm hoping we'll be able to open again by then."

"Why can't you open now?"

"The Crime Scene people. Lieutenant Quinn's waiting downstairs for them. If they ever get here, they're supposed to look for physical evidence first. That's why I'm making this coffee. It's for them—and for Lieutenant Quinn. He's used to the cheap stuff, and I'd like to convert him."

"Clare, tell me something about Anabelle's fall. What makes you think it was a *crime*?"

"My gut. The way I found her. Things don't add up. And by the way, what do you know about Anabelle that you wouldn't tell Quinn? I know you well enough to know when you're holding something back."

Matt shifted uneasily. "I knew there was something wrong between Anabelle and her boyfriend."

"How?"

"She said so. She told me she was trying to figure out some major issues."

"What sort of issues? Think back. Try to remember exactly."

"It was about six weeks ago, when I was last in New York. I was having an espresso downstairs and she sat down at my table and said she and her boyfriend were having some problems and she wanted to know about men."

"*What* about men?"

"Things like . . . what makes them want to get married."

"She asked *you* for advice about marriage?" I did my best not to burst out laughing. "What did you tell her?"

"What do you think, Clare? I told her I wasn't the best person to ask about that stuff. I barely know what makes *me* tick. But she pressed, said she heard I was a confirmed bachelor, and asked if I'd ever consider getting married, and I told her I *had* been married. So she asked what made me commit, and I told her."

"Joy."

"Yes."

"Then what did she say?"

"Then she said, 'Thanks, that helps a lot,' and that was it."

"That's a pretty big deal, Matt."

"I don't see why."

"It sounds like she was trying to figure out whether to get pregnant to get her boyfriend to marry her, that's why."

"So what if she was. That's none of the detective's business."

"It is if her boyfriend is the one who pushed her down our stairs."

"You see, that's why I didn't say anything to those cuff-crazed cops. One remark in a passing conversation and they'd have me incriminating some poor innocent kid."

"But, Matt, what if he isn't so innocent? Have you ever met him?"

"No."

"Neither have I, but I really wish you'd said something to the lieutenant. Clearly Quinn thought you were holding something back. Officer Langley did, too."

"Let them! I don't like either one of them."

"So I noticed. Why not? Other than the handcuff thing. Remember, I thought you were an intruder, and they were trying to protect me at the time."

"They're probably dirty cops."

"That's ridiculous!"

"You think so? Mark my words they'll never mention that vial of white powder again. Quinn or Langley will probably pass it around at some cop bar tonight. That or they'll barter it on the street to some skell junkie for information to make themselves look good at the precinct. Only the joke will be on them because you can't get a cocaine high from sniffing *caffeine*."

"Matt, you've been spending too much time in banana republics. Those guys are good cops. Lieutenant Quinn especially—"

"Quinn I *especially* don't like."

"Why, for heaven's sake?"

"For one thing, I don't like the way he looks at you."

"And how is that?"

"Like he's interested."

"Really? . . . He does?"

Matt stared at me. "My God, Clare, you're interested, too."

"Of course not!" I said, "Don't be stupid. He's married."

"So?"

"What do you mean *so*! Do you honestly think I'd get involved with someone who's married? Well, I'm not you, Matt. Get *that* straight. And you know what? My interest in any man is not your business. Not anymore. You think you can just waltz in here and—and—"

I ran out of gas. It had been a long morning. I turned away, walked to the window, and crossed my arms. The rain that had been threatening all morning had finally begun to fall.

Matt didn't move for a few moments, then he finally let out a disgusted grunt and headed for the stairs. "Guess it's time for me to finish getting dressed, before I get any *more* of a chill."

Five seconds later I heard a sharp thump, and I knew on the way up the steps, he'd sent his fist into a wall.

Ten

In 1849, four Sisters of Charity founded St. Vincent's as a thirty-bed hospital for the poor in a small brick house on Thirteenth Street.

Today St. Vincent's has 758 beds, and the only trauma center below Fourteenth Street in Manhattan. It's also a teaching hospital—something I have firsthand experience with because its medical residents are outstanding customers.

I figured at least one of the red-eyed young residents who regularly stumbled into the Blend for double-tall lattes, triple espressos, and grande Italian roasts during their periodic thirty-hour on-call shifts would be able to tell me about Anabelle's condition. So, as soon as the Crime Scene Unit left the shop and Tucker arrived to help Matteo open the coffee bar again, I grabbed an umbrella and trudged up Seventh Avenue South, through the pouring rain.

When I neared the hospital's entrance, I paused at one

of the building's walls. Cold rain streaked the dark gray stone, trickling like tears down its smooth blank face. Just a few years ago, this gray wall wasn't so blank.

I could still see the hundreds of photos—the faces, the names, the desperate messages scrawled beneath: "Have you seen . . . ?" "Please, please call . . ." "Looking for my . . . wife, husband, son, daughter, brother, sister, lover, friend . . ."

On the morning of September 11, 2001, I had been in New Jersey, watching the breaking news on television like most of the country, but I still remember how hard it was to contemplate the details: the cut throats of stewardesses, the terror of passengers as commercial jets were turned into guided missiles, the horrible deaths of the Trade Center workers—people from all nations, all beliefs, all income levels, people who'd simply arrived early to get the job done—office workers, restaurant staffs, banking executives, security guards, and maintenance men.

Many of those killed had lived in this Village neighborhood. They had woken that morning unsuspecting, unaware it would be the last morning of their lives, the last opportunity to feel a new day's sunshine, smell and sip a cup of freshly brewed coffee.

People forget as years go by, but this city will never forget. The terror, the tragedy, or the courage . . .

The firemen running up as others ran out. The businessman who wouldn't leave his friend stranded alone in a wheelchair. Two figures in a window, high above the street, a man and a woman with locked hands, jumping together, like so many others before and after them who decided a falling fate was better than burning up alive amid the toxic cloud of melting office furniture and hundreds of gallons of jet fuel.

When the reality hit that morning and most of the city felt paralyzed, Madame Dreyfus Allegro Dubois descended from her Fifth Avenue penthouse, just a few blocks from this spot, and marched straight to the Blend, instructing the staff to brew coffee nonstop around the clock—and deliver a fresh thermos every two hours to every nurses' station at St. Vincent's. The Village hospital had treated over 1,400 patients, including some of the most severe trauma cases.

"At such times, you do what you *can* do," Madame had said to me. "And we can do coffee, so that's what we *will* do."

And we did. Joy and I dropped everything to help. In the weeks that followed, we even helped Madame transport urns down the West Side Highway, to Ground Zero, the smoldering site of the collapsed World Trade Center, where firemen, iron workers, and hundreds of volunteers toiled tirelessly for months to recover remains and clear away the tons of smoking, twisted wreckage near the tip of Manhattan island.

Nothing would end the heartbreak of that fall and winter, certainly nothing as trivial as a cup of coffee. Yet every time Joy, or Madame, or I placed a hot paper cup into the hands of an exhausted volunteer, I understood why Madame wanted to take urn after urn down there.

What cheered and warmed these weary people for a few minutes wasn't the liquid extraction of a handful of beans, but the idea that someone had made it for them. Someone had cared. Someone had loved—an essential reminder for anyone who must daily face the gray, twisted evidence of someone else's hate.

"The coffee almanac said it best," Madame liked to remind us at the end of those long days. And then she'd quote words written at the beginning of the last century:

"Coffee makes a sad man cheerful, a languorous man active, a cold man warm, a warm man glowing. It awakens mental powers thought to be dead, and when left in a

sick room, it fills the room with a fragrance. . . . The very smell of coffee terrorizes death."

To Madame, a cup of morning coffee was more than a pick-me-up, it was fortification against whatever the world was about to throw at you, be it the best or the worst.

Which brings me back to my fears for Anabelle. After my silent moment at St. Vincent's rain-streaked wall, I entered the hospital and found its elevator bank.

The ascent took the usual four months with orderlies, nurses, and visitors entering and exiting on their appointed floors. During one of these brief stops, the elevator doors opened and I caught a glimpse of a familiar face down one of the hospital corridors—

Madame was sitting in a wheelchair and chatting with a gray-templed white-coated doctor. Before I could step out, the doors closed again.

"Excuse me, what floor was that?" I asked the tall Filipino orderly, who was standing beside me with an empty wheelchair.

"Cancer treatment," he said.

My stomach dropped.

Cancer treatment. My god.

Madame had indeed seemed more tired lately. And the contracts she'd tricked me and Matt into signing. *My god,* I thought again, it all made sense now: She was ill. That's why she wanted the legacy of the Blend in our hands. That's why she'd had the nerve to give us both permission to live in the duplex—she wanted to see us get back together before she . . . before she . . .

My god.

My mind was still processing this awful revelation when the elevator door opened on the floor for the intensive care unit. While I was still reeling from this news about Madame, I knew Anabelle was in even more serious trouble, so, like a triage nurse, I did my best to put my worries about Madame on hold and refocus my attention on Anabelle.

Venturing into the ICU waiting area, I noticed a young woman with a mass of frizzy dark hair and baggy clothes standing at a large observation window, staring at a ward full of beds. It was Anabelle's roommate, Esther Best (shortened from Bestovasky by her grandfather, she'd told me when we first met).

Anabelle's bed wasn't far from the observation window. She appeared to still be unconscious, plugged into an array of daunting-looking medical machines. A nurse sat near the foot of the bed, watching the monitors. Next to the bed, a slender blond woman stood, her back to us.

Through her trendy black-rimmed rectangular glasses, Esther glanced over at me. Like the mother I was, I found myself thinking how lovely the girl's features were, how beautiful her skin, and yet they were hidden by that too-long mass of frizzy, unconditioned hair and those clunky black glasses.

The truth was, I actually had a soft spot for Esther Best because I'd been just like her in my teen years (albeit a might less hostile). Eventually I grew out of it. I lost weight, made an effort with my appearance, dealt with my anger, and accepted the things I could not change, as the saying goes.

The biggest issue for Esther, as it had been with me, was her attitude. The giant chip on her shoulder usually fell on anyone within earshot, especially members of the opposite sex, whom she puzzled about on a fairly regular basis. From what I overheard in her conversations with poor Tucker, she was "totally perplexed" as to why the few boys who asked her out were so "hostile" after only an hour or two with her.

I greeted Esther. She nodded, and then she glanced back to the window, offering one of her characteristic observations—

"I thought she was supposed to be graceful."

Gee, how charitable, I thought with a sigh. "Anabelle *is* graceful, Esther. She's a dancer."

"I know she's a dancer. Everyone does. My god, it's the first thing that comes out of her mouth in case you haven't noticed—especially with men—'I'm a dancer!' But geez, Clare, I don't call slipping down a flight of stairs and ending up here graceful. I'd call it stupendously klutzy."

You know that old saying, *If you've got nothing nice to say—then slide over here and sit next to me.* Well, Esther was definitely comfortable on *both* sides of that couch.

"Who's to say she slipped?" I asked Esther.

"What's that supposed to mean?"

"I mean, she may have been pushed," I said, watching Esther closely for a reaction. "I think somebody pushed her."

Esther's eyes narrowed. "Like who?"

Okay, so the truth is the New York Police Department's Crime Scene Unit hadn't uncovered a darned thing to support my "pushing" theory. The only "physical evidence" they found was that JFK luggage tag from the back alley, which to my chagrin, Quinn handed over for the Crime Scene folks to file (even after Matteo identified it as coming from his luggage) along with Anabelle's jacket and purse.

For a grand total of about thirty minutes, they'd inspected the overflowing garbage can above the staircase, as well as every other potentially clue-filled surface. They found the smudged fingerprints of over a dozen people. Clearly, there was no way to get any leads from prints—unless someone who worked at the Blend had figured their prints would prove nothing.

I cleared my throat and raised an eyebrow to Esther,

trying to look shrewd. "I don't know who pushed An-abelle. But I'm going to find out."

Esther rolled her eyes.

"By the way," I said, "where were *you* last night?"

"At the *Words on Eighth* poetry reading, why?"

"Then where to?"

"Sheridan Square Diner with some friends. Then back to the apartment. Alone."

"And when was the last time you saw Anabelle?"

"What are you? Working for the NYPD now? Those cops already asked me that stuff."

"Just answer me."

"I last saw her before I left for the poetry reading. She said she was going to the Blend for an eight-to-midnight shift."

"And?"

"And what?"

"Anything else you can remember? Did she mention seeing anyone?"

"Like I told the cops. No, *nyet, nada*, zippo!"

I sighed, out of questions already, and made a mental note to speak to Lieutenant Quinn about interrogating suspects. Maybe he could give me some pointers.

I looked through the ICU observation window at An-abelle again. The blond woman moved around the bed to talk to the nurse, and I got the first good look at her face.

She was distraught, that was clear. And the lines, creases, and shadows confirmed she was a lot older than her youthfully slender body appeared, probably late for-ties. The hair that fell just past her shoulders was blond but the roots were dark, and she'd pulled it into a tasteful ponytail. The skin was too tan for a New York autumn and her clothes—tight black designer slacks and a white silk blouse—appeared tailored to fit her perfectly.

"Who's that woman?" I asked.

"Anabelle's stepmother."

"Her stepmother? I didn't know she was in the New York City area. Anabelle's employment forms say her next of kin is in—"

"Florida, I know," said Esther.

"So what's with the stepmother?"

"She came by the apartment a few days ago. Anabelle didn't look too happy to see her, I can tell you."

"Do you know why?"

"*Money.* I don't know the particulars, but I do know Anabelle borrowed five thousand dollars from her stepmother to get started here in New York last year. Mommy Dearest was passing through here on some sort of business. I think she wanted it paid back."

"What happened between them?"

Esther shrugged. "They just kept arguing. Actually, they've been arguing back and forth about money for about two months now."

"Was Anabelle arguing on the phone yesterday, before she left for the Blend?"

"Come to think of it, she was—I forgot about that. She got a cell phone call about an hour before I left. I forgot to tell the cops, but now I remember. She had a pretty big fight, too—"

"Why? What did her stepmother want?"

"It wasn't her stepmother she was fighting with. It was The Dick—"

"The what?" I said.

Esther rolled her eyes. "Anabelle's *boyfriend,* Richard."

"What do you know about Richard, anyway?"

"Richard Gibson Engstrum, Junior. Total asshole. Dartmouth senior this year. But this past summer he was living at home."

"Where's home?"

"Upper East Side."

"Where does he work in the summer?"

"He doesn't. Ever hear of Engstrum Systems? Daddy made a fortune on the NASDAQ run-up. They cashed out before the dot-bomb. The Dick's got his lifestyle covered."

"And his parents let him laze around all summer?"

Esther shrugged. "All I know is what Anabelle told me. Since she met him in July, he hasn't worked."

"Do you know where they met?"

"He was slumming with some friends at an East Village dance club—Nightrunners or Rah, one of those Alphabet City places. He saw Anabelle moving on the dance floor, and that was that. In case you haven't noticed, guys drool over the girl."

"I noticed, Esther. And it's pretty hard not to notice that you're incredibly angry about it."

"About what?"

"About Anabelle—and her ability to attract male attention."

"Hey, listen, I'm not like one of those nicey-nice Barbies who hides what she *really* thinks while she proceeds to stab you in the back each and every chance she gets. That's what Anabelle liked about me—or at least she said so. She liked that I told the truth—and the truth ain't always pretty. And the truth about me and Anabelle is that I've never been angry at her, I've just been *jealous* of her. So at least get that straight."

"And what are you jealous of, exactly?"

Esther shrugged, turned away to stare at the girl in the ICU. "She's just so beautiful and it's always been so easy for her to just . . . I don't know"—Esther shrugged again—"get what she wants."

"Esther, tell me the truth now. Were you jealous enough of her to argue with her at the Blend last night and maybe accidentally cause her to fall down that flight of stairs?"

"*No*. No way. I may be jealous of Anabelle, but I'm also her friend. I mean, okay, we aren't that close, but I'd *never* in a million years hurt her. Not like this."

The distressed look in Esther's eyes made me believe she was telling the truth.

"Besides," she added with a sigh, turning toward the observation window again, "suspecting me of something like that doesn't even make sense."

"Why not?"

She shrugged. "I was nowhere near the Blend all night. And we share an apartment. Don't you think if I was going to go postal on her, I'd have done it in the privacy of our own living space, like most domestic violence stuff?"

The girl did have a point, I thought.

"Have you been in to see her?" I asked.

"Just when they first brought her in. But the ICU is pretty strict. They wouldn't let Richard's mother in, either."

"Where is she?"

"Oh, she left. Probably to give her son the update. I called Richard at school and didn't get an answer so I called his parents' apartment, and she came for him. They'll only allow one visitor in there at a time. I was the one who called Anabelle's stepmother, too, to tell her what happened, and when she got here, I got booted out."

"It's nice that you stayed here so long."

"I don't mind."

I was just beginning to think the girl had a selfless streak I'd never before appreciated when I noticed her rapt gaze had shifted from Anabelle to another bed, farther up the ICU ward. A handsome young Chinese-American doctor in a white coat was finishing up there and swiftly walking toward the exit. Esther's eyes followed him like a cartoon mouse watching a ripe hunk of traveling cheese.

"That's John Foo," I told Esther.

"You know him?"

"He's a Blend regular."

"Why haven't I seen him before?"

"Because he's an opener—he's in and out by six-thirty in the morning, right after his martial arts workouts. And you, my dear, insisted on no shifts before noon."

"I admit it, I'm a sleep whore," said Esther, watching the young well-built doctor's every move. "But *he's* almost worth getting my butt out of bed for. Almost."

Dr. Foo moved through the set of double doors that led out of the ICU and came directly toward us.

"Esther, you're still here?"

"Oh, yes, Doctor," she said, rushing toward him. "I was hoping Anabelle might wake up."

I felt my eyebrows rise at that. For all Esther's talk of being a direct individual, I had a hunch she was dulling the edge there for the good-looking Dr. Foo. Her tone, I noticed, had even softened to a perceptible purr—a marked departure from the usual snarl.

"Yes," I said, stepping toward them. "Has she woken up at all?"

"Clare Cosi. Nice to see you."

Dr. Foo held out his hand, and I shook it.

"Nice to see you, too, Doctor."

"You weren't open this morning," he said. "I came by at the usual time."

I pointed to Anabelle. "Your patient was our opener."

"Oh, I see. I'm so sorry."

"How is she, Doctor?"

"Not good. She's in a coma."

"Is she assigned to you?"

"No. I believe Howard Klein is taking care of her."

"I don't know Dr. Klein. Does he ever come to the Blend?"

Doctor Foo laughed. "Klein's an anti-caffeine fanatic."

"I see. Well . . . would you mind doing me a small favor?"

"What's that?"

"I need some information."

ELEVEN

⟨⟨⟨⟨⟨⟨⟨⟨⟨⟨⟨⟨⟨⟨⟨⟨⟨⟨⟨⟨⟨⟨⟨⟨⟨

"EXCUSE me? Did you *get* that? A mochaccino with *skim* milk?"

"Is my latte coming this *year*?"

"Double. Double espresso!"

"What's the holdup?"

"Is *someone* going to take my money?"

Coffee drinkers were usually very "on" people—ambitious, fast-thinking, fast-moving, aggressive, aware, and involved. I liked them, and I liked serving them. But gourmet coffee drinkers who had to wait an excessively long period to get their fix were not the most patient people on the planet to be wading through.

"Hi, Tuck," I called over the crowd. "Need a hand?"

"Clare! Thank the lord you're back!"

Tucker Burton was my afternoon barista. A gay thirtysomething actor and playwright, he'd been born in Louisiana to Elma Tucker, a single mother with a few Hollywood screen credits who had returned to her home state claiming her only son was the illegitimate offspring of Richard Burton. Thus, upon turning twenty-one, Tucker moved to New York City and legally changed his name from Elmer Tucker to Tucker Burton.

Maybe it was his Southern roots, but when especially agitated, Tucker seemed to take on the inflections of a revival tent preacher. He was also tall enough for me to see his mop of light brown hair and angular face over the bevy of bodies lined up three deep at the blue marble counter.

"Clare is here and we are saved! Hal-le-lujah!"

This was the lunchtime crowd from the offices located a few blocks away on Hudson: Assets Bank workers, Satay & Satay Ad execs, and Berk and Lee Publishing people. The neighborhood regulars were here, too, and I exhaled with relief.

Who knew what sort of rumor hit the streets at the sight of an ambulance in front of the Blend—botulism could not be ruled out. Bacteria-laden half-and-half or salmonella in the cream cheese strudel.

Now that the police had allowed us to reopen, I was overjoyed our customers had not flocked elsewhere. It was a satisfying affirmation that the Blend served the best damn cup in town.

"Can I get my latte this *decade*!"

"Clare Cosi!" Tucker shouted. "Will you get your blessed booty back here and help me!"

"Coming, Tuck! Excuse me, excuse me!" I snaked through the bodies, slipped around the counter, and tied on a white chef's apron.

"Take over the register," I told him. The register position took the order, collected the money, and poured the regularly brewed coffees into our paper cups with the Blend signature stamp.

I took over the barista position. This division of labor made perfect sense. While Tuck was competent enough at making the Italian coffee drinks, I was better at pulling shots and less flustered under pressure. Besides, as a stage actor, Tuck was a pro at working a crowd.

"All right, people! Line it up! Work with me, work with me! Make a queue, for lord's sake! C.C.'s back and she's gonna make magic!"

Espressos are the basis of most Italian coffee drinks. The dealer who'd sold Madame this gleaming, low-slung machine claimed a good barista could pull 240 shots every sixty minutes, but speed wasn't the objective because an espresso made in under thirty seconds was *merde* (excuse my French). So no matter how many customers screamed to be served faster, I wasn't about to sacrifice quality.

"Clare, got that cappuccino?"

"Working!"

Freshly drawn shot of espresso, fill rest of cup with one part steamed milk, one part frothed milk.

"Latte!"

Freshly drawn espresso, fill rest of cup with steamed milk, top with a thin crown of frothed milk.

"Mochaccino!"

Pour two ounces chocolate syrup into the bottom of the cup, add one ounce shot of espresso, fill with steamed milk, stir once around lifting from the bottom to bring the syrup up, top with whipped cream, lightly sprinkle with sweetened ground cocoa and curls of shaved chocolate.

Sure, it looked easy from the other side of the counter. But how many of those demanding gourmet coffee palettes knew there were over forty variables that affected the quality of their espresso alone? Forty ways to mess up the perfect cup, including machine cleanliness, ground coffee portion, particle size distribution, porosity of caked grounds, cake shape, cake moisture, water quality, water pressure, water temperature, extraction time, and, oh, about thirty others.

Just last year the industry issued a report saying only approximately five percent of coffee bars in America operated their machines properly. Only five percent gave their customers a true espresso experience.

I was appalled, but not entirely surprised. Take "Perk Up!," the rival coffeehouse that went into business across the street from the Blend a few years back then swiftly went out again the very same year, and for a very good reason—they bragged about making their espressos in record time, seven seconds.

Now most people in the food and beverage service business would agree that speed in making your product and getting it into the customer's hands is usually a lucrative idea, but here's the problem: To produce a quality espresso, you've got to have nearly boiling water at pressures of eight to ten bars. Creating hot water at these pressures is the basic function of an espresso machine. Unfortunately, at these high pressures, water can be forced through the ground coffee too quickly if the barista does not make sure that the coffee is ground fine enough or the grounds are packed tightly enough into the filter-holder cup.

If the grounds are too coarsely milled or too loosely packed, coffee practically gushes out of the portafilter spouts. This rapid process extracts only the soluble components of ground coffee, making it *brewed* coffee, *not* espresso.

Thus are standards lowered, and as Madame says, when we lower our standards, we lose our soul—not to mention our returning customer base.

When I make an espresso, I slow down the extraction process by using a finer grind and a *very* packed filter-holder cup. That way the espresso *oozes* out of the portafilter like warm honey (as it should) instead of gushing out like water. When it oozes out, you know that oils have been extracted from ground coffee and not just the soluble components as in brewed coffee.

A quality espresso should consist entirely of rich, reddish-brown crema as it flows easily out of the portafilter spout. Crema, or coffee foam, is the single most important thing to look for in a well-made espresso. It tells you the oils in ground coffee have been extracted and suspended in the liquid—the thing that makes espresso, espresso.

"Got that mocha?"

"Got it!"

"XXX!"

Triple espresso.

"Skinny hazelnut cap with wings!"

Cappuccino with skim milk, hazelnut syrup, and extra foam.

"Caffé Caramella!"

Latte with caramel syrup, topped with sweetened whipped cream and a drizzle of warm caramel topping.

"Caffé Kiss-Kiss!"

Otherwise known on our menu as Raspberry-Mocha Bocci. One of my favorite dessert drinks. "Got it!"

"Americano!"

Also known as a Caffé Americano. An espresso diluted with hot water.

"Grande skinny!"

Twenty-ounce latte with skim milk.

"Double tall cap, get the lead out!"

Sixteen-ounce cappuccino with decaf.

Decaf.

A shudder ran through me as I glanced up and saw the wane, pale, overanxious face of the man ordering the decaf.

Okay, I'm sorry, but decaf drinkers *annoy* me.

Expectant mothers I can understand, but lifelong decaf

drinkers give me the creeps. They're usually the sort who have a half-dozen imagined allergies, eat macrobiotic patties, and pop Rolaids like M&Ms when their acid reflux kicks in from anxiety over the Chinese restaurant's delivering white instead of brown rice.

Look, I'm not saying anyone should overdo ingesting caffeine, but let's face it, researchers have already declared too much *water* is a bad thing. So overdoing anything isn't particularly good idea. All I'm saying is that I find it difficult to believe the bedtime story that true "health" completely hinges on the number of milligrams of salt *not* consumed, always and forever ordering bernnaise on the side, and—god forbid—ever letting yourself enjoy a warm, satisfying beverage in the natural state it's been consumed for, oh, about a thousand years.

Okay, lecture over, back to work—

"Mocha-mint cap, vanilla lat, espresso, espresso, espresso!"

During a typical day, when things were in control and enough hands were on deck back here, I took the time to talk to the customers, savor the look on their faces as they took that first sip.

But for a solid forty minutes there was no time to enjoy their enjoyment. Not even any time to ask Tucker where the hell Matteo had disappeared to. Eventually, however, the crowd thinned. A dozen or so bodies lingered at the marble tables on the first floor, but the bulk of the waiting customers had gone, returning to the offices whence they'd come—whether cramped cubicle, receptionist desk, or the plushest of executive suites. (All hail mochaccino!—the great equalizer.)

With the lunch rush over, I fixed Tucker and myself double espressos. Most espresso drinkers like their shots black or with sugar. Some like lemon zest (gratings of lemon rind) or a twist of lemon and sugar.

Matteo drinks it straight black. Tucker and I like a bit of sugar.

(The thing to remember when adding sugar is to use white granulated—it desolves much faster and smoother than cubes or brown sugar.)

Some of my customers even add a bit of frothed milk, but this version of espresso "stained" with a bit of milk is technically called a caffé macchiato (*macchia* being Italian for stain, spot, or speckle).

As I finished making our drinks, Tucker put a New Age instrumental CD into the sound system. The mellow music was a tradition I had reinstated.

Before I'd returned to managing the Blend, Moffat Flaste, the previous manager, had driven customers away not only from his lack of attention to store hours, his improper cleaning of the espresso machines, and his laziness in keeping the seating areas tidy—but also with his exclusive and incessant playing of Broadway show tunes on the coffeehouse sound system.

As Madame put it: "How can one read, write, cogitate, or converse with Ethel Merman caterwauling in the background!"

Unfortunate but true. I mean, Broadway musicals are fine things, but their raucous tunes are distracting: worthwhile when ensconced in a velvet theater seat or cleaning the refrigerator, but downright irritating when trying to relax with a cup of cappuccino.

So about four weeks ago, on my first day back managing the Blend after more than ten years, I instructed the staff to return to the routine that the Blend had maintained for decades: classical, opera, and New Age instrumentals in the morning and afternoon; jazz and world music in the evening.

In less than a week, the old customers began to return. And with word of mouth traveling as quickly as it does in the Village, the customer base was now almost back to a profitable level.

"So where the hell did Matt go?" I finally asked Tucker.

He shrugged. "All I know is that he was helping me get ready to open when he said he'd be right back. He went up to the manager's office, came back down about fifteen minutes later, said he had to take care of something very important, and left."

"He said it was very important?"

"*Dire* was the word Matt used."

"*Dire*," I repeated and took a fortifying sip from my cup. The stimulating warmth reached out to rally every weary nerve ending in my weary body.

Tucker had no way of knowing this, but *dire* was a loaded word for me, especially when it involved my ex-husband.

When we'd been married, and Joy was very little, Matt had described as dire the various "business networking" events that to me sounded more like they were ripped from a page of Hugh Hefner's daytimer, e.g.: "It's dire that I attend that club opening," or "It's dire that I stay in Rio another two weeks," or "It's dire that I accept that coffee broker's invitation to his hot tub party."

Eventually I realized my Peter Pan husband was simply dropping the letters *es* in the word *desire* to get the desired reaction from his little wifey, home taking care of the little daughter and managing the little coffeehouse.

I put up with it for almost a decade, mainly for Joy. But after a few major epiphanies in the wake of a few minor discoveries, I finally realized the fool I was and moved Joy and myself to Jersey, leaving a simple note behind: *Dear Matt: It's dire we divorce.*

Thus ends my unhappy history with the D word.

Unfortunately, in this case, Matteo had not been exaggerating. What he'd discovered in the upstairs office *was* dire. But I wouldn't find that out until I saw him later that day.

It was still early afternoon and a few surprises were about to come through my front door, starting with a cacophony of yips and barks attached to a stampede of long legs.

"I'm no wildlife expert," quipped Tucker, his head deep under the counter, checking on supplies, "but that's either a pack of roving hyenas or the Dance 10 crew."

TWELVE

~~~~~~~~~~~~~~~~~~~~~~~~~~~~~~~~~~

THE herd of too tall, too thin, and too toned young women, and a few lean and muscular young men, stampeded through the door as if they'd been stranded for weeks on the Sahara and just discovered the great oasis.

Sporting leotards and water bottles, the chattering pack usually showed in the afternoons and evenings, during their breaks between dance classes or show rehearsals at the Dance 10 studio just a few blocks away—the same studio at which Anabelle Hart had studied.

"Tucker, do me a favor," I said, watching them swarm the counter.

"What?" he asked. "Help you serve this rabble? You already pay me to do that."

"No. Something else." I often saw Tucker laughing it up with Anabelle and other groups from the studio—he was usually after the attractive male dancers, but that didn't matter at the moment. Tucker was in the arts and close to their age, so many of the girls seemed to treat him as a trusted friend. He wasn't a direct competitor for dance jobs, and because he was gay, he wasn't going to become some sort of unwanted male pursuer. The perfect friend to confide in—so, I asked Tucker—"After they sit down, I want you to introduce me to Anabelle's friends."

"Her *friends*?" Tucker raised an eyebrow. "Clare, among dancers that term is a fluctuating one at best."

"Why?"

"Jealousy, of course."

Nevertheless, Tucker did as I asked, calling me over after we'd served the group and they'd settled in at various tables.

"Come on over, C.C.!"

Actually, before he'd even called me, I had made a point of closely surveying the pack. Though I felt a little guilty for thinking it, Tucker's comparing them with those hungry scavengers of the African veldt persisted—helped considerably by one girl's zebra leotard and another's leopard print headband and jacket.

They'd been in here many times before, laughing and whispering, gossiping and dishing, but I seldom made a point of listening to their conversations. (Most of my eavesdropping efforts leaned toward the older crowds—writers, painters, professors, and the occasional stock broker with a hot tip.)

Today, after lending an ear, I better understood Tucker's "Wild Kingdom" comparisons. Why? Well, to start with, the dancers' conversations included such genteel and eloquent remarks as—

"She's a slut!"

"He's a whore!"

"The bitch thinks she's all that!"

"Can't balance for shit—"

"No timing. No style. No talent!"

"I'll break her legs before she upstages me again!"

And that was just in the first ten minutes.

"Hey, C.C.," said Tucker, motioning me over to a table where five young women sat—three double tall lattes and two teas. He introduced me to the two teas first—

"This is Petra and Vita. They were both born in Russia and studied ballet in Moscow."

Ahhh, I thought, *that's why the tea.* Matteo had told me, after a trip to Moscow and Leningrad, that tea was the most popular nonalcoholic drink in that country, usually consumed during midafternoon breaks or after meals.

"Nize to met you," said Petra. Her eyes were two black pearls and her straight black hair was cropped into a severe dominatrix-style cut. "You have nize place here," she said. Her chin rose to gesture toward the end of the room. "Nize samovar, too."

On the mantel shelf above the fireplace and next to Madame's French lacquered coffee urn was an antique Russian samovar.

"Excuse me, but what's a samovar?" asked one of the latte girls.

"It makes very strong tea called *zavarka,*" said Petra. "It is Russian tradition to serve tea after supper. You clean supper table, put samovar in center of table, and whole family gathers round for tea."

"How interesting," I said, although I knew this already. I also knew, from one of Madame's afternoon chats way back when, that the word *samovar* meant "self-heater" and the device was thought to be a modification of a Mongolian fire-pot, which had been used by the trans-Urals for cooking. With Petra's haughty demeanor, however, I thought it best to keep my mouth shut and let Petra assume the role of expert.

"And you're Vita?" I said instead.

"Charmed," said Vita, "I am sure," although she looked anything but. Petra's companion appeared to be the "yang" to Petra's "yin" (or was it the other way around?). Anyway, where Petra was dark, Vita was light—pale blue eyes and yellow-blond hair pulled so tightly into a ponytail I thought for a minute she'd had a face-lift at the age of twenty-three.

Tucker gestured to the first latte. "This is Maggie."

This one reminded me of a Vegas showgirl. Long legs. Tiny waist. Big red hair. Bigger breasts. Wide, heavily lashed eyes with a color green that does *not* appear in nature—contact lenses, or I'm twenty-five.

The second latte and fourth girl came next. "This is Sheela," said Tucker.

"S'up, Clare," said the statuesque African-American girl with sculpted shoulders and a hip-hop attitude as sharp as her long aquamarine fingernails. "Your place is phat."

(I thanked her, grateful that Joy and her young friends had enlightened me on the MTV lexicon. Otherwise, given the recommended dietary allowances from the health mafia for the last thirty years, I wouldn't have guessed calling something "phat" was good.)

"And this is Courtney," said Tucker. She was the one who had asked about the samovar.

A pale-skinned, frail beauty with a dainty nose and long blond hair in a ballerina bun smiled shyly up at me. She shifted in her chair, all arms and elbows, as if she were uncertain of what to do with them in polite company. She definitely seemed the wallflower of this group.

Before Courtney could muster the courage to say hello, Petra turned to me, shaking her head and loudly pronouncing: "Zat vas terrible, vot happened to Anabelle."

The others nodded as one. If I hadn't already figured out the pecking order of this pack by Tucker's introduction, I couldn't miss it now. My eyes locked on Petra.

"Do you think it was an accident?" I asked straightaway. "Or did Anabelle have enemies?"

As I expected, the directness of the question was not

unlike a bulldozer slamming the trunk of an apple tree. I waited with my bushel ready to collect whatever might come down—while assuring myself I could dodge anything aimed directly at my head.

For a solid minute, mouths gaped, but nothing came out. Even Tucker, eyes wide, looked shocked by my frankness—but within a few seconds, they narrowed with interest.

The other eyes began to dart around the table until, finally, they all settled on the Russian émigré with the black eyes and the blunt haircut.

"You zink there vas maybe foul play?" Petra said slowly.

"Yes," I said. "I think it is a little peculiar that a girl as graceful as Anabelle could suddenly plunge down a flight of steps."

"*Oh*, is *dat* all," said Vita with a nudge to her Russian companion. "Do not stress yourselv. Anabelle vasn't that good."

"Oh?" I said.

"She was good enough," Sheela said to Vita with a finger to the girl's shoulder. "Good enough to get that spot *you* said you and Petra nearly got in Moby's Danse."

That news surprised me. Though not a follower of modern dance, even I had heard of Moby's Danse, a troupe with a small theater in Soho. They mounted a few shows in New York City a year, and *The New York Times* dance critic loved them. Fawning write-ups usually made their shows overnight sensations with sold-out performances for months, providing the necessary buzz for subsequent national tours.

I was even more surprised that Anabelle hadn't mentioned this accomplishment to me.

"When did she get that spot?" I asked.

"Just last week," said Sheela.

"Well, she von't be danzing for zem now," Petra said, her black eyes narrowing.

"That's cold," Sheela said, cocking her head.

"No colder zan you ver to Vita when she beat you out of zat spot for Master Jam J. music video."

"That was different," said Sheela, eyes blazing.

"How?" asked Petra.

"Well, for one thing, Vita ain't in St. Vincent's sucking on a respirator. She's sittin' right here sucking down a tea!"

Vita and Maggie snickered at that.

But Petra seethed.

And Courtney shifted uncomfortably.

"What about you, Courtney?" I asked. "Do you have an opinion?"

"She *should*," Maggie drawled, her Vegas showgirl lips perfectly outlined with pink lipliner. "She's the one who's gonna get Anabelle's spot. Aren't you, Courtney?"

Courtney just stared into her double latte and nodded.

"Is that right, Courtney?" I said, trying to coax her into saying *something*. "Are you going to be joining the Moby's Danse troupe?"

The girl's pale skin and delicate features reminded me of Anabelle. But that's where the resemblance ended. This girl was much shyer and far less hardened than my assistant manager—whose street smarts, energy, and confident way of expressing herself could have easily kept up with the other girls at this table.

After a few silent moments, Courtney's flushed face looked up. There were tears in her eyes. "Trust me," she whispered, "I didn't want to get into the troupe this way."

There are good actresses and bad actresses, and this one was no actress at all. Courtney's eyes were telling the truth. I was certain of it.

Then I glanced over at Petra. The contrast was so marked I drew in a sharp breath. Where Courtney's soft blue eyes were brimming with tears of sorrow, Petra's cold black pearls were as hard and unmoved as a predator's.

But before I could continue questioning any of them, the front door opened and a harsh, direct voice cut through the mellifluous piano stylings of George Winston, one of Tucker's favorite instrumental CDs—

"Who owns this place."

Trouble. You know it when you hear it.

I sighed.

Before turning from the Dance 10 table, I nodded my thanks to Tucker. I had gotten what I wanted—a lead on a motive. Tomorrow I'd visit the studio myself to find out more.

"Did anyone hear me?" the voice demanded again. "Who owns this place!"

"May I help you," I said, knowing at once I was going to need more than one double espresso to get through this afternoon.

ThIRTEEN

~~~~~~~~~~~~~~~~~~~~~~~~~~~~~~~

The demanding voice came out of a killer body.

Tailored designer slacks on mile-high legs. Gucci boots and a black jacket of butter-soft leather over a white silk blouse. Blond hair tied back into a tasteful ponytail. Coach bag and skin too tan for a New York autumn with makeup applied in artful layers—lipstick, eyeliner, mascara—like talismans meant to ward off the curse of lines, creases, shadows, and any other betrayer of an otherwise youthfully slender appearance.

I'd seen this blonde at the hospital, I realized: Anabelle's stepmother.

"*You* the one owns this place?"

The accent and phrasing were rough—lower-middle-class, not quite what I expected to hear coming out of such a finished and fashionable façade.

The voice was deep and rattled a bit in her throat, signs of a hardcore lifelong smoker, the sort of woman I used to see laugh-coughing amid marathon gossip sessions back in the hair salon next to my grandmother's grocery in Pennsylvania.

"Well," I began, "I'm a *part* owner, and the full-time manager—"

She cut me off. "I want *the* owner. *Now.*"

The increasing volume on that last statement drowned out the various conversations that had been buzzing all over the room. I glanced around to find dozens of pairs of eyes blinking in our direction.

A scene. Great.

Years ago, my grandmother gave me the best advice when dealing with hostile people—a situation she encountered quite a bit during her lifetime, given the hot tempers of her grocery's working-class clientele and her son's (and my father's) knack for bringing more trouble to her doorstep than a barrel full of bad luck charms.

I didn't realize until later, after the two years of college I managed to finish before becoming pregnant with Joy, that my grandma actually had a lot in common with Socrates, not to mention Abe Lincoln.

"Clare," she would say, "if you want to win an argument with angry people, don't argue. Just ask the kind of questions that will make them think you agree with them. Pretty soon, you're both on the same side."

That part was Socrates.

She also liked to say—"Remember, you catch more flies with honey than with vinegar. Try to make them see you as a friend."

That part was Lincoln, the president who'd said over one hundred years ago, "It is an old and true maxim that 'a drop of honey catches more flies than a gallon of gall.' So with men, if you would win a man to your cause, first convince him that you are his sincere friend. Therein is a drop of honey that catches his heart; which, say what you will, is the great high road to his reason."

I stepped closer to the blonde to (hopefully) discourage her from yelling again—and in a calm, quiet voice asked: "You're Anabelle's stepmother, aren't you?"

Her bloodshot blue eyes with perfectly applied brown/black liner and mascara stared, the slight surprise for a moment unbalancing her predetermined indignation. "How did you know that?"

"I saw you at the hospital—"

"I'm her stepmother, that's right," she said. "I'm her closest relative, too. And that's why I'm here—"

"Do you mean Anabelle sent you?" I asked excitedly. "She's *awake*?"

The woman's shoulders drooped a bit. "No. She's still in her coma . . . But I heard she got that way because of your crappy managing of this place."

"I'm sure you're tired," I said as soothingly as I could manage between clenched teeth. "And I'm as worried about Anabelle as you must be. Wouldn't you rather we go somewhere more private to discuss this?" I gestured to the crowd of staring eavesdroppers. "What do you say?"

The woman glared back at the audience. "Screw them," she said.

"How about a fresh cup of coffee?" I asked.

"I drink tea. Not coffee."

"We have tea. How about a nice Earl Grey—"

"Green. Decaffeinated. Better for the skin," she said as she began to dig into her Coach bag for a pack of Camels.

A chimney. Great. There was no smoking in the coffeehouse. Or in any coffeehouse, for that matter, ever since the city's new statutes against smoking in public places. So I thought fast.

"How about we go up to the second floor?" I suggested. "We don't open it up until evening. It'll be nice and private."

And, I added silently, I can sit you and your pack of Camels beside an open double-pane window to prevent your smoke from driving out half the customers down here.

"Fine," she said. "But I don't have all day."

So far so good, I told myself. At least four yeses and she hadn't once threatened fisticuffs—a routine occurrence in my old neighborhood, where use of brawn was preferred to use of brain by a margin of at least two to one.

After I prepared the coffee and tea, we settled in at a table on the deserted second floor. I learned her name was Darla Branch Hart. I told her my name was Clare Cosi. And the accusations instantly resumed—

"Anabelle is in the hospital for *one* reason—*negligence,*" the woman said, stabbing the air with her unlit Camel. "She had a workplace accident. So I expect you to pay Anabelle's hospital bills."

"Anabelle's covered, Mrs. Hart," I said, watching her place the cigarette between her lips and fire it up. (Why was I suddenly picturing the small burst of flame igniting the fuse of a cannon?)

"What do you mean, she's covered?"

"When I promoted Anabelle to assistant manager," I said, "she received health insurance and hospitalization coverage under our HMO plan. The bills will be paid. Except for the fifteen-dollar copayment. And there might be some deductibles—"

"Well, *you* have to cover all that. In fact, I'd like that fifteen-dollar copayment. Right now."

I stared at her. "Fifteen dollars?"

"Yes," she said, sucking in a lungful of tar and blowing it out the side of her perfectly lined lips. *"Now."*

I suddenly found myself reconsidering the use of fisticuffs as a conflict resolution strategy. After all, as I'd already mentioned, it *was* preferred two to one in my old neighborhood. And in the words of Joe Pasquale Cosi (aka my father), who was often forced to collect his fair share of earnings from one deadbeat business partner or other: "Cupcake, you just can't beat the purity of communication in a simple punch to the nose."

But Grandma would have disapproved.

"Mrs. Hart, I'll gladly give you fifteen dollars if it will make you feel better." I dug into my Old Navy jeans and came up with a ten and a five. I moved to place them on the table between us. She snatched them up and stuffed them into her Coach bag before the worn green bills even touched the coral-colored marble.

"Where's my daughter's things?" Darla next demanded. "The hospital told me she didn't have a purse when they brought her in—and her roommate, that ethnic-looking girl, what's her name? Esther? She told me Anabelle must have left the purse here."

"The police have it," I told her, trying to hold my temper ("ethnic-looking" could pretty much describe me as well as Esther and I didn't appreciate the insulting tone she'd used in stating it).

"The police?" Darla Hart's face looked stricken. I made a significant note of that. "Why would the police have it?"

Why would you look stricken at the mention of the police? I wanted to ask, but saved that question and instead asked—

"Why do you think the police think Anabelle's fall wasn't just a workplace accident?" I asked. (Okay, so I fudged the facts—the police *did* think it was a simple accident. But the Petty-Cash Queen here didn't know that.)

Darla's mouth turned down, her eyes widened, then shifted to stare out the open window. She took a long drag. The white of the cigarette paper against the blood-red polish of the woman's manicured nails reminded me of a line from Clare Booth Luce's play *The Women*: "Looks like you've been tearing at somebody's throat."

"What do they think?" she asked, still staring into the afternoon rain clouds. Her fingers were slightly trembling.

"Well, the police called it a 'crime scene,'" I said. "They took fingerprints, collected evidence, that sort of thing. Seems like she could have been pushed."

Darla turned back, stared hard into my face. "*Who* do they think would have pushed her?"

I didn't know, of course. So my instinct was to turn away, but I didn't. I forced myself to hold her gaze. "Whoever they suspect. They wouldn't tell me."

Darla frowned again. Abruptly, she rose to her feet, almost spilling her untouched green tea. "I have to go."

"Where can I reach you?"

"The Waldorf."

She searched the table a moment and, after finding no ashtray, carelessly dropped the burning butt into her teacup. I grimaced, watching the pale rolled paper rise to the top of the green liquid and float there, dead and cold.

"I want you to know—and you can let all the owners of this place know—I'm hiring a lawyer," she said. "I don't care if all Anabelle's hospital bills are covered by insurance. My stepdaughter deserves some money for her pain and suffering, and I'm gonna see she gets it."

With that, Darla shoved the short handles of her fashionable Coach bag onto her shoulder, turned on her Gucci boot heel, and headed for the exit.

I watched her go, noting that her movements were as graceful as her stepdaughter's. A former dancer, no doubt.

I leaned back, averted my eyes from the cold, dead butt floating in the green tea, sipped my house blend, and considered the fact that Darla was staying at the Waldorf yet snatching up a worn ten and five like she was down to her last dime. And I remembered Esther had said something about Darla showing up a few days ago to take care of some sort of "business." I needed to find out what exactly that "business" was.

As I cleared the table, I quietly thanked my Grandma Cosi. I guess her method (not to mention Socrates's and Abe's) was really the best way to go—at least when you were trying to gather information from an angry source. Hostility handled and channeled through reason and strategy—

"Clare? Are you up here? It's *dire* I speak with you!"

It was Matteo. Back from god knows where, doing god knows what. And using the dreaded *D* word again.

I sighed, wishing my grandmother were still alive— then maybe she could tell me why, when it came to my ex-husband, I almost always wanted to use the more straightforward conflict resolution strategy my father employed—and (need I add) preferred two to one in my old neighborhood.

Fourteen

~~~~~~

A few hours later, I was heading up the back stairs to my new second-floor apartment. Everything was under control downstairs. Tucker was on duty as assistant manager, and our evening barista, one of our many part-time workers, had just arrived.

After the events of the day, I really needed a few hours off. Joy was coming for dinner, and I wanted the time to clean up, set a nice table, and listen to some Frank Sinatra.

When I unlocked the door to the duplex, Java greeted me with her usual ear-piercing jaguar yowl. She wasn't used to her new surroundings. Well, neither was I. But at least Java's problem could be solved by a scratch or two behind the ears and a can of Fancy Feast Chopped Grill Platter. My dilemmas weren't so easily solved.

After I presented Java with the attention and the food, the little ball of coffee-bean-brown fur chowed down, then contentedly sprawled across Madame's living room Persian and began to groom.

I decided to groom as well. My first shower of the day was a dim memory—back in my former New Jersey home. It felt like another decade. I entered the bathroom (small but tastefully designed with a terra cotta floor, Mediterranean-aqua tiles, a marble sink, luxuriously large tub, and two watercolor originals from a student of twentieth-century American Realist painter Edward Hopper—"Boats in Brooklyn Harbor" and "Long Island Sea Foam").

I dropped my clothes in a heap and jumped into the marble tub. The shower nozzle above had a spa-quality massage head. No time for that, unfortunately, just a hot spray and a quick soaping. After drying my hair, I stood before the closet pondering my wardrobe. I'd moved most of it in batches over the last few weeks. I'd done some shopping recently, too. What to wear suddenly had me stumped. I considered my ex-husband, remember he liked me in skirts—

Oh, god, what am I doing!

Disgusted with myself for giving Matt's preferences even one moment's consideration, I quickly grabbed the first clothes I saw—a pair of black slacks and a red blouse.

I finished dressing and set the table in the dining room. I pulled out the handmade lace tablecloth Madame had bought in Florence and put tapers in the crystal holders. Madame's finest china was displayed in an antique cabinet in her Fifth Avenue dining room. Her second best was stacked in her Fifth Avenue kitchen. Here she kept a set of her third best dishware. But to be honest, I liked it the most: Spode Imperialware's "Blue Italian" pattern, which has been in continuous production since 1816. I think I liked it best because it felt so cozy and homey, and the blue Northern Italian scenes set against the white earthenware matched the cheerful blue color in the marble of the Village Blend's main counter.

I set three places.

Next I headed for the kitchen, complete with finished oak cabinets and brass fixtures. The dishwasher was small, but the refrigerator/freezer was large, and the stove was huge, with six burners and a double oven—all with shiny stainless steel finishes.

I'd stocked the tall wall cabinet last week with essentials like sugar, flour, oils and assorted can goods—everything I needed for the dessert I had in mind, Clare's Cappuccino Walnut Cheesecake, one of Joy's favorites.

I had phoned Madame earlier and invited her to join us for dinner. She loved to spend time with Joy, and my daughter loved Madame, too. But Madame had declined, claiming she was feeling tired.

The way she had said it—hesitating between "feeling" and "tired"—made me want to cry. It sounded like an excuse, like she'd wanted to say "ill" instead of "tired" but had caught herself. After seeing her in a wheelchair at St. Vincent's cancer ward, I wasn't going to press her. I'd wait until she chose to reveal the truth. I certainly wasn't going to tell her a thing about our problems at the Blend.

Earlier today, I'd told Matt my worries about his mother's health. I felt bad doing it, but he might have otherwise burdened Madame with the Blend's problems, and his mother had enough troubles. She didn't need to know about Anabelle's fall, the threats made by Anabelle's stepmother to sue, or the highly disturbing news Matteo had brought to my attention a few hours ago.

There would be other dinners, I told myself, even if Madame was ill and even if, God forbid, she wouldn't be with us much longer. With that thought, I promised myself that I would make sure Joy and I had dinner with her in the very near future. Perhaps at her penthouse instead of here—so she wouldn't have to travel.

For now, however, I had a dessert to prepare.

Fortunately, the rest of dinner was taken care of. Matt had insisted on making Joy's favorite appetizer, which sent him on a shopping trip: first to Dornier's, a gourmet butcher shop in the meatpacking district; and then to Carbone's, a local Italian market that specialized in homemade mozzarella cheese and pastas.

Joy, of course, was bringing her "surprise," which I took to be yet another dish she had learned to prepare at culinary school. All of Joy's recipes were fully tested before she brought them home to share, so I had no doubt that we were in for a gastronomic delight. And in any case, Matt was also planning a quick side dish—one substantial enough to be a main course in itself.

That thought alone spurred me into action. Matteo would be arriving within the hour, and when he was cooking, he always (and I mean always) completely dominated the kitchen. I was in no mood to fight for elbow room in my own place, so I got right to the cheesecake.

After tying back my hair, I preheated the oven then began pulling ingredients from the refrigerator and spices off the oak rack. The great thing about my Cappuccino Walnut Cheesecake was that you could whip it up fast. After rummaging through a stack of boxes still piled in the corner—my own well-used supply of cooking equipment, shipped from New Jersey a few days ago—I located my nine-inch springform pan.

I blended the walnuts, butter, and sugar for the crust. Then I poured the mixture into the pan and patted it down. Next came the food processor—another item I'd brought from New Jersey. As I spooned cream cheese into the hopper, my mind went back to the unpleasant meeting I'd had with Anabelle's stepmother—who had threatened to sue the pants off the Blend for what happened to her daughter—and the ironic surprise Matteo brought me a few minutes later, when I'd heard Matteo's voice calling, *"Clare? Are you up there? It's dire I speak with you . . ."*

I was still angry at Matteo for rushing off and abandoning Tucker to deal with the afternoon crowd alone, and I planned to let him know it.

"Up here," I called, not wanting my staff to see me argue with my ex. After all, he was still the Blend's coffee buyer—and now he was part owner, too.

I heard his heavy tread on the stairs and a moment later he appeared, his face flushed. It looked as if he'd been running.

"We've got trouble," he announced. *No surprise there,* I thought. *Whenever Matteo's around, trouble follows.*

"What?" I said, my voice tinged with anger. "It couldn't be nearly as much trouble as leaving the Blend during lunchtime rush with only one person to handle everything. Tucker was swamped when I got here. What the hell were you thinking, Matt, disappearing like that, and—

"Clare, listen! I've just seen Gordon Calderone. You know, Gordon from Parasol."

My face must have gone blank because my mind sure had.

"Parasol Insurance," Matteo said. "You know: 'Your Umbrella in Times of Need'? He's been the Blend's insurance representative for over two decades now."

"Oh, *that* Gordon from Parasol." I did remember the man. Short and stocky, built like a football player (with an outgoing personality to match), Gordon used to stop by at least once a week, back during the ancient history around here—when Joy was a little girl and Matteo was still my husband.

"How is Gordon?" I asked. "I haven't seen him in years."

Matteo sat down in Darla Hart's seat. I was glad I'd cleared away the mess because cigarette butts gross out Matteo almost as much as they do me.

"There's a reason you haven't seen him," Matt said, his voice even. "It seems that when Moffat Flaste was managing the Blend, he failed to make the quarterly insurance payments. Gordon sent notice after notice, but they were ignored. He stopped by and Moffat brushed him off, implying the Blend had found another provider. Can you believe that? I could kill the guy. The liability insurance on the Village Blend lapsed months ago. In case of accident or personal injury, we're not covered—not for liability."

I sank down into the chair opposite Matt.

"Oh, no. No, no, no, no . . ."

I told Matt about Darla Hart's visit, and her threat of legal action. After that we sat silently, just staring.

"My god," I said, "for once you weren't kidding. The situation *is* dire."

"She could own this place by the time she's through," said Matt.

"What do we do?" I asked.

"I've renewed the insurance coverage," Matteo said. "It just about emptied my checking account, but it could have been worse. I was honest with him about what happened, and he did what he could, which is sign us up to cover anything that happens in the future—"

"So we're *not* covered for Anabelle?" I asked, even though I knew the answer.

"No, we're not covered for her," Matteo said. "But when the police report about Anabelle's accident is filed, it will be too late for the parent company to deny our renewed coverage or raise our rates. We owe Gordon big time for this favor!"

I nodded in agreement. At least the business was now covered in case another barista took a tumble down the stairs, or a customer slipped on a wet napkin. That was something, at least.

But for me the real surprise was Matteo. I was always the level-headed, pragmatic adult in our relationship, he was always the Peter Pan, yet I didn't even think of checking with the insurance company—something I should have done immediately after the incident (I still didn't think it was an "accident"). Matt, however, was right on it, and he may have saved our butts and our business—at least from future liability. His generous gesture of paying the insurance bill was doubly unexpected.

"We can't tell Madame," I admitted to Matt during that same conversation. "Not about Anabelle, not about the insurance. Not now."

"Why not?"

I told him about St. Vincent's cancer ward, about her saying she was too "tired" to come to see Joy for dinner. Matteo nodded, his face grim.

"No, we can't tell her," he agreed.

I sighed, remembering the look on Matt's face as he said that. Then I slid the cheesecake into the oven, and set the timer.

Maybe Madame would beat the cancer, I told myself.

And Anabelle . . . maybe Anabelle would wake up tomorrow, tell us all what happened, and everything would be solved. Maybe.

But then I recalled the girl's butterfly pulse, her pale face, her twisted rag-doll body at the bottom of the steps, and I felt my heart despair.

Suddenly, a series of rhythmic knocks sounded at the front door. There was only one person who knocked that way—my pride named Joy. I smiled, my spirits lifting.

Fifteen

~~~~~~~~~~~~~~~~~~~~~~~~~~~~~~~~~~~~~~

I opened the door to the apartment, fully expecting to find Joy standing on the threshold. Instead I found Matteo, arms weighted with grocery bags.

"Thanks," he muttered. "I bought so much stuff I couldn't get to my keys."

"I thought you were Joy," I said.

"Why?"

"The knock," I said. "Rat-tat-uh-tat-tat. That's Joy's knock."

"Who do you think she picked it up from?" he said, breezing by me and making a beeline for the kitchen.

I could smell the freshly grated Pecorino Romano wafting up from the grocery bags. Two crusty brown loaves of baguettes rustica protruded from another paper sack.

"It's dinner for three, not thirty," I called over my shoulder, closing the door.

"I only bought a few essentials," he replied. "If I'm going to stay here, I'll need some staples."

Except you're not *staying here*! I thought. *At least not for long.*

"Fine" is the word that actually came out of my mouth.

"I *know* what you're thinking," Matt called. "And don't worry. You can have the bedroom. After dinner I'm going to clean out the storage room upstairs. It used to be my bedroom when I was a boy. I can haul up the fold-away bed from the basement, and I should be set for the week."

Then Matt threw me a teasing leer. "Unless of course you've got a better idea for the sleeping arrangements."

"No," I said. "Sounds like you've got it figured out just fine."

Matt rolled up his sleeves and checked his watch.

"You still have that thing?" I asked, surprised.

"I *love* this thing," he said with a smile.

It was a sporty self-winding duograph chronometer from Breitling (list price new: $5,000; "gently" used price at Torneau's resale shop: $1,500). I had scrimped and saved during our first year of marriage and even borrowed some money from Madame so I could surprise Matt on our first anniversary. It moved from time zone to time zone with ease and even displayed the correct time in two zones at the same time—the perfect timepiece for a globe-trotter traveler like Matt.

"Wow, it's late! I'd better start cooking," he said.

"Well, don't open the oven," I warned. "You'll ruin dessert."

While I prepared the items for the cheesecake topping, Matt went to work behind me, bumping and elbowing me the entire time. God, he was annoying in the kitchen!

First he set a pot of water on the stove and lit the fire

under it. A moment later I heard the crinkle of shopping bags as he dumped his plunder onto the counter.

"They had Maytag Blue Cheese—for once," Matt said as he tossed a blue-marbled brick of soft cheese into the refrigerator.

I arched my eyebrow. "'*Essentials*,' you said. Frightfully expensive blue cheese is an *essential*?"

"It is—in *my* house," he said.

Just let it go, I chanted to myself. *Don't take the bait. Just let it go.*

"And here," he added. "Look at this!"

Matt proudly displayed a slab of bacon the size of Rhode Island.

"So you've brought home the bacon at last," I blurted. *Whoops.*

"Very funny."

Matt loaded the crisp green leaves of Romaine lettuce into the vegetable bin, and plastic containers of grated cheese onto the refrigerator shelf next to a pint of heavy cream.

"So," he said, "speaking of, uh, 'bringing home the bacon'—is that why you came back here from New Jersey to manage the Blend? Are you having money problems?"

"No." I bristled. "I was doing just fine, thank you very much."

"So what's the reason then? Why did you come back?"

Matt leaned a hand on the counter. With his rolled-up shirtsleeves, his muscular forearm caught my eye. Tanned by the Peruvian sun and slightly dusted with fine black hair, it reminded me of the first time we'd met on a brilliant June day along the Mediterranean.

I was a college student at the time, spending the summer with my great-uncle's family while studying Italian art history. He was backpacking across France and Italy, heading for Greece. I'd thought he was a Michaelangelo statue come to life. *Stop it, Clare.* I warned myself. *Stop it.*

His dark brown eyes locked onto my green ones—he was waiting for an answer.

"I, uh . . . I guess I wanted a change," I told him, attempting to change something else in that moment—my focus. I forced my eyes to shift away from his forearm and over to a two-pound bag of Carbone's homemade fettuccini. "The suburbs were nice enough, don't get me wrong. I mean, New Jersey has its charms—"

Matt snorted.

"It *does.* And it's a good place to raise a child. I was happy there, at least in the beginning. But now that Joy's gone away to school—never to live with Mom again—I thought I should try making a change, take Madame up on her offer to start again."

"That's it?"

"What do you mean, 'That's it'? Gail Sheehy created an entirely revised version of her book *Passages* based on that premise alone."

Matt stared blankly.

"You know," I said, *"New Passages?"*

Matt continued to stare blankly.

"Longer life spans," I explained. "Second Adulthoods that begin after children leave the nest? You've never heard of this?"

Matt shook his head.

"Well, *you're* older now, too," I reminded him. His eyebrow rose, as if to say *duh.* "What I mean is: Haven't you thought about the changes that come with reaching middle age?"

Matt dismissively waved his hand. "I never think about that stuff."

Of course you don't, I thought, because you're another type that Sheehy writes about—the man who wakes up one morning on the Dark Side of Forty and realizes his bright future full of possibilities has dimmed and narrowed. That he's too old to be a young . . . Well, a young *anything*.

Matt would never admit it, but I was pretty sure his sprint to Parasol Insurance earlier today was evidence he was reaching that Dark Side of Forty stage. The *old* Matt never thought ahead, never took responsibility, and never, ever took cash out of his own pocket to help clean up a mess.

The old Matt would have taken the first plane out of town—waved *aloha* to me and Madame and let us pull out the buckets and mops while he made a deal at a *luau* for five hundred bags of Kona.

Sure, I could chalk up the change to Madame's ownership deal. Even experiments in public housing (according to one of my customers who worked for the City of New York) have suggested that if you give people a way to own a thing, they suddenly find the time, energy, and money to invest in protecting and improving it.

And yet . . . that ownership theory didn't really hold water when it came to Matt. For one thing, I was sure Matt had already assumed he'd inherit the Blend anyway—yet his actions had always been aloof where the Blend's business was concerned. All he ever seemed to care about was the freedom to come and go as he pleased.

And—in terms of ownership theories—what about me? I found myself thinking. When I was *his* exclusively, he took me for granted. Just like the Blend.

Whether it was the new part-ownership status or the Dark Side of Forty change-in-perspective thing, I didn't know. All I knew was that Matteo Allegro was showing positive signs of change.

Change is (usually) good. And ten years ago, I would have rejoiced at it. But I couldn't rejoice now. Now our child was grown—and I wanted *my* freedom. After all the years of pining away for the man, I had finally reached an emotional point in my life where I wanted to be free of Matteo Allegro and all of his heartbreaking patterns.

Madame wouldn't understand or accept my decision, but that was just too bad. Even with her cancer scare, I'd find a way to gently tell her. A tricky scheme (even one as well meaning as Madame's) wasn't going to erase years of pain, frustration, and resentment. Not for me anyway.

"Heads up," Matt said, tossing me a bundle of fresh garlic. I caught it.

"It goes in the hanging basket behind you," he said with a wink.

God, this was infuriating. My ex-husband knew my kitchen better than I did—and wasn't shy about making sure I knew it. Well, I reminded myself, he *had* lived here as a boy with his mother before Pierre had moved them up to Fifth Avenue. Resentment rose in me anyway. I checked my watch. For Joy's sake, I reminded myself yet again, I wasn't going to start any battles with her father. Not before dinner anyway.

"So what's on the menu?" I said, changing the subject to one that was nice, safe, and neutral: Food.

"I'm going with the fettuccini carbonara," he said. "It's rich—especially when I make it with fettuccini instead of thin spaghetti—but Joy always loved it when I cooked it for her. And it's probably the only dish I can still cook better than my soon-to-be-chef daughter. She's probably a real pro now that she's been formally trained."

"Matt, she just started culinary school. She's years from graduation," I said. "In fact, she confessed to me that she's having a little trouble in one class. Apparently a hollandaise broke and the guest instructor humiliated her in front of the rest of the class."

"Maybe she needs a few pointers from her dad."

"You think you could help her?" I asked hopefully.

"Sure. And this should cheer her up, too." Matt

reached into his pocket and withdrew a small, square box. "Check this out," he said.

I opened the box.

"I picked it up in Mexico," said Matt.

I looked down and almost winced. *Not again.*

When Joy was nine, Matt brought a bracelet back from one of his endless trips and gave it to her. The bracelet was lovely, its delicate links made of pure, fourteen-karat rose gold. Since then, Matteo had presented her with various charms, distinctive little items he found over the years in foreign lands on his never-ending quests for the richest coffees, the bluest waves, the tallest mountains—and (I'm sure) other sorts of stimulation as well (cocaine and women).

For a lot of years, those seemingly thoughtful little baubles from Dad, transported from faraway lands, delighted Joy. In grade school she wore the bracelet constantly. In junior high less so, and by high school . . . Well, the truth was, Joy hadn't worn that charm bracelet in public since the junior high school prom—not that Matt was ever around enough to notice.

"It's a charm," Matt explained. "For Joy's bracelet. Think she'll be wearing it tonight?"

"I don't know . . ."

"Like it?"

"It's . . . interesting," I said diplomatically. What I was looking at was a little nugget of gold shaped like an incredibly stout woman wearing a bowler hat and holding an ear of corn over her prodigious breasts.

"It's supposed to be Centeotl, the Aztec goddess of corn," Matt explained, after noting my puzzled expression. I nodded, not quite *up* on my religions of Mesoamerica.

"And the significance is?" I asked.

"Corn was central to the Aztec diet. Their corn goddess was a harvest god. And since Joy is going to be a chef, I figured, you know . . . food, harvest . . ." Matt's voice trailed off, and he shrugged his broad shoulders.

"How very Joseph Campbell of you," I said, trying to be positive. I handed the box back to him and laughed as I added, "as long as it's not some sort of *fertility* goddess."

Matt stared down at it. His brow wrinkled. "Actually I think it is."

We were interrupted by another rhythmic knock—the identical one Matt had used.

"Joy!" I said.

She'd finally arrived. The two of us ran a sort of short foot race (which looked about as embarrassing as it sounds) to see who would be the first to greet her.

I won—by virtue of being short enough to duck under Matt's arms, just as he was pulling open the door.

"Hello!" I said, reaching up to hug my daughter, who either had grown another two inches since the last time I saw her or was wearing stacked heels.

"Mom," she cried, hugging me back. "I saw Tucker downstairs and he told me about Anabelle. How terrible!"

"Hi, kiddo!" Matt said. Joy rushed into his arms.

"I missed you so much, Daddy," she said, squeezing him tightly.

I was about to close the door when the shadow of another figure fell across the threshold.

"Mom. Dad," Joy said, bursting with excitement. "Here's my *surprise*! I want you to meet Mario Forte."

A young man stepped into the room. He was tall for an Italian. That's the first thing I noticed. Taller even than Matteo. (Now I knew why Joy was wearing stacked heels!) His hair was black and long and tied back in a loose ponytail. His lips were curled into a slight smirk which, to my mind, marred his otherwise good features. He wore black slacks and a long-sleeved black shirt, unbuttoned far enough from the neck to show a gold chain dangling between sculpted pecs. The sleeves of the shirt were rolled up and I glimpsed some sort of tattoo around his bicep—it looked like barbed wire.

Joy looked up at the young man with something akin to hero worship. *Uh-oh*, I thought. She was smitten. And my ex-husband tensed the moment he realized it.

So much for a relaxing evening.

"Mrs. Allegro," said the young man, taking my hand. "It is a pleasure to meet with you at last. Joy has told me so much about you."

Is that right? I thought, then why didn't she mention I'm "Ms. Cosi," and no longer "Mrs. Allegro"?

"And you must be *Mr.* Allegro," Mario said, stepping up to Matteo and reaching out to shake his hand. "I did not expect to meet you so soon—"

"I'll just bet you didn't," Matt muttered, his jaw muscles working. They shook hands, but neither seemed to put much enthusiasm in the gesture.

"Joy told me that her father was a mystery man," Mario said with a little chuckle. "The 'mystery' was when you were going to finally make an appearance at home."

Matt looked like a pressure cooker ready to blow. Thank goodness Joy was canny enough to step between the two men.

"Something smells good," she said, her voice a little too high-pitched. "What's for dinner?"

"Carbonara," Matt said through clenched teeth.

"And my cappuccino walnut cheesecake!" I added in a pitch even higher than my daughter's. My god, in an effort to cut through the tension, I was actually chirping like Doris Day.

Joy looked at me. "Surprise!" she said feebly.

"Not the surprise we expected," I said with a look that

told her: *You should have warned me.* "Well, I'd better set another place at the table. Why don't you both make yourselves comfortable."

Though I don't consider myself a superstitious person, as I set a new place at the dining room table, I cursed Centeotl, the Aztec goddess of corn and fertility, along with my ex-husband for bringing that golden witch under my roof.

Sixteen
∿∿∿∿∿∿∿∿∿∿∿∿∿∿∿∿∿

I returned to the kitchen to find Mario and Matteo having a little disagreement about something. Matt clutched a meat cleaver in one white-knuckled fist—not a good sign.

"Fettuccini carbonara should be prepared with pancetta," Mario was saying. "Never with American bacon."

"Carbonara is a Depression-era dish created by Italian-Americans," Matt stated. "How many of them had pancetta? Anyway, Joy likes carbonara prepared with *bacon*." He turned to Joy for some support. "Don't you, kiddo?"

Joy turned to me, her eyes pleading.

(It occurred to me in that moment that the first young man my daughter chose to introduce to her elusive father was a tall-dark-and-handsome Italian cook with an arrogant attitude. Even their names were similar. My, my, how Freudian.)

My heart went out to my daughter. But it was *her* mess. And she was a big girl. (Even bigger with those heels.) I shook my head and showed her my empty palms. *No tricks up my sleeve for this one, honey.*

"So what sort of bacon then?" Mario asked, the smirk defining his level of sincerity. "Sugar cured, hickory smoked, or do you prefer those bits you find in the supermarket jars?"

"Don't be a jackass," said Matt.

Joy was about to jump in, but I stopped her.

"Well, you must admit," said Mario, "the dish does sound like something you get at the House of the International Pancake."

"It's IHOP—the International House of Pancakes," said Matt. "You obviously don't know everything."

I sighed, considering the scene. Here I was in New York City, an international center for art, commerce, intellect, and culture. A prime symbol of Western Civilization. And what was I doing? Watching two alpha males argue over a greasy slab of pork fat.

As the barbs continued, I pulled Joy aside. "Your first lesson in understanding men," I whispered. "There will often be times like these—when they act as if they've been evolution-proof for the last fifty thousand years."

The baking timer went off, startling everyone into silence.

"Saved by the bell," I whispered to Joy. She smiled with grateful relief as I announced: "Mario, Joy, it's time to clear out! I have to make the cheesecake topping, and your father has to make dinner."

I reached into the wine cooler and clutched the first bottle I could feel.

"Here!" I said, thrusting it into Joy's hand. "Why don't you go into the dining room with Mario and open this."

"Wow! Mom!" Joy shrieked at seeing the label on the bottle. "Proseco, 1992. What's the occasion?"

Ohhhhh, nooooo, not the Venetian champagne. That was a mistake. But too late now.

"Just happy to see you," I chirped, still channeling Doris Day. "And of course—your bringing Mario is an occasion," I managed to choke out for Joy's sake.

I heard a disgusted grunt from behind me. A loud slam came next, as Matteo crushed a half-dozen whole cloves of garlic with one flat-sided blow from his meat cleaver. Chunks of the powerful-smelling herb bounced off the walls.

Mario leaned close and took my hand again. "Thank you so much, Mrs. Allegro."

It's Cosi, you idiot!

With a wet slam, Matteo slapped his slab of good old American bacon onto the thick wooden chopping block near the sink. With quick, angry jabs, he began mincing the smoked pork into tiny shards.

"Let's go into the dining room," Joy said, seeing the flash of disgust cross Mario's face.

After they'd quickly retreated, I turned to Matteo.

"You!" I hissed in my most grating ex-wife voice (a harridan tone so annoying I actually annoy myself when I use it). "Make your damn pasta and keep your mouth shut. Your one and only daughter has brought a man home to meet her parents, and you are not going to ruin this night for her!"

Matt stared at the garlic scattered across the cutting board. I took his silence for defiance.

"You are going to behave yourself or leave right now," I added.

Matteo crushed another clove of garlic—this one with his fist.

"The pasta will be ready in half an hour," he said, turning up the fire under a large pot of boiling water. "When you're finished with your cheesecake, you can make the Caesar salad."

"Oh, I'll get right on it," I replied tersely. As I knew already, there was no kitchen large enough!

Fortunately, things went somewhat better from then on. During dinner, Joy talked about school, and about how she aced her last saucier project—with Mario's help.

Mario, it turned out, was from Milan, but had spent the last three years in New York City, joining a cousin who had emigrated years before to work in the restaurant business here. Mario himself had worked in a series of restaurants in both Italy and France—first as a dishwasher, then a waiter, then as a sous-chef. He was twenty-five years old and had landed a full-time kitchen staff position at Balthazar, one of the top restaurants in Soho.

I asked how he'd met Joy. Apparently, he'd been friends with the guest saucier instructor who'd balled Joy out for ruining her hollandaise sauce. Mario had been observing the class in support of his friend, and after the class, he'd approached Joy.

"My heart went out to this pretty little girl. She looked as though she was going to cry—and I remembered how *stupido* I felt when I had made a mistake at my first job in a four-star restaurant. I was hired the day I applied because the chef was on the spot. He handed me the house recipe for cream of mushroom soup and told me to prepare it for Sunday brunch. I went to work, and when it was done, the chef tried some."

"He didn't like it?" I asked.

"No, no," Mario replied. "The soup was superb, and for a very good reason. Along with the cultivated mushrooms, I had diced a thousand dollars' worth of truffles. I felt so like an ass because I had made the most expensive pot of soup in history! I explained to the head chef that I had never taken classes, that I always learned on the job. But the little restaurants I had worked in . . . Well, they didn't serve truffles. I got fired anyway. Of course, that was a long time ago."

"Oh, so you don't make mistakes anymore?" Matt said.

Mario's eyes met Matt's. "No."

Joy hung on Mario's every word. The boy's arrogance would be interpreted by her as confidence. I knew this because I had been young and in love with a guy like this, too.

In Mario's defense, however, he was otherwise polite, lively, intelligent, and when it came to Joy, clearly considerate. Of course Matteo hated him already, even after Mario diplomatically asked for seconds on the carbonara (that was a nice surprise) and repeatedly complimented the Venetian champagne.

By the time dessert rolled around, things were far more congenial than they had been when the long evening began, though Matt still eyed Mario warily and answered most of the questions asked of him with a monosyllabic grunt.

Along with the chilled cheesecake, I served a hearty espresso made with a dark-roasted Antigua bean. Its smooth nutty flavor perfectly complemented the walnut crust of the cappuccino cheesecake.

To my delight, Mario went on and on about the quality of the espresso. (Okay, I admit it. The kid managed to work his way onto my good side.)

By eleven o'clock, Joy said it was time to go, claiming she had an early class tomorrow. With a final hug, she and her new boyfriend were gone.

"She sure can pick them," Matteo said miserably.

"She's a chip off the old block," I replied.

Matteo looked at me, puzzled for a moment.

"Our daughter managed to find a guy who is self-assured to the point of arrogance, something of a know-it-all, but smooth and charming as they come. Sound familiar?"

"No," Matteo said.

"No? You idiot! He's just like you!"

"What? You're crazy! He's nothing like me!" Matteo threw up his hands. "I'm going to clean out the second bedroom so I don't have to sleep on the couch."

"Fine," I replied. "I'll clean up here, then go down to the Blend to close up with Tucker."

I hadn't forgotten the sad events of this day. And I remembered that I still had to prepare a list of employees and their addresses and phone numbers for Detective Quinn—which I didn't want to mention to Matt, considering his opinion of our local gumshoe. I also had to juggle everyone's work schedule to cover Anabelle's absence.

When the kitchen was clean, the dishes done (except for a single espresso cup that seemed to be strangely missing), I bagged up the garbage to carry it downstairs. On the landing just outside the front door I found a second plastic bag full of stuff—boyhood items Matteo was tossing to make room for the foldaway bed. I peered into the bag.

There were a few dog-eared magazines, mostly, dating back to the 1970s, including vintage issues of *Playboy*. There was an old board game, Risk, which I thought quite appropriate, and a battered copy of Ernest Hemingway's paean to the bohemian life in Paris, *A Moveable Feast*—undoubtedly a seminal influence on Matteo's young mind.

Amazing what someone's garbage will tell you.

Then it hit me. Garbage—specifically the garbage in the can in front of the Blend's basement steps this morning, the garbage that Anabelle supposedly slipped on before she was sent down the stairs and into a coma.

I dropped my own sack of kitchen garbage on the landing and hurried down the steps. I wanted to grab the bag in question before Tucker carried it outside to be collected. The crime scene unit had already examined the bag and dismissed it as evidence, but they didn't know this place as well as I did.

Within that Blend garbage, there might be something that they'd overlooked, some clue that would help me prove what I knew in my gut: That Anabelle's "accident" was no accident at all. It was a slim hope, perhaps, but given the news of our insurance fiasco, I was close to desperate.

As I entered the Blend from the back staircase, Tucker was just locking the coffeehouse's front door. "Garbage!" I cried out like a madwoman. "Where is this morning's garbage?"

"Lined up in the basement with the rest," Tucker replied. "I was about to put it outside."

I took the basement stairs two at a time, and scanned the line of dark green plastic bags lined up against the stone wall. After singling out the one with lingering flakes of fine grayish white powder still clinging to its waterproof surface—the one the crime scene unit had dusted for prints—I dragged it directly underneath the fluorescent lights.

I was surprised they hadn't impounded the whole mess, but I guess they didn't need foul old garbage stinking up their evidence room. And anyway, Detective Quinn had made it clear that everything about the scene and Anabelle's body made the incident appear to be an accident, not a crime.

I gingerly unwrapped the wire tie on the top of the bag and opened the mouth. Inside was a second bag sealed with a wire tie as well. This was standard for the Blend. Coffee and espresso grounds, as well as tea leaves, are moist, so we use two bags behind the counter—one inside the other—as double protection against breakage or spillage.

After opening both bags, I peered inside, not quite sure for what I was searching. At first glance, the contents seemed typical enough. The bag was filled with off-white paper filters stained with coffee grounds, loose grounds, and caked grounds dumped from espresso baskets— some still retaining their packed circular shape hours after being discarded. Most of the paper filters were encrusted with dark black grounds that shined like oil under the harsh light. These were the remains of our famous French Roast—the Blend's Brew of the Day on that unfortunate evening.

Pie-pan-sized paper filters from another urn were lined with a lighter, brown mass that resembled mud—which told me a Colombian bean had been brewed at one point (and that the beans had been ground too fine, which probably resulted in a bitter cup. I made a mental note to lecture the staff yet again on the proper grinding techniques).

Soiled napkins, disposable plates, and half-eaten pastry sat amid crushed cardboard cups, stirring sticks, paper towels, and other refuse, but none of it could be considered unusual—let alone incriminating.

I sighed.

So much for intuition.

And yet . . . I couldn't dismiss my feeling that there was something here in this garbage bag that could shed some light on what had really happened a little over twenty-four hours ago.

I stared down at the contents of the plastic sack and realized that this foul garbage was possibly the last thing Anabelle saw before her tumble down the stairs. The morbid thought sent a slight shudder right through me, which is the reason I screamed like a banshee when I felt strong fingers grip my shoulder.

After the bloodcurdling noise echoed off the thick stone walls, a voice spoke—

"Good god, relax. It's me."

"Matt!"

"Didn't you hear me coming down the steps?"

"I was lost in thought," I said, my voice still shaking a bit from the scare. "What the hell are you doing down here anyway?"

"I found this bag of kitchen garbage leaking on the landing," Matteo said, tossing the sack onto the pile. "I brought it down before it ruined the parquet."

"I guess I dropped it when I came down here."

"You dropped the garbage on the way downstairs to put the garbage out? Clare, are you feeling all right?"

"Forget it," I said, facing him. It was then that I noticed the tiny espresso cup Matteo gripped in one hand.

His eyes followed mine. "I found it on the end table in the hallway," Matteo explained. "Mario must have left it there after dinner. Joy was showing him the apartment, I guess."

"So put it in the dishwasher," I replied. "Unless you think it's so polluted by that boy's touch that you're planning on throwing it away."

There was a pause as I waited for Matt to say something.

"I think they were kissing," he said.

I blinked. "That's what two people who like each other tend to do," I said evenly. "Usually they do it every chance they get."

"So, you really think she likes him?" Matteo asked.

There was a touch of anguish in Matt's voice that, to be honest, I couldn't share. I had lived through too many of Joy's grade school crushes, her junior high school dates, a summer fling, and even a serious high school romance to fret over yet another romantic interest in my daughter's life. Of course, Matt was there for none of it, so this was all new to him. Poor man.

"Don't you know how to read coffee grounds?" Matt asked.

Now that was a silly question, and certainly a leading one. My ex-husband knew perfectly well that I read coffee grounds the way some read tarot cards. I learned it from my grandmother, who learned it from hers.

I know, I know! It sounds ridiculously medieval. Yet it *is* an ancient art, and coffee ground and tea leaf divination—collectively known as tasseography—is a little like interpreting a work of art.

Coffee residue or tea leaves dry at the bottom of a cup to form a "picture." Interpreting that picture is similar to gazing at clouds and trying to see the shapes of bunnies, locomotives, sheep, what have you. And as with cloud gazing, two people may see the same cloud and interpret it entirely differently.

One might see a mushroom, for instance, and another a mushroom *cloud*—which makes tasseography a kind of Rorschach test, too, since the person seeing the mushroom and the one seeing the nuclear detonation might just have *slightly* different worldviews.

In any event, to "divine" tea or coffee, you study the "picture" created by drying tea leaves or coffee residue on the bottom of a cup. You then let your subconscious loose to freely associate ideas.

When I was young, I thought it was a good party trick, and I often used it as a way to meet people, including boys. As the years passed, however, I learned that my divination skills with coffee grounds could be uncannily accurate. A few things happened that scared me. And I now did it only rarely.

"What do you see?" Matt said, waving Mario's used espresso cup under my nose.

I wanted to turn away, but despite my better judgment I gazed into the depths of that cup. The remains of the coffee grounds had dried to form the distinctive shape of a hammer in the center of the cup. Around that hammer was a halo of stains shaped like licks of fire.

"Don't be silly," I said, pushing the cup away. "You know it's just a parlor trick. And I haven't done it in years. I can't tell you anything more about that boy than you already know."

"I know I don't like him."

"Fancy that."

Abandoning my quest, I tied the garbage bag again. Out of habit, I tied the inner bag first. But as I was about to close the outer bag, I noticed a bulge on one side of the sack. A wad of garbage had ended up wedged between the two layers of plastic. From working behind the counter myself, I knew that happened sometimes, usually when some last-minute trash turned up after the inner bag, filled to the brim, had already been sealed.

I opened the outer bag wide and reached down between the plastic layers.

"What are you doing *now*?" Matt said, clearly repulsed.

"Reading garbage," I replied. "A whole other brand of divination."

"Not if you count the supermarket tabloids. Didn't they go through the late JFK Junior's garbage on a fairly regular basis?"

"I guess that's why they call it muckraking," I said, poking around until my fingers closed on what felt like a mushy mass of cold, wet spinach. Steeling myself, I drew out the sloppy blob.

Matt watched over my shoulder as I opened my hand. A hand that was stained with a wad of used tea leaves. Green tea leaves, just about enough for a grande cup's worth.

Anabelle herself was not a tea drinker, so she must have brewed it for someone else. No doubt, the tea leaves were wedged between the two bags because she'd already tied the first bag for the night when she'd tossed the leaves away. So brewing that tea must have been one of the last things she'd done that evening.

If I was correct, and someone *had* entered the store and assaulted Anabelle that night, then said person was a *tea drinker*.

My mind raced. Tea drinkers were not common at the Blend. But just today I'd spoken to four—Letitia Vale, who had no motive; Anabelle's stepmother, Darla Branch Hart, who either had a motive or was simply an opportunist in the face of her stepdaughter's tragedy; and the two Russian dancers, Vita and Petra, who certainly did have a motive.

"What's up?" Matt asked. "What are you thinking?"

"That maybe I should have learned to read tea leaves instead of coffee grounds."

Seventeen

~~~~~~

THE next morning, I opened the Blend on time. At ten minutes after six, Dr. John Foo was through the door like clockwork.

"Good morning, Clare," he said.

"The usual, Dr. Foo?"

"Yes, thank you."

As I pulled the two espresso shots for the double tall latte, I made the usual small talk with the handsome young Chinese-American medical resident. After his morning workouts at the dojo down the street, he was usually in a chatty mood. For the past four weeks, since I began managing the Blend again, I listened and learned.

The first time we met, he'd told me one of the forms he studied was Wing Chun Gung Fu. "It was actually invented by a Buddhist nun named Ng Mui," he'd said.

I knew nothing about martial arts, or Buddhism. But any form of self-defense invented by a nun was definitely worth learning more about in my book, so I'd been chatting about it with him ever since. Dr. Foo had even showed me a few simple moves, encouraging me to take it up at his dojo—but finding free time had been a challenge over the last four weeks. The struggle to get the Blend back on its feet had been all-consuming.

"So how are things at the hospital?" I finally got around to asking as I gave him his latte.

"They're going well," he said. "I'm learning a lot on this rotation in the intensive care unit."

He took his first sip, closed his eyes and smiled. "Great cup, Clare. As usual. Thanks."

"You're very welcome."

As he picked up the protective cardboard sleeve and slipped it onto the very hot cup, I asked, "Have you learned anything more about Anabelle Hart?"

"Oh, yes," he said. "I got the information you wanted. But this has to stay confidential, agreed?"

"Agreed."

What Dr. Foo said about Anabelle's condition shocked me, but it didn't change my plans. So, a few hours later, at just after 10 A.M., Matt took over managing the Blend and I ventured out.

The Dance 10 Studio was located in a refurbished office furniture warehouse on Seventh Avenue South, a bustling thoroughfare that cut through the heart of Greenwich Village's historic district.

Lined with bars, restaurants, off-Broadway theaters, and cabarets, the wide, high-traffic avenue attracted high-spirited crowds nightly. On some Friday and Saturday evenings, it reminded me of Mardis Gras in the French Quarter. Anything went.

On a Friday morning, however, the wide avenue was quiet. The windows of the bars, restaurants, and cabarets were dark, and the vehicular traffic relatively light as I crossed the street.

I actually wanted to approach Dance 10 from the *op-*

posite side of the avenue from where it stood. According to Tucker, there was a little bar located there, and randy college boys, cheap beers in hand, were said to use the vantage to drool up at the dance studio's wall of windows, where honed female forms floated across the wood floor during the last rehearsals of the night.

"The straight little boys start their pub crawls there," Tucker explained to me, "because if they don't manage to get lucky during the course of the night, then at least they've got a female form or two to fantasize about in the wee hours."

I decided to see for myself if there was any truth to that particular rumor—and, unfortunately, there was.

Directly across the avenue from Dance 10 were the tall front windows of Mañana, a little dive of a bar with a fake south-of-the-border motif—the prerequisite sombreros, horse blankets, and piñatas dangled from hooks on its walls and over its stained wooden bar.

Mañana survived for four reasons, according to Tucker:

1. It caught the overflow from the much bigger Caliente Cab Co., a huge bar/restaurant with its most memorable characteristic being a giant-size margarita glass hoisted over its doorway.

2. It served the cheapest beers in the area. (The stuff tasted like "piss," so said Tucker, but it got you drunk for far less money.)

3. The name *Mañana* meant "tomorrow" and was sometimes used among college freshmen who enjoyed showing off their knowledge of high school Spanish. Consequently, "See you Mañana" would confuse their half-drunk friends who hadn't studied the language and they'd end up stumbling into this eponymous dive. And last but not least—

4. The view.

Standing outside the little bar, I pretended to be a twenty-one-year-old college junior with a frosty mug of urine bought during half-price happy hour. Looking up, I could see a clear-as-crystal view of Dance 10's large third-floor practice room. In the early evening with the lights blazing inside, I figured those young men probably fogged up Mañana's front windows pretty good.

This opened up yet another possibility for a motive and a suspect. If college boys were using this vantage to drool from a distance at the beautiful girls in the window of Dance 10, then what were the odds one of them might have become obsessed with Anabelle from afar?

Perhaps one of them had tried to make a pass and failed, and somehow Anabelle ended up falling down the stairs when she tried to get away.

That theory would hold water *if* the front or back door to the Blend had been left unbolted, but it hadn't.

No sign of a window escape, either.

Someone had obtained a key—or made a copy. I sincerely doubted that any of Anabelle's coworkers had any real motive to hurt or kill her. Which sent me right back to Dance 10, where Anabelle rehearsed for hours and a jealous codancer might have slipped the girl's key ring away to make copies.

I climbed the stairs to the studio, bribe in hand—a cardboard tray snugly filled with four double tall lattes (who doesn't like lattes?).

According to the schedule posted in the lobby, Jazz Dance had just finished. Anabelle had attended this class religiously. Typically, she would open the coffeehouse at 5:30 A.M., leave at 9:30 to make the 10 A.M. jazz class, and continue taking dance classes for another four to five hours. Then she'd come back to the Blend to put in another three to five hours.

That's why I'd promoted her to assistant manager. The girl was working the equivalent of a full-time schedule for the Blend, and in the short time I'd known her, she'd been a reliable opener.

"Can I help you?"

A woman in her late twenties with an abundance of good posture spoke to me with the sort of sharp-edged tone that really means, "Who the hell are you? And what do you want?"

She wore a large burgundy sweater over black tights, and her light brown hair had been pulled back into a tight bun. She sat alone at a small wooden desk inside a tiny office covered with schedules, announcements, and show posters. The back wall was lined with old file cabinets and a tall column of stacked chairs.

This must be the second floor "reception and registration office," I decided. According to the building directory in the lobby, this floor also held practice rooms A, B, and C. I could hear piano music filtering out of one closed door, a hip-hop beat out of another.

"I'm looking for the teacher of the ten A.M. Jazz Dance class," I told the young woman.

"You can leave your delivery here," said the young woman. "What do we owe you?"

"I am *not* a delivery person," I said with just enough haughtiness to cow her attitude (a fraction anyway). "I'm the manager of the Village Blend, where Anabelle Hart works."

Her eyes grew wide—as I had expected. Tucker assured me that gossip among show-people traveled "faster than Louisiana lightning."

"What do you want?" asked the young woman, all curiosity now.

"I told you. I want to speak with the teacher of the ten A.M. Jazz Dance class. The one Anabelle attended daily."

"You'll find her in the large recital room. Third floor."

"And her name is?"

"Cassandra Canelle."

An array of leotards and leg warmers thundered down the squeaky wooden staircase as my black boots climbed up. Lord, I thought, these girls may have been light on their feet when it came to performing on stage but off they sounded like a herd of buffalo.

Giggles and chatter receded as I stepped onto the landing. The walls were stark white, as they had been downstairs. Framed black-and-white photographs of dancers leaping and posing hung in a level line. I followed that line to a single doorway. Strains of contemplative classical music grew louder as I moved closer, and I expected to find another class in progress.

To my surprise, I found a single dancer in motion.

She was graceful, lithe, and as elegant in appearance and bearing as Anabelle had been, though her skin was mocha rather than milk-pale, and her age was closer to forty than twenty. I didn't know much about dance, but I knew enough to know her movements were not modern, hip-hop, or jazz. In her violet-blue leotard and skirt, she appeared to be performing the pirouettes of traditional ballet.

Hesitant to interrupt her, I simply watched. The composition accompanying her was tuneful, lucid, and emotional. The opening strings were sad and brooding, the dancer's movements heavy and posed, then came a flurry of almost manic energy. Leaps and twirls matched the tempo with astonishing speed and grace. A bluebird on the wing. An orchid spinning madly.

She seemed so focused in the dance, I was utterly startled when, amid a final high leap, she looked straight at me and sharply called—"What do you need?"

From the doorway I held up the tray of cups. "I hoped we could sit down and talk about one your students—Anabelle Hart—"

The dancer stopped. Her body sagged. A weeping willow.

In the background, the music played on, reaching an emotional intensity that was almost unendurable.

"That's Schubert, isn't it?" I asked.

"What do you *want*?" The accent had a slight Jamaican lilt.

"I want to know who from this studio might have been angry enough or jealous enough to push Anabelle down my service staircase."

Eighteen

〰〰〰〰〰〰〰〰〰〰〰〰〰〰〰〰〰〰〰〰

CASSANDRA Canelle glared at me. Then, with light, even strides, she crossed the polished hardwood floor, placed hands on hips, and inches from my nose, said, "How dare you! What evidence do you have for such a charge? Who of my girls are you accusing?"

"No one. Yet," I said. "I just know that Anabelle's fall was not an accident, and I know dancing is a competitive arena. Do you care about Anabelle?"

"Of course I care about her. She is one of my star students! I am devastated she is lying in hospital. How dare you come here and—"

For the next five minutes, the dance teacher balled me out to the strains of *Der Tod und das Mädchen* (Schubert's "Death and the Maiden").

Boy, did I feel like a heel.

My blunt approach had yielded me useful information—with the young dancers. But it sure as heck was the wrong approach with their teacher.

"Please understand," I said when she finally let me get a word in. "I also care about Anabelle, and I'm determined to find out who did this to her. That's the reason I'm here. And I'm sorry I've upset you. I just need your help to get to the bottom of this. To find out the truth of what happened."

The anger slowly left Cassandra. Her crossed arms relaxed, her wrinkled brow smoothed. She sighed and rubbed the back of her long, slender brown neck. With her dark hair cropped close to her scalp, the perfect swan-like line of it was shown to advantage.

She closed her eyes, shook her head, and murmured, "All I want out of life is perpetual music and an unending expanse of smooth and level floor."

It sounded like a mantra. One I understood. "Don't we all," I told her.

She looked up, spied the cardboard tray in my hand. "How 'bout you give me some of that coffee."

We sat on folding chairs in the corner of the recital room. Her next class was due in ten minutes, and she gave me that time to answer questions.

"How badly did your students want that spot in Moby's Danse?" I asked. "The spot Anabelle won."

"Very badly, Ms. Cosi—"

"Clare."

"Fine, Clare. Moby's Danse is a prestigious modern dance company that tours nationally. They have auditions only a few times a year for the troupe's Young Dancers' Program. If a dancer makes the cut, she has the chance to participate in some of the most exciting choreography being produced in the world today."

"That sounds like a strong enough motive to try getting rid of the competition."

"You're crazy. That's *not* how dancers operate."

"Am I? I spoke to five of Anabelle's fellow dance students yesterday, and a few of them struck me as capable of pretty ruthless tactics."

Cassandra laughed. "Let me guess. You spoke with Petra and Vita, didn't you?"

"Yes. Do you suspect them, too?"

"Only of being Russian émigrés who've had a very tough life. They've got a street attitude and they're brutal competitors, but they would never do that to Anabelle."

"How can you be so sure?"

"For one thing, hurting Anabelle would have done them absolutely no good. Neither of them was even in the running for the spot in Moby's Danse."

"What do you mean? They told me they were—"

Cassandra shrugged. "They lied. Wanted to make themselves look good in front of their friends. Score sheets are private, so they could say what they like, but I know the truth and so do they. Their scores were far too low to get them even among the top ten of the fifty who auditioned."

"Well, who did have something to gain?"

"You talkin' 'bout Courtney now?" said Cassandra, her surprise bringing out the Jamaican lilt. "That slight girl! The sweetest girl I've ever had take a class here?"

"Sweet girls can have a dark side," I pointed out.

"You think that little girl pushed Anabelle down a flight of steps to get her spot in Moby's Danse?" Cassandra asked.

She stared.

I stared back.

She burst out laughing. "You're crazy."

"Why?"

"Ms. Cosi—Clare, these are *dancers,* not mobsters. With the exception of maybe that Tanya Harding ice dancer nut who hired a brute to knee-cap Nancy Kerrigan before the Olympics, there is no sense in hurting your rival physically. There are far too many good performers to think hurting *one* will help you in any way. No, the way to win this game is to perform to your very best. To achieve excellence. As competitive and as catty as dance sometimes is, these girls know that."

I sighed. Cassandra made sense, but I hated giving up a good theory.

"You're sure Courtney couldn't have done it?"

"When was she supposed to have done it?"

"Two nights ago. On Wednesday evening. Anabelle would have been closing up about midnight. It most likely happened around that time."

"Well, I can tell you that Courtney was with me all evening right up until midnight. You see, Moby's Danse loved Courtney, but they didn't like the choreography she chose. She scored so high that they agreed to consider her for a very rare standby spot if she reauditioned with a modern piece, and she hired me to tutor her privately. We quit after midnight, and I dropped her at her home myself in a cab."

"And where does Courtney live?"

"In Brooklyn, not far from my mother. I have an apartment here in the Village, but my mama needed help with some shopping the next morning."

"I see."

"It's preposterous what you suggest," said Cassandra. "You cannot tell me the girl rode all the way to Brooklyn in a cab after an exhausting class, then turned around and took a subway all the way back to the Village to try pushing Anabelle, who is taller and stronger, down a flight of steps."

I sighed. Cassandra was right. On all counts. She'd provided the answers I'd come for, and yet I was still full of questions. Mostly about Anabelle. I had known the girl only four weeks—but Cassandra had been teaching her for twelve months.

"What can you tell me about Anabelle, then?"

"The girl is a natural talent," said Cassandra as proudly as any mother. "She simply never got the training

she deserved. The girl's father died when she was twelve.
After that, her stepmother moved her from town to town
so often there was never any way to have a consistent
course of study. Anabelle told me she had gone to see
Moby's Danse when they'd been on one of their national
tours. They'd given a performance in Miami, and Anabelle waited at the stage door, naively asking if she
could join them. Can you imagine? A teenage kid with
little formal training? She had guts.

"Well, lucky for her they didn't laugh in her face,"
Cassandra continued. "Instead, a kind member of the
company explained to her that she was too young to join
and that the troupe only took members by audition. They
suggested she study here in New York at Dance 10, which
is where the troupe rehearses, and perhaps one day she
might audition on an open call."

"And that's why she traveled to New York," I said.

"Yes," said Cassandra. "She borrowed money from
her stepmother, came to New York a year ago, enrolled
here, and worked her ass off. She auditioned twice in the
last year, but third time's a charm, and last week she got
the spot she'd wanted so much—a Cinderella story."

"Except for the trip down the castle steps."

"Sadly, yes."

"What did Anabelle tell you about her stepmother?" I
asked.

"Oh, that one's a piece of work!" Cassandra blurted.
She rose from the folding chair. Latte in hand, she glided
across the smooth wood floor and gazed out the floor-to-
ceiling windows that stretched the length of the room.

"How so?" I asked.

"Anabelle's stepmother was a nude dancer," said Cassandra. "Anabelle didn't want anyone to know. And neither did her stepmother. The nude dancing brought in
enough money for them to buy nice things, you know? So
she'd do it in one town, then move to another, try to pre-

tend she was classy, hook up with a man with money. When that didn't work out, and it never did, she'd move along to another town, where they didn't know her. She'd go back to nude dancing again, to get the cash built up once more. Then they'd leave again—and so on. You get the picture?"

I nodded. After personally experiencing the costly façade and classless behavior of Darla Branch Hart, I got the picture in living color. What kept me silent a few moments was the sadness I felt on behalf of a talented little twelve-year-old girl being carted from town to town without regard to her well-being—

A thought suddenly occurred to me. An ugly thought—

"Did Anabelle's stepmother encourage Anabelle to . . . you know, do the nude dancing, too?"

"She did, I am sorry to tell you. About six months ago, Anabelle broke down during an evening class. She had noticed the college boys in the bar across the street. Saw them gawking up at the dancers as they sometimes do. After the class, she confided in me—"

"I was wondering if you knew about that bar," I interrupted. "Why don't you install shades or drapes up here?"

Cassandra waved a dismissive hand. "Dancers must learn how to concentrate before an audience. Any audience."

"But you said the gawking boys bothered Anabelle."

"Only because they reminded her of another audience. A much baser audience."

"I don't follow—"

"They made her feel as if she were up here nude dancing. That feeling led her to admit to me how conflicted she felt. I urged her to quit the nude dancing, and she did. The next week, she took the job at your coffeehouse to make ends meet. She told me it was harder work for the money, but it was honest work, and it allowed her to stop debasing her talent.

"You see, the nude dancing forced Anabelle to put up walls between her outside self and her true self. Art does not do that. Art brings you closer to your true self. As Anabelle progressed in her studies here, she came to that awareness."

"I think I understand," I said.

"The things that exploit you—they are the things that harden you. Anabelle had seen such things harden her stepmother, and she confessed to me that she would do almost anything to avoid that kind of life. She wanted her dancing to mean more—as she remembered it meant to her when she first saw Moby's Danse—to uplift the spirit, bring it closer to the true self, not alienate it, bring it down."

I rose and stood with Cassandra. We looked at the darkened windows of Mañana below us. "Life is like that, isn't it?" I said, "Filled with base brutishness as well as higher callings. The vulgar and the sublime."

"Yes," said Cassandra. "And the sooner these girls understand that, the better. The choice is ours to make."

"Not always," I said. "Sometimes the choice is forced down upon us."

"In my view," said Cassandra "that is what art is for: To lift us up again when we are pressed down."

I nodded.

Outside the door, the sound of eager feet echoed down the hall then swarmed the rehearsal room. Leotards and leg warmers: my cue to depart. After a thankful wave to Cassandra, I did.

Nineteen

~~~~~~~~~~~~~~~~~~~~~~~~~~~~~~~~~~~~

"**M**s. Cosi."

"Detective Quinn—"

A lanky beige wall was the last thing I expected to be colliding with upon returning to the Blend. For a moment, I was mortified.

How the heck was I supposed to know Lieutenant Quinn had been sitting at a Blend table waiting for me for the past fifteen minutes? Or that he had moved to greet me at the door like any well-mannered gentleman?

Well, he was. And he did. The man's worn-out raincoat effectively became a coffee-stained toreador's cape, and I'd embarrassingly butted it head-on.

What can I say? My mind had been preoccupied.

I'd *like* to tell you I'd been engrossed in rejiggering the suspect list. After all, my view of the Dance 10 girls as potential assassins was now passé. That left Mommy Dearest, boyfriend Richard Gibson Engstrum (affectionately referred to by Anabelle's roommate Esther as "The Dick"), and . . . ? Could there be others?

As I said, I'd like to tell you that was what I'd been thinking about when I'd collided with Quinn. And I had been sorting through these remaining suspects during my walk back uptown from Dance 10. However, right before I walked through the Blend's beveled glass door, I slipped a hand into my jacket pocket and rediscovered the rectangular piece of cardstock I'd shoved in there the day before. It was the $105 parking ticket I'd pulled off the windshield of my Honda, which had been parked too close to a fire hydrant for most of the morning.

I cursed upon rediscovering the thing, but the truth is I was supremely lucky that the city tow trucks had been behind schedule yesterday; otherwise I would have found the ticket—and my Honda—at the impounding lot in the Bronx.

So there I was, walking back into the Village Blend, reading the small-print instructions from the City of New York about how and where to contest the darned thing, when I'd collided with the lanky beige wall.

I immediately looked up—away from Quinn's brown pants (presumably a different pair from yesterday's identical ensemble)—and beyond the starched shirt and striped tie (sporting today's colors of brown and rust).

Quinn's jaw was still as square as I remembered, his dark blond hair still as short but the stubble was gone. He'd managed to shave close without a scratch. And the shadows under his eyes were less pronounced this morning, though their intense color was still blue enough to require a conscious effort on my part to take a breath.

"How are you?" I asked after regaining my balance and a small portion of my dignity.

The question was simple enough, but it seemed to fluster the detective—as if my asking about his personal well-being was as odd to him as someone asking if he'd enjoyed his recent trip to Mars.

"I'm fine," he answered after an awkward silence. His voice sounded less wrung out today, but his clipped words still had the bite of burnt coffee.

"You look better," I said, trying to lighten things up. "Like you got some sleep, at least, since we last saw each other."

"I'd like to speak with you," he said, chipping each word out of ice.

Okay, so the man had beige walls *inside* as well as *out*. Fine. I wasn't going to dwell on it.

I scanned the room for a place to sit. We had about an hour before the lunchtime rush and only a few tables were occupied. Two customers stood at the coffee bar, behind which I noticed my ex-husband staring at me and Quinn.

To be honest, Matt's dark eyes were shooting us more of a glare than a stare.

I ignored him.

"How about we sit in the corner. Over there," I told Quinn, gesturing to a table near the exposed brick wall— and far from listening ears.

"That's fine."

As I walked him over, I asked, "How long have you been waiting?"

"Not long. Ten, fifteen minutes."

"Did Matt get you a cup of coffee?"

"No."

My jaw clenched. "Well, please sit down. I insist you have a cup with me. I'll be right back."

"What the hell does *he* want?" Matt groused the second I stepped behind the coffee bar. He was putting the finishing touches—whipped cream and chocolate shavings—on two mochaccinos for the only waiting customers.

"Lower your voice," I told him, shedding my jacket. Matt eyed my cashmere blend sweater, bought at Daffy's fall sweater bonanza. (Daffy's Fifth Avenue store was a real treasure trove—designer clothes remaindered at outlet prices, and without having to travel to the typical New Jersey outlet locations.) The sweater's soft pine color brought out the green of my eyes, and the way it fit my petite figure didn't do my breasts a disservice, either.

"Answer my question," Matt demanded. "What does he want?"

"A cup of coffee, for starters," I said. Hands on hips, I waited for Matt to oblige. After all, he was the barista on duty.

"Come off it."

"Why else do people come to the Blend?" I asked.

"Clare, what does he want?"

"I swear, Matt—I can't believe he's been waiting here fifteen minutes and you didn't at least offer him a cup of the house blend on the house—"

"Why, for God's sake? You know these cops will drink anything that's brown and in a paper cup. Half of them aren't even particular about its viscosity level, as long as it's under a dollar."

"You're being insulting to someone who is trying to help us—"

"Us? Or *you*."

"Temper. Temper," I said. "Just make us a couple of lattes."

"No."

"C'mon, just singles."

"I am not wasting my talent on a Robusta-drinking philistine. And neither should you."

With a sigh of disgust, I nudged Matt aside and smacked the switch on the automatic grinder. I took hold of the handle on the espresso basket, dumped the wet grounds, rinsed the basket, and packed the freshly milled coffee beans tightly in.

"He probably keeps a jar of Sanka in his desk drawer," muttered Matt.

"That's uncalled for," I said as I began the extraction process.

"Or better still," Matt whispered into my ear. "Folgers instant crystals."

"Go to hell!" I whispered.

"Temper. Temper."

After the extraction process was finished and the espresso had properly oozed out of the two spouts into separate shot glasses (remember, it should ooze like warm honey, otherwise you've got a brewed beverage— not espresso!), I poured the contents of each glass into their individual serving cups.

Because the lattes would be consumed in the dining room, I eschewed the paper cups and instead used the tall cream-colored ceramic cups stacked in neat rows on a shelf against the back wall. Next came the steamed milk, splashing into the dark liquid like a white tsunami.

I placed the lattes on a cork-bottomed tray, held it high like a good barmaid, and sashayed on over to our corner table, letting Matt watch my hips deliberately swing for good measure. With veiled glee, I could feel him seething silently behind me.

Tray held high, I weaved through the coffeehouse's obstacle course of small marble-topped tables. I noticed Quinn watching me approach from across the room.

He was staring at my swaying jean-clad hips. I couldn't read the guarded expression on the man's square-jawed face, or the cool look in the depths of those dark blue eyes: Not as they watched my hips. Not even as they traveled north, up my pine-colored sweater, pulled tight from my upraised arm.

Now, another woman might have been delighted with this undivided male attention, and I *thought* I would be— but I wasn't. In fact, Quinn's blank stare was making me more than a little self-conscious and my steps slowed mid-room.

What the hell am I playing at? I asked myself. *I'm no flirt. This is really, really stupid.*

I brought the round tray down from its Bavarian beergarten level and began carrying it with two hands, strategically positioning it to block any further view of my pine-colored breasts.

Sure, I may have started the day making a sweater selection with the hopes of seeing Quinn again, but the reality of having him stare at it (or rather *me* in it) suddenly felt like way too much to handle—as if petting my cat in the morning could remotely prepare me for feeding a tiger in the afternoon.

Why in the world did I think I could take on something as uncontrollable in my life as lust? (I mean, beyond the fantasy arena.) And with a married man!

After mentally kicking myself across the room, I set the lattes on the coral-colored marble surface of the table. Quinn still hadn't said a word. Just kept staring.

"Remind me never to play poker with you," I said, trying to break the tension.

"What do you mean?" he asked, continuing to stare.

"Forget it," I said. And then, in an effort to battle my schoolgirl nerves and get back down to business, I launched into the story of my life for the past twenty-four hours. I recounted the conversations I'd had with Esther Best, Cassandra Canelle, and last but not least, Darla Branch Hart.

As I told my story, Quinn watched me wildly gesticulate with the same intense expression he'd given me as I came toward him from across the room.

When I finished, he said, "So . . . you've been working the case."

I nodded.

He sipped his latte. A long sip. Then he leaned back and allowed a mild look of emotion to change his features—a cross between astonishment and admiration. But he said nothing. Not one word of encouragement. Not even a compliment on the latte.

That hurt.

"Well," I said, trying to hide my disappointment, "given what I've discovered—what do you think?"

"What do *I* think?" he said. "*You* conducted the interviews. What do *you* think?"

"I'm not the professional here."

"When you spoke with these women, you saw how they spoke to you—their body language, their tone of voice. What was your impression?"

"My impression . . ." I sipped my latte. Thought about it. "To tell you the truth, I do have an impression I can't shake. Well, really more of a vision than an impression."

"What is it?"

"You really want to know?" I asked.

"No. I like to waste my breath."

"God, you're a tough audience."

"Just tell me, Clare—Sorry, Ms. Cosi—"

"It's okay, you can call me Clare. What's your first name, by the way?"

He shifted uneasily. "It's Mike. Michael Ryan Francis if you count the confirmation name."

"Well, I'll tell you my vision, Michael Ryan Francis, for all the good it will do . . . I see an image of Cassandra Canelle leaping through the air like a blue-violet bird, and telling me all she wants out of life is 'perpetual music and an unending expanse of smooth and level floor.' And then I see Darla Branch Hart's expensive manicure snatching up two wrinkled bills and saying, 'My step-daughter deserves some money . . . and I'm gonna see she gets it.'"

"You see them both?"

"They intertwine in my mind. The images twirl, kind of like dancers on a ballroom floor . . ." I shrugged. "Sounds crazy, right?"

Surprisingly, Michael Ryan Francis Quinn didn't in fact offer me a ride to Bellevue's psyche ward. Instead he said I reminded him of an article he'd read a few years back about the strangeness of our universe.

"Excuse me?" I said. "The strangeness of our *universe*?"

Now who needed the ride to the nuthouse? I thought.

"No, listen," said Quinn. "It applies. In the article, an astrophysicist explained how he was able to see a black hole in the darkness of space. He said, 'Imagine a boy in a black tuxedo. The boy is the black hole. Now imagine he's twirling with a girl in a white dress. The girl is the light from a nearby star. Now imagine the girl and boy are in a dark room, the room is the vast darkness of space. How do you locate the boy dressed in black if he's dancing in a dark room?'"

Quinn paused, waited.

"You look for the girl in white," I said. "The light gives away the dark."

He nodded. "Darkness can't hide. Not forever. Not even in the vastness of space."

Twenty

~~~~~~

"**S**o what are you saying?" I asked Quinn. "That in my vision Cassandra is the light, the good mother, and she's revealed Darla as the bad one—the one who kept Anabelle down and maybe literally pushed her down, as well?"

"We look for motive—and opportunity," said Quinn.

"Well, the motive could be the money she'd get from suing the Blend for a supposed accident. Or she could have been arguing with Anabelle about the five thousand dollars she'd lent her to come to New York. Esther said Darla wanted it back. And if Anabelle didn't have it, it's possible Darla pressured her stepdaughter to go back into nude dancing for it. Darla's obviously too old for that now—so her only quick-fix for absolving the debt would have been to convince Anabelle to go down the low road again. Anabelle could have refused, Darla could have come here to argue further, cornered her, maybe ended up causing her to fall down the steps."

"That's motive enough. What about opportunity? Do you know *where* Mrs. Hart was the night Anabelle fell?"

"No, but I can try to find out."

"That's your best bet. And don't rule out other possibilities. A theory might look pretty on its face, but it doesn't mean you should marry it. I've learned that one the hard way, I can tell you, and not just in my work—"

The admission came with a frustrated sigh that surprised me. I wanted to ask about his loaded implication (that his marriage was going badly), but he just continued with his comments about police work, so I dismissed it as some sort of trivial husbandly annoyance over credit card bills or house chores—one sigh didn't mean his marriage was on the skids, not by a long shot.

"Facts," he continued. "Facts and evidence. This place was locked up tight. Whoever got out of here had a key. Do you have that list of employee names and addresses for me today?"

I pulled the folded paper out of my jeans pocket. I hadn't noticed I'd pulled the parking ticket back out too until Quinn had taken the papers from me.

He glanced at the list of names.

"Tucker is my only other full-time employee besides Anabelle," I told him. "The rest are just part-time workers and full-time students. I already spoke to all of them—Esther face-to-face, and the rest I called late last night to readjust their work schedules, and I honestly can't see any of them as real suspects. None had a plausible motive for hurting Anabelle."

Quinn nodded. "I'll run the names anyway, along with Mrs. Hart. See if there are any outstanding warrants or criminal records."

"Good. But can't you do something in the meantime about Mrs. Hart?"

"Do something? Like what?"

"Like keep her away from Anabelle for one? If she hurt her once, she might try to hurt her again."

Quinn paused a moment. "Anabelle is in the ICU," he said. "She has supervision around the clock. No one's going to harm her there."

"You mean there's nothing you're willing to do to restrain Darla Hart? Aren't you even going to take her down to the precinct and interrogate her?"

"Clare—" Quinn began with a sharp tone. Then he paused a moment and spoke again, this time with the sort of tone you might use when trying to explain calculus to a preschooler. "Clare, you have no evidence to prove she's guilty of any criminal act. Or even that there *was* a criminal act. So the answer to that would be *no*."

God, I thought, that tone was insufferable! "Then what *are* you going to do?" I demanded. "Have you at least questioned Anabelle's boyfriend? I haven't gotten around to him yet."

Quinn frowned and shifted in his seat. "To be honest with you, my work on this case—what I mean to say, *official* police involvement in this case—is going to be limited. My superior knows that the Crime Scene Unit found no evidence that Anabelle's fall was caused by foul play—"

"Yeah, I know. And the rape kit and physical exam proved negative on evidence that there was any attempt at sexual assault."

Quinn's blue eyes widened. It was the first moment he'd showed open emotion since he sat down (surprise, followed by annoyance).

"*How* in the world do you know that?" he asked.

"I have my sources," I said. Mike Quinn grimaced. I added: "I also know that Anabelle is pregnant, which makes her condition even more tragic."

"And how did you find *that* out, too?"

"I told you, I have my sources—"

"Who, Clare?"

His cheeks were actually flushing red.

I shook my head. "No way."

Quinn took a deep breath, exhaled it. "All right, fine. Like I said, there is no evidence of foul play. My boss wants this shut, but he's willing to let me keep it open while there's still a chance Anabelle can wake up and give an eyewitness account to some sort of assault. Meanwhile, I'm supposed to be working on another case—a shooting and therefore a clear-cut homicide."

"So what are you saying, you're going to help me investigate this, but on the side? Why? What's it get you? Free coffee?"

Quinn stared at me with no expression, then he looked away, shrugged. "I like your coffee."

"Really? You didn't say anything yesterday when I gave you your first cup of our house blend—"

"I don't gush. Not as a rule. Certainly not over coffee. But I'll tell you now since you're asking—it was the best damned cup I've had in my entire life of coffee drinking . . . and that's a lot of coffee drinking."

I smiled. "Thanks. What about the latte?" I asked, pointing to the tall cream-colored cup. "Bet that's your first one, isn't it?"

Quinn peered down into it. "Never thought I'd like the fancy drinks—they always seemed sort of—well, you know, sort off—"

"Gay?"

He laughed. "What does that make me if I like it?"

"Not gay. Just . . . oh, I don't know . . . *Continental,* I guess. You know like that Dashiell Hammet detective. The Continental Op."

Quinn laughed again. Then he grew serious. Exhaled. "If my boss gets wind of my helping you out of school, I'm off the case, okay?"

"Okay," I said.

"So whoever your source is, make sure my helping you stays quiet."

"Will do."

Quinn looked down at the papers in his hand, noticed the parking ticket beneath the employee list. "What's this?" he asked, quickly reading it. "A parking ticket—"

"Oh, sorry. You shouldn't have gotten that. Here, I'll take it back."

"One hundred and five dollars? Hydrant violation. What happened?"

"It's no big deal," I said, embarrassed. "I mean, I didn't think I was that close to the hydrant. There was just no other place to put the car for a few minutes. I was going to move it right away, but then I'd found Anabelle, and with all the activity, the car just sat for hours."

I expected Quinn to return the ticket to my outstretched hand with an accompanying cop lecture about traffic safety or fire prevention. Instead, he shoved the ticket into the pocket of his stained trenchcoat and simply said, "I'll take care of it."

"What? No!" I was mortified. The man was already going out on a limb helping me in his spare time. I didn't need him ponying up to the traffic division for my sake, too. "It's okay. Really. I didn't mean for you to trouble yourself—"

"I insist. You were involved in a police action. I can void this for you. Let me."

I really did hate the prospect of having to either write a 105-dollar check, or take off an entire morning to appear in traffic court.

"You'd do that?" I asked. "It's no trouble?"

"Well, it's a little trouble. But it's okay. I don't mind."

"Oh, thank you, Lieutenant, I could just kiss you!" I blurted.

For barely a second, his eyes met mine. Then he

looked away, as if he'd suddenly realized he wasn't supposed to want me to kiss him. Or worse, show me that he wanted it.

Ohmygod, I thought. *Something just happened. Lightning or fireworks or a radioactive mushroom cloud, but for sure something.*

Now it was his turn to fight the awkwardness. He rose quickly from the table, completely draining the cup of latte. "Better go."

"Would you like one for the road?" I asked.

He eyed the empty cup and nodded. "Sure. Okay."

I cleared the table, picked up the tray, and walked back to the coffee bar with an extreme feeling of relief—and renewed confidence.

Now that I knew the attraction was *not* a complete schoolgirl fantasy on my part, I could hold my head up. It was really a matter of pride more than anything. I mean, this wasn't the movies. Simply recognizing an attraction meant absolutely nothing—especially at this stage of life. A flirty spark didn't obligate a man and a woman to act on it, go to bed, get married, have children, divorce, remarry, whatever, for the purposes of some two-hour family drama.

No, in real life, a man and a woman might flirt until the cows come home. They might appreciate each other, be attracted to each other—but that was the end of it. Boring as all get-out, but that was as far as these relationships usually got.

I knew that was all there was between me and Quinn—a mutual appreciation. I was also sure it would lead to absolutely nothing. It was just gratifying to know I wasn't the only one wrestling with feelings that made me feel as awkward and giddy as a high school kid on a first date.

I was just finishing up Quinn's grande latte when the front door opened on a new arrival. Silver-gray hair, rosy cheeks, and a familiar Chanel pantsuit. In black. Still mourning black.

"*Bonjour,* my dears!"

"Madame!" I called. "You look so—" I was about to say "healthy" but caught myself. I'd promised myself not to give away what I knew about her cancer. "—happy."

"Oh, yes! Oh, yes! I have *excellent* news. Two friends canceled on my charity auction tonight. They already bought tickets—a thousand a seat, which they consider a donation. With my Matteo back, I can pass them on to you both . . . Where is he, Clare?"

"Is that my mother here to give me grief?" called Matt, cresting the service staircase with a new bag of freshly roasted house blend.

"Giving you grief is Clare's job, my errant boy," she said as he lugged the heavy bag behind the coffee bar's counter. "Yours is to come here and give your mother a proper greeting."

Matteo swept around the counter, and his mother held out two hands, ready for the customary shake and polite Continental kiss on each cheek. Instead, Matt opened his strong arms and enveloped the frail, impeccably tailored woman in a big old American bear hug.

Madame's pale blue eyes widened with flabbergasted shock as her Fendi heels left the ground, but then her features transformed into a state of surprised pleasure I hadn't seen since Pierre had been alive.

"What's all this?" she asked. "Oh, I know! You need a loan, don't you?"

"A loan? Sure. How about a million five? I always wanted my own jet."

"Can't do," said Madame. "But I'll let you have my frequent flyer miles. I think you can get half a coach seat."

"Nope. It's my own air bus or nothing." Matt released his mother then all of a sudden hugged her again. The sight nearly melted my heart.

"Espresso, Madame?" I asked.

"Please—" she said, her expression of happy surprise now changing to one of puzzlement. "Matt, enough!" she cried, downright dumbfounded by her son's unusual out-pouring of affection. "What's got into you?"

Matt released her, turned abruptly, and headed back behind the coffee bar. "Can't a man miss his mother?"

"No," said Madame, "not when *you're* the man." Her eyes narrowed and bored into mine with a *What gives?* look.

I glanced away quickly, finished Quinn's latte, and handed him the paper cup with the plastic sip lid.

"What do I owe you?" Quinn asked quietly.

"Are you kidding?" I said just as quietly. "You've just saved me a hundred and five dollars and all the pleasures of traffic court. Your money's no good here."

He nodded in thanks and took the cup. "Hot."

"Oh, sorry. Here you go—" I snatched a heat sleeve from the pile near the pickup area. The regulars knew the drill, so we saved time behind the counter by putting the sleeves right where the customers could reach them.

"Thanks," he said, taking it. Then he stopped and stared at the two-inch swath of folded cardboard. "Uh. What's this?"

"What do you mean?" I asked.

"I mean—" He turned it around in his hand, staring at it so helplessly I nearly burst out laughing. Clearly, Quinn needed a tutorial.

"Here, let me show you. First you open the cardboard, then you drop the bottom of the cup in. See, it slips right in, a nice snug fit through the hole—"

Quinn looked uneasy. Embarrassed even. "What's wrong?" I asked.

He shook his head. "Forget it. I mean, thanks, but I gotta go—"

I glanced back over my shoulder. Matt was standing there, arms folded across his chest, a smirk on his face.

"What?" I snapped to my ex.

Matt's eyebrows rose. He lifted his hands, palms up.

Quinn gave Madame a polite nod as he passed, heading for the door.

"You two should come by about eight," said Madame, leaning on the counter. "The auction starts at nine, but we'll have some fabulous music and food, of course, and—"

"Matt should go," I said. "But I can't."

"And why not, for heaven's sake?" asked Madame.

Because the last thing I need right now is to be pushed into a "date" with my ex-husband, thank you very much!

"It's Friday," I said. "The Blend will be packed. I should be here."

"Nonsense," said Madame with a wave of her wrinkled hand. "It's only a few hours. And you have reliable assistant managers. At least you told me that you have them. Let that sweet girl handle it. What's her name? Anabelle—"

I drew in a breath, looked toward the door. Had Quinn left?

Oh, god! I realized he hadn't. He'd stopped by the door. He'd heard Madame. His eyebrows rose and he looked about to speak. I grimaced at him—gave a few quick silent shakes of my head. *Don't say a* thing!

"The Blend is my responsibility now," I said as gently as I could to Madame. "Matt can go tonight—"

I noticed Quinn motioning me to come over to him. "Excuse me, Madame," I said, then I turned to Matt. "Please make your mother that espresso."

"What does he want now?" Matt asked quietly as I passed.

"I don't know," I said.

"More help slipping something into a hole, no doubt," he muttered, disgusted.

I shot Matt the angriest look I could summon.

At the door, Quinn looked down at me. He seemed so tall now that we were standing so close to each other.

"I forgot to tell you something," he said quietly. "Funny. It's the reason I came by to see you in the first place."

"What?" I asked.

He took my hand in his. My throat closed on me and my heart began pounding so hard, I was sure he'd think I was having an attack. But it wasn't anything close to what I'd imagined was happening—

"Here," he said.

I felt a small, hard object being placed into my palm.

"It's caffeine," he said.

I looked down. Cradled in my hand was Matt's vial of white powder. The one Langley thought was cocaine— and Quinn thought could go either way.

"So there it is," said Quinn, lifting his chin in the direction of Matt. "He was telling the truth."

I nodded. "Thank you."

"S'okay," he turned. "And, uh, thanks for the coffee."

"You're welcome," I said, then watched his tall, trenchcoated form exit the Blend and negotiate the traffic across Hudson. I held up the vial and found myself wondering why the man almost forgot to tell me something he'd come here in the first place to tell me—unless he didn't *want* to tell me.

"It's at the Waldorf," said Madame.

He didn't want to tell me, I continued to consider, but he'd told me anyway.

"What's that?" I asked, walking back to the coffee bar.

"I said you must come, Clare. The auction tonight. It's at the Waldorf."

Matt looked at me, mouthed "Anabelle's mother is staying at the Waldorf," and smiled. I nodded, thought of Quinn, and smiled for my own reasons.

"Okay, then," I said. "I'll come."

Twenty-one

"**M**UMBLE, mumble, mumble, LOVELY AFFAIR, mumble, mumble, BUT . . ."

Ah, yes, I thought with a tight smile. *After the compliment, always beware the BUT.*

The gaunt-cheeked Vera Wanged, second wife of a Fortune 100 executive, paused after her "BUT" and smiled. A small treasure in orthodontia now gleamed at me amid the itinerant babbling and clinking glasses of the Waldorf-Astoria's four-story grand ballroom, site of state dinners, gala weddings, and historic press statements.

Above us, luminous chandeliers hung within a gilded balcony perimeter. Below us, the plushest burgundy carpet framed a blond wood dance floor. And on the horizon surrounding us, one hundred tables of ten were adorned in white raw silk, calla lilies, and glowing tapers.

The bartender was just finishing my Black Russian when this woman cornered me. Apparently, amid this crush of overdressed society types seeking alcoholic sustenance, she had overheard a friend of Madame's compliment me on my recent article on U.S. coffee consumption for the *Times Magazine,* thus, I was deemed "worth" speaking to.

I didn't much want to speak to her, however, but I was unwilling to excuse myself (because, frankly, given what Matt and I were about to do, I *really* didn't want to leave the bar without that black Russian!) so I found myself forced into playing Madame's mumble game.

The mumble game was a handy little party tool Madame had taught me when I was a mere twenty-something newlywed. I was attending one of my first grand social functions and my nerves were about as steely as an underdone bread pudding.

"Listen for the HOT words," she'd said.

"What do you mean, HOT words?" I'd asked, wringing the neck of my wine spritzer to within an inch of its life (wine spritzers and Asti Spumantis were about the extent of my cocktail repertoire back then).

"The hot words are the ones you can readily understand amid the mindless chatter and cacophony of party music," she'd said. "They contain the actual meaning."

"Oh, yes!" I cried with the zeal of a college sophomore. "My rhetoric professor talked about that! Isn't that Marshall McLuhan? Hot and cold words? The medium is the message—"

"I'm not talking academic analysis, dear," Madame had said with a dismissive wave. "I'm talking social intercourse. When you hear an annoying string of mumbles, don't bother asking the people to repeat themselves. Mumbles are pointless parsley. Empty dressing. Listen for the meat, the heat—the words you can unequivocally hear. Respond to *that.* And don't be excessively nice. These people are born bitchy. Show some backbone."

So here I was almost twenty years later, continuing to practice what Madame had preached.

"Mumble mumble WOULD HAVE USED A DIF-FERENT mumble," continued the thirty-one-year-old debutante with the unused Ivy League degree and the blinding pair of Bulgari earrings that could readily have paid for my daughter's entire culinary education. ". . . LIKE THE mumble mumble AT MY MOTHER'S mumble mumble. THAT WAS A SPECTACULAR mumble. UNFORGETTABLE. NOT THAT THIS ISN'T."

"Well," I said, "this IS a CHARITY auction, so I guess the important thing is that we REMEMBER to be GENEROUS."

"OH, WELL, mumble, mumble. MY HUSBAND'S COMPANY mumble, mumble FORTUNE 100 AND HIS mumble is GENEROUS WHEN IT COMES TO mumble!"

"FABULOUS!" I told her. "Because, you know, *THE NEW YORK TIMES* is here."

"Oh, really?" she said with the same level of feline disinterest my Java would show toward a thick piece of bloody prime rib. "Are they?"

Yeah, sure, the entire Sunday Arts & Leisure section. Metro is holding their coats in the lobby.

"Clare!"

The call of Madame. Thank goodness. "Will you excuse me——"

I might have gotten away if the woman hadn't dug her French manicure into my forearm.

"Did they send a PHOTOGRAPHER, do you know? *THE TIMES*?"

Curious. No mumbles there. Every single syllable perfectly pronounced.

I gave her a wide-eyed I-just-don't-know shrug, unhooked myself from the white-tipped claws, and with Black Russian firmly in hand, made a beeline for Madame.

Really, since the stock market's turn-of-the-century

plunge this sort of scene felt a lot more desperate. More like verbal hockey than a mumble game. Maybe I should take my inspiration from the Pittsburgh Penguins smacking it around on the Civic Arena ice of my youth—or as my prodigal father might put it—*What I wouldn't give to high-stick some of these people.*

Don't get me wrong. Conversations at these things weren't always so vacuous. Ask a Cooper Union professor to name his top ten favorite buildings in the world, and you've got an entire course in architecture appreciation in one thirty-minute conversation.

Or ask a dignified older couple how they met and before your eyes they've melted into twenty-year-olds reliving a chance meeting in postwar Paris or a nervous blind date in Central Park.

Ask a heart surgeon from Cedar Sinai to name the most important medical breakthroughs over the last five years; a Chase banker which types of small businesses are applying for loans this year; or a Berk and Lee publishing executive what books are on his or her nightstand, and presto! you have a fascinating quarter hour.

All I'm after is a person who is a lively *participant* in this world. The PAP is what I can't abide. Park Avenue Princess. (And Prince, of course; the male version is just as bad.)

This type is either (1) new money and therefore filled with a missionary's zeal to prove they have lots of it along with the high connections and refined tastes that go with it, or (2) old money and so content with their pedigree and trust fund they feel no need to make any effort on their end of the conversation.

The number twos are pretty much self-evident: They don't speak. They just nod.

As for the number ones, Madame advised me to watch for name dropping and carping. According to her: "These people are operating on the theory that simply criticizing is criticism. That the more books, plays, artists, clothing designers, and restaurants they simply abhor (for no thoughtfully articulated reason), the more you will see them as being hard to please and therefore having the best of taste."

Among the PAPs, there are also those who secretly realize they've failed at any real-world accomplishment beyond stockpiling loot and drawing down annuities, so they've solved their problem of having nothing to talk about by making conspicuous consumption their profession.

The following topics tend to dominate their conversations: pursuit of the perfect fill-in-the-blank (spa, tan, resort, hotel, golf course, restaurant, clothing designer, plastic surgeon, therapist, prescription drug); the care and feeding of your fur; and who's purchased what house in the Hamptons.

Given that set of slap-happy topics, I for one didn't have the bank account to play anything *but* the mumble game!

As I made my way over to Madame, black Russian in hand, I admired how regal she looked tonight. Her energy level was as amazing as ever, too. Despite her condition, she had decked herself out in a floor-length Oscar de la Renta with the loveliest lacework at the neck and sleeves. The mourning black wasn't out of place here. Most of the women had worn it tonight, including me.

I hadn't been to a function like this in years, of course, and tried to squeeze into an old cocktail dress—as embarrassing as that was. Madame took one look at me on her doorstep and snapped her fingers. Before I knew it, her personal maid was helping me don an off-the-shoulder Valentino of gauzy silk, twisting up my hair into a neat chignon, and adorning my exposed neck with a delicate antique necklace of emeralds, diamonds, and rubies crafted to appear as tiny linked rosebuds.

Now, at least, I *looked* as if I fit into a thousand-a-plate charity gig. This was crucial, considering what Matt and I had planned.

After we'd met Madame at her Fifth Avenue penthouse—and she'd dressed me with the glee of a vintage Barbie collector—we'd rode up here together in her private car and helped her check in.

"It will be a late night," Madame had told us. "And I'd much rather take an elevator to my room at the end of the evening than a car downtown. Besides which, brunch is always a delight in Peacock Alley." (One of the Waldorf's classy-as-they-come restaurants. Really, their chestnut soup is to die for.)

Madame's decision to check in for the night was actually very good luck for Matt and me. With access to a Waldorf-Astoria room key card, our plan was now foolproof. Or so we'd hoped.

"Clare, we're at table five," said Madame as I approached her.

Five out of one hundred, not bad, I thought. But it made perfect sense, given Madame's high place on the ten-member organizing committee for this benefit.

"Which zip code?" I asked. There were one thousand attendees here. I feared I'd need a road map.

She gestured toward the front of the vast room, near the high stage, on which the silent auction items were being displayed next to individual boxes where bidders would deposit their written offers by the end of the evening. All the items had been donated by patrons. The bulk of them were antiques, objets d'art, or promised services (including a famous Food Channel chef who'd agreed to cater your next dinner party, and a celebrity singer who stood ready to serenade you tonight in a carriage ride around Central Park).

The funds raised would benefit various special programs at St. Vincent's Hospital, a charity for which

Madame's earnest efforts now made more sense to me than ever since she was being treated for cancer there. In fact, as she and I approached table five, I was surprised to see her oncologist rising to greet us.

"Clare," said Madame. "I'd like you to meet Dr. Gary McTavish."

It was Doctor Gray-Temples all right. I had caught only a glimpse of the sixtyish man the other day, talking with Madame in the hospital corridor, as I rode the elevator up to see Anabelle in the ICU. He still had distinguished gray temples in a head of salt-and-peppered hair, boldly chiseled facial features, and a sturdy build, but tonight he'd exchanged his white coat for a black tie, red plaid vest, and black dinner jacket.

"Charmed, my dear," he said, the slight Scottish brogue sealing the Sean Connery impression. "I've heard many good things about you."

"Nice," I blurted as he bent over my hand. "I mean, uh . . . nice to meet you."

Gray-Temples gave me a polite smile, then quickly focused his warm brown eyes back on Madame's now-glowing face. "She's charming, Blanche."

Blanche, I thought. *Hmmmm. Doctor and patient certainly have gotten chummy.*

Gray-Temples then moved to the chair next to his, gallantly pulled it out, and gave Madame a flirty wink. "May I?"

Madame practically giggled. "You certainly may, Gary."

Gary! Not even Doctor *Gary.* Another *Hmmmmm* on my part.

The good doctor pulled out my chair next, but his eyes never left Madame's.

I nervously glanced about, making sure Matt hadn't arrived yet. He had a short fuse and a terribly protective streak with every woman in his life. Who knew what he'd do if he suspected his mother's oncologist was trying to make time with her.

"Greetings, all," said Matt about ten seconds later. He plopped into the empty seat between me and his mother. "Ready?" he whispered to me.

I took a fortifying sip of my black Russian.

"Now we're all present and accounted for!" exclaimed Madame. "Everyone, this is my son Matt, and his wife, Clare—"

EX-wife, EX-wife, EX-wife!

No, I didn't actually shout this over the tinkling piano music, burbling conversations, and discordant rhythmic bleepings of cell phones. Maintaining my composure, I tried instead to refocus my attention on sending another hit of coffee-flavored alcohol down my esophagus. Loving Madame as much as I did, I figured what the heck else could I do?

"—and let me introduce everyone else—"

There were seven other people at the table besides me, Matt, and Madame: Dr. Gray-Temples; Dr. Frankel, a middle-aged African-American doctor, and his corporate lawyer wife, Harriet; a St. Vincent's administrative director named Mrs. O'Brien; a deputy city commissioner from the New York City Department of Health and Mental Hygiene named Marjorie Greenberg and her psychologist husband; and finally—

"Eduardo," said Madame, gesturing to the man on my left. "Eduardo Lebreux."

Why did the name sound familiar? I asked myself.

"Eduardo worked for my late husband," Madame answered before I could ask.

Now I remembered! Eduardo was also the man Madame had said "highly recommended" that idiot Moffat Flaste, undeniably the worst manager in Blend history.

"And now that we've all been introduced," continued

Madame, "I see our first course coming. Waldorf salad. *Bon appetit!*"

I haven't met a lot of fans of the mayonnaise-covered apples and celery salad, which is the original version of the Waldorf (the recipe now includes chopped walnuts), but it was a nostalgic choice for the evening, considering the salad was created at the Waldorf-Astoria Hotel back in the 1890s. Of course, back then, the hotel was located over on Fifth and Thirty-fourth, the very spot where the Empire State Building is now located.

As the salads were being served, I turned to the man on my left. Middle-aged, but how old was hard to tell. Fifty? Sixty? Short of stature, like Pierre, but not nearly as handsome. He had dark hair, thinning on the top and a little too long at the back, a mustache that needed trimming, and a pensive look to his pale green eyes. No wrinkles but the sort of blotchy skin acquired from drinking and smoking to excess since nursery school. He was the sort who could easily appear aged beyond his years. Yet his evening clothes were gorgeous. Possibly Italian. Definitely expensive.

"Excuse me, Mr. Lebreux," I said, "but what did you do for Pierre Dubois?"

"Oh, a little bit of this, a little bit of that—"

Slight French accent. French last name. But first name *Eduardo*?

"Were you raised in France?" I asked.

I felt Matt's hand rest lightly on my arm. I ignored it. There was something shady about this guy, and my gut urged me to do some fishing.

"My father was French," said Eduardo. "My mother Portuguese."

"That's why Mr. Lebreux was so helpful to Pierre in the import-export business," Madame said, leaning toward us. "His connections in France, Portugal, and in Spain, too."

"Yes, that's right. You know how it goes. A shipment here or there, of champagne, port, perfume, whatever, may go missing on its way to America if the right wheels are not—how you say—*greased*."

"Clare—" Matt whispered. His hand moved to my elbow, squeezed.

"How interesting," I said to Lebreux. "Tell me more."

"Really, it's boring stuff. . . . I just helped Pierre with his business."

"And now that Pierre has died and his business is closed," I said pointedly, "what do you do?"

"Oh," he said, looking away as if bored. "A little bit of this. A little bit of that."

"Clare!"

The entire table jumped and turned. Now every one of our dinner companions was staring at us.

Smooth, Matt. Smooth.

"Excuse me, everyone," said Matt with a sheepish smile. "I, uh, left my Palm Pilot in Mother's room, and it's vital I retrieve it. Clare, I'm sure you'll remember where I set it down. We'll be right back—"

I was reluctant to leave off my questioning of Eduardo, but I was even more reluctant to be parted from my right arm, which was being aggressively tugged upward by an ex-husband whose carved marble biceps were no match for me.

"Go on, then," said Madame, who looked oddly pleased by this announcement. I didn't know why until we'd taken two steps away. "Matt's father used to make excuses to slip away from parties, too. Matt is so romantic! Just like his father!"

"Matt," I whispered. "Did you hear that? Your mother thinks—"

"Let her," he said. "Better she suspects us of having a sexual fling than what we're really going to do."

I myself wasn't so sure.

Twenty-two

〰〰〰〰〰〰〰〰〰〰〰〰〰〰〰

THE elevator door slid open. I inhaled, exhaled, and wrung my clammy hands.

"Don't worry," Matteo had told me back in Madame's suite. "Everything has gone smoothly so far, hasn't it?"

"If by 'smoothly' you mean that no hotel detective has caught on yet and handcuffed us, then I guess you're right."

Matt actually laughed at me.

"Clare, you've seen too many film noirs. Or maybe episodes of *The Three Stooges*. And I can just imagine you watching the Stooges on the local Podunk, New Jersey, channel out there in suburbia."

"Ha, ha."

We had gone to Madame's suite, just as we'd said. I had to make the call from an actual guest room—given the advances in telephone technology, the hotel staff could easily see where you were calling from, and I couldn't risk using a house phone because they might get suspicious.

"Don't worry about Darla Hart showing up, either," Matt insisted. "Before I came to the table downstairs, I called your friend Dr. Foo at St. Vincent's. He told me Darla's still at Anabelle's side, so there's no chance you'll be caught in the act."

Somehow his words didn't comfort me. After all, I was the one who had to be the con artist here. Matt— who, in my experience, was so much smoother at misdirection than I—couldn't do it this time.

"Go ahead, make the call," Matt said, indicating the telephone on the night table. "Nobody who picks up that phone will believe that *I'm* Darla Hart."

"I know, I know," I said.

I cleared my throat, lifted the receiver, and pressed the button marked HOUSE KEEPING. Someone answered on the first ring.

"Hello," I said. "This is Darla Hart, from Room 818—" (As Madame was checking in, I had asked the desk clerk if "our friend Darla" had checked in yet—and then asked for her room number so we could visit. The clerk was reluctant to give out a guest's room number because it wasn't the hotel's policy to give out such information. But I pressed, and since Madame was a familiar guest, she gave it up.) "I'm visiting Mrs. Dubois on twenty-six, but I'm about to return to my room for a nice long bath. Please send up extra towels."

"Certainly, Ms. Hart. Right away!" said the male voice on the other end of the line.

"Thank you," I said. And for a split second, I imagined the same male voice dialing the police the second I hung up.

"This will never work," I told Matt.

"Of course it will," Matteo replied, pushing me out the

door. "Now get going and watch for the maid to enter Darla's room. Ring me here when you get inside, and I'll come up. And don't forget this."

He thrust Madame's key card into my hand. "Hold it in your hand, as if you were about to unlock the room," Matt reminded me. "But don't let her check it in the door lock or you might be spending the night on Riker's Island."

"What do you mean *you;* don't you mean *we*?"

Matt's dark eyebrow lifted, and he crossed his arms. This unfortunately emphasized how beautifully his broad shoulders tapered down to his narrow hips, all of which were handsomely defined by the smooth lines of his exquisitely tailored Armani dinner jacket. "I don't know. You look pretty hot tonight," he said. "Seeing you handcuffed in this little Valentino number might be worth it."

"Fine," I said, more irritated by my momentary attraction to Matt's damned irrepressible masculinity than his bawdy little joke, "but if I get caught, I'm cutting a deal. You're the one who masterminded the operation—the DA's going to want you, not me."

"You *have* been watching too many film noirs."

"All right, I'm going."

"Clare—"

"What?"

The teasing laughter left his eyes. "Don't worry."

"Too late."

Darla's floor seemed to be deserted when I got there. Good, I thought.

I walked down the hallway, which was pleasant but not plush. This was a business-class floor, after all, the floor for the more budget-minded guests. Since Darla Hart seemed to be nearing the bottom of her cash barrel, that made sense. What didn't make sense was why she chose the Waldorf-Astoria in the first place. Even a "cheap" room in this place could run three to five hundred dollars a night. Why not seek more economical digs?

Well, Clare, I told myself, *that's what you're here to find out* . . .

I turned a corner in time to see a young Hispanic woman in a maid's uniform stepping out of Darla Hart's room.

"Hello!" I said, brandishing Madame's key card as I hurried forward. "Thank you so much for the extra towels."

I brushed past the maid and stuck my foot in the door.

"This is for your trouble," I said as I produced a ten-dollar bill. I pressed it into the woman's hand.

"Good night," I said.

Slipping past the maid, I entered the room and closed the door behind me. Bolted it, too. Then I peered through the peephole until the woman pocketed her tip and vanished around the corner.

So far, so good. *I'd like to thank the Academy for this award* . . .

I dived for the phone and called Matt.

"I'm in," I said and hung up.

The décor was what I expected of a 2,000-room hotel—what I called "Commercial Colonial Moderne." Of course, Darla's "Business Class" room here on the eighth floor was much smaller than Madame's "Astoria Level" suite up on twenty-six, which had a foyer, a separate bedroom, living area, a wet bar, French doors, a spectacular view of Park Avenue, and access to an executive lounge that served complimentary evening hors d'oeuvres.

Tourists to New York City are often surprised at the small size of hotel rooms even in grand hotels like the Waldorf. But real estate comes at a premium price on Manhattan Island, and spacious living, even in hotels, is a rarity indeed.

Well, I thought, at least it wasn't Tokyo, where Matt

tells me an economy room can be as small as a horizontal phone booth. The Waldorf's Business Class wasn't *that* small, more like 200 square feet, nothing compared to Madame's 700-square-foot suite upstairs. But it was well appointed, if not up to the lush opulence of the grand lobby.

The furniture consisted of a queen-sized bed with a dark wood headboard. The cream-colored coverlet had been turned down and a foil-wrapped chocolate placed on the fluffy white pillows. There was a nightstand, a matching dresser, an upholstered armchair draped with a floral-print slipcover that reached down to the thick-pile carpet, a large wood-framed mirror, a few lamps, and a desk in the corner.

Darla was pretty neat. There were a few pieces of clothing draped over the armchair (a lovely satin negligee and thigh-high silk stockings) and some shoes next to the bed (Manolo Blahnik Alligator pumps, retail $850), but otherwise the room was well kept. On the desk was a tangerine Mac laptop computer, plugged into the phone jack. That surprised me. Somehow I never pictured Darla Hart as a computer user, but this was, after all, the high-tech yet still-violent twenty-first century; everyone was either getting plugged or plugging in.

A familiar rhythmic knock interrupted my search. *Rat-tat-uh-tat-tat. Tat. Tat.* I opened the door, and Matt slipped inside. I bolted it again.

"I told you it would be easy," he said.

"We're not out of the woods—or the room—yet," I countered.

It occurred to me that Matteo's little plan was so foolproof in his mind, he might have used it successfully before. Probably to slip into some other woman's room, I figured. Three guesses why.

"We don't have much time," I announced, opening the drawers and riffling through them. All were full of neatly folded clothing. "Donna Karan, Miuccia Prada, Dolce & Gabbana . . ." I muttered, "Well, it's easy to see where her money goes."

"A laptop!" Matt said, moving to the desk. "Shit, it's a Mac."

"I like Macs," I said. "Need help?"

"No. I can use them. I just don't like them. We've *had* this discussion."

"Yes, let's not go there again. Wouldn't Darla have a password or something?" I asked, still tossing drawers.

"Maybe," Matt replied. "But you'd be surprised at how many people don't bother with—presto!"

I turned. Matt had opened the cover on the computer, pressed the space bar, and the machine had come to life.

"She actually left it running!" Matt said. He couldn't hide his boyish glee at doing something naughty.

I continued my search while Matt examined the contents of the files on Darla Hart's computer.

"She's got a security password set up on her banking program," Matt said. "No chance I can get in."

"Don't worry about that," I replied. "Judging by her behavior, there are no secrets lurking in Darla's bank account. It's empty."

Behind me, Matt continued tapping the keyboard.

After more searching, I found Darla's suitcases—monogrammed Louis Vuitton leather with polished brass trim—tucked in the back of the closet. I dragged them out and opened one after the other. The first bag was empty. The second, a small beauty case, contained cosmetics. The lipsticks were all pinks and neutrals and perky pastels that were more appropriate for a much younger woman—or a woman who wanted to look much younger. Ditto the mascara. Darla certainly wasn't wearing this kind of makeup the day I met her. Could it belong to someone else? Perhaps Anabelle?

I closed the cosmetics bag and opened the third case.

Inside I found buried treasure—a wad of papers clipped together with a black metal clamp. I pulled them out.

"I'm going to access her Internet files," Matt said. "There's a dedicated line here and it looks like she automated the password to her AOL account."

I sat on the edge of the chair and paged through the paperwork. One of them—dated just a few months ago—was actually an official court document with the title "Darla Hart vs. The Penn Life Insurance Company." I turned the pages, wading through the legalese.

As far as I could puzzle out, about eighteen months ago Darla Hart had—or claimed to have had—an on-the-job injury that occurred while she was employed as an "artistic dancer" at a "place of business" called The Wiggle Room in Jacksonville, Florida.

Darla claimed her injury prevented her from working and demanded disability payments. The manager of the establishment, one Victor Vega, disputed her claim and the matter was settled in a court of law.

Not in Darla's favor, as it turned out. Not only did she lose her case to the insurance company, but the State of Florida denied her disability claim. The last few letters were from her lawyer, demanding payment for legal fees that were in arrears.

At least now I knew that Darla had learned what my dear old dad had called the "slip-and-fall" ploy—a variant of which she was now threatening to use against the Blend.

Clearly, Darla was an opportunist. But just how far would she go to exploit an opportunity, that was the question. As far as pushing her pregnant stepdaughter, who'd just made the dance company of her dreams, down a flight of stairs?

As unpleasant as she was, it was still difficult to picture even Darla stooping so low.

"Bull's-eye!" Matteo announced. He turned around

and faced me, a dazzling grin on his handsome face. "Wanna know why Darla's in New York?"

I raced to his side. "Why?"

"There are about thirty e-mails to a guy named Arthur Jay Eddleman, who appears to be the partner in the accounting firm of Eddleman, Alter, and Berry."

"I found something, too."

I showed Matteo the legal papers. Then I pointed to the list of e-mails on the computer screen. "Are these e-mails part of another lawsuit or something?"

"More like *or something*," Matt said with a bawdy tone.

"What?" I asked. "What!"

"I opened a few of the more recent e-mails in Darla's download file first. By then they were Darla and Arthur. But when their relationship began, they were called 'Muffy' and 'Stud366'—their chat room names."

"You mean an Internet romance?"

"And a hot and heavy one, too. The first e-mails date back about three months, the last few were sent yesterday and today."

I sat down and read the letters. It was obvious that once Darla had discovered the real identity of the affluent "Stud366," she set out to hook the fat fishy and reel him into her net.

Darla's e-mails made her out to be a respectable woman of independent means—not exactly the broke, unemployed ex-stripper she really was.

Yet from the letters themselves—barely literate with misspelled and misused words—Mr. Arthur Jay Eddleman would have had to be pretty darned gullible to be fooled into thinking Darla was even a high school graduate, let alone a cultured woman of wealth.

Some of her e-mails were vulgar and explicit enough, however, to get any male's attention. And Darla Hart clearly had succeeded in getting Mr. Arthur Eddleman's.

With an explicit e-mail of his own, outlining all the things they might do together (and I'm *not* talking Central Park carousel rides and trips to the Statue of Liberty), he'd agreed to meet her when "she came to New York City on business."

That's why Darla had taken a room at the Waldorf-Astoria! It fit her false front as an independently wealthy woman, thereby assuring Mr. Eddleman she wasn't after him for his credit cards, stock portfolio, or four-bedroom apartment on the Upper East Side.

Finally, Matt showed me an e-mail that was sent by Darla at eight o'clock in the morning on Thursday, the very day I found Anabelle lying broken at the bottom of the Blend's steps—a letter gushing with happiness at the wonderful evening they'd spent together, and the night they'd spent together, too, right here in this room.

So while Anabelle was tumbling down stairs, her mother was tumbling in Waldorf sheets here with Mr. Arthur Jay Eddleman of Eddleman, Alter, and Berry, Accountants. Or at least it *looked* that way. She could easily have sent the e-mail as a ploy, to cover her ass.

"God," I cried. "That name. *Eddleman.* I think he's on the list!"

"List?" said Matteo. "What list? Who's on the list?"

I pulled the silent auction program out of my evening bag—a little black lizard double-strapped Ferragamo knockoff, bought from an Eighth Street sidewalk vendor for $20 (as opposed to eBay for $650). The slick booklet included information on the items being auctioned as well as information on the St. Vincent's programs for which the benefit was being held.

"Look, here at the back of the program is an extensive guest list for the dinner downstairs . . ." I pointed to the pages where the thousand names were listed in alphabetical order, table numbers printed beside each name. "See, under the letter *E* . . . Mr. and Mrs. Arthur Jay Eddleman.

Looks like Stud366 is one of the guests at your mother's charity ball. *And* he's married. Bet Darla didn't know that."

"Curiouser and curiouser," Matt said, eyebrow arched. "And how the hell did you remember seeing his name anyway? What did you do, memorize a thousand names?"

"I took a chance and looked up the name *Engstrum* earlier. Eddleman is two names away on the list. Look— Eddleman, Eggers, Engstrum."

"I see," said Matt. "But who are the Engstrums?"

"That's the family name of Anabelle's boyfriend— Richard Engstrum, Junior. You know what Esther calls him, don't you? 'The Dick.'"

"Oh, right."

"The Engstrums have money and connections," I told Matt. "So I thought someone from the family might be here tonight. We know Anabelle was pregnant, but we don't know anything about how her boyfriend felt about it."

"Right," said Matt, looking closer at the names in the booklet. "Engstum is listed here all right."

"Yeah, and it's a jackpot, too. See . . . Mr. and Mrs. Richard Engstrum, Senior, are listed at table fifty-eight, along with their son, Richard, Junior."

"Am I reading this right?" said Matt. "That boy is here partying when his pregnant girlfriend is lying in an ICU?"

"Yes."

"The little shit." Matt's jaw worked a moment and his fists clenched. "Yeah. I'd like to *talk* to him all right."

"Agreed. After we finish up here. Anything else we should check?" I glanced around the small room.

Matt rubbed the back of his neck. "I guess we could jot down some of the Web sites Darla bookmarked. Then we'd better get out of here."

I loaned Matt a pen and small notebook I'd brought

along. He jotted down Web sites while I put Darla's papers in the suitcase and put everything back into the closet pretty much as I'd found it. I scanned the room one more time.

"That's weird," Matt said.

"What now?"

"We just talked about Richard Engstrum, didn't we? Anabelle's boyfriend."

"Right."

"Well, Darla has been doing some heavy research into—guess what?"

I hurried over to the laptop screen.

"Engstrum Systems," I said.

"Yeah," said Matt, "And the subsidiaries like Engstrum Investment. And look at this—newspaper articles about Richard Engstrum, Senior, the CEO."

"Wow, the woman really is an operator," I said. "Anabelle got pregnant with Richard Junior's baby, and it sure looks like Darla was preparing to blackmail the kid into getting the money from Daddy."

"*Preparing* to blackmail. You don't think Darla could have started blackmailing Anabelle's boyfriend already?"

"No way. Darla's too desperate for cash. If she *is* in the process of blackmail, there've been no payoffs yet."

"In any case, Darla may have an alibi," Matt said, closing the lid on Darla's computer. "Looks like she was here having a romantic tryst the night her stepdaughter got hurt—if it *was* attempted murder, and not just a stupid bloody accident."

"It wasn't an accident, Matt. Don't even say that."

"But that's what it still looks like, Clare." Matt shook his head. "And we're in deep trouble. Darla's workplace injury claim was denied in Florida. Then her next money-making scheme to blackmail Anabelle's boyfriend went bad because with Anabelle's accident the girl's pregnancy is now in jeopardy anyway. The woman's got no money-making prospects left but to sue the hell out of us."

"She's still got one," I pointed out. "You forgot about Arthur Jay Eddleman."

A soft knock suddenly sounded at Darla's door.

"Matt!" I rasped. "Who the heck is that?"

"How should I know?"

"Do you think it's the maid again?"

"If it is," said Matt, "you better answer."

"What if it *isn't* the maid?"

I pictured NYPD uniforms and nickel-plated badges again. A wall of blue dragging my evening-gowned ass through the Waldorf's elegant lobby.

The knock came again.

"Clare," whispered Matt, "go answer it!"

I frantically shook my head. "Silver bracelets don't go with vintage Valenino, Matt. *You* answer it!"

Suddenly, we heard a man speak.

"Muffy," called the voice in a seductive coo. "Open up. It's me. Stud366."

Twenty-three

༄ ༄ ༄ ༄ ༄ ༄ ༄ ༄ ༄ ༄ ༄ ༄ ༄ ༄ ༄ ༄

I stared at Matt. He stared at me. Arthur Jay Eddleman knocked again, this time more insistently.

"Come on, Muffy honey," he said with a mixture of sweet talk and wheedling. "Don't hide from your Studdly-bunny. I saw the floor maid. She told me you'd just retired. How about we take that bed of yours for one more spin?"

"Matt, what do we—"

Matt put his finger to my lips.

"Follow my lead," he said. Then he winked. I hate it when my ex-husband winks. Trouble always follows.

Before I could stop him, Matt flung open the hotel room door.

On the other side stood a very startled older man wearing a suit of evening clothes. He had delicate features, pale skin, and a receding hairline. Though short and thin, Mr. Eddleman could almost be considered distinguished, except for the bottle-thick, black frame glasses that were too large for his head.

"Sorry," he stammered, his pale face flushing. "Wrong room."

"Mr. Eddleman," Matt said in an authoritative-sounding voice. "Arthur Jay Eddleman?"

The man froze in his tracks. "Yes?"

"Step inside, Mr. Eddleman."

Matt stepped aside. To my surprise, Arthur Jay Eddleman entered the hotel room of his own free will.

Then, in one smooth motion, Matteo slipped his passport out of an inside jacket pocket and flipped it open. A split-second later he snapped it closed again and tucked it back.

"My name is Special Agent Matt Savage of the International Drug Interdiction Task Force, and this is my assistant, Agent Tiffany Vanderweave."

Vanderweave? I knew it was spur of the moment, but couldn't he have come up with a better name that that? *And Tiffany! Do I look like a Tiffany?*

"Oh, goodness!" said Eddleman, clearly shaken. "Goodness."

"We were going to pay you a visit down at Eddleman, Alter, and Berry, but you saved us the trouble," Matt continued.

"D-Do you m-mind if I s-s-sit," Mr. Eddleman asked, pointing to the floral-print chair with the satin negligee draped on it. Matt nodded and sat down across from him on the edge of the bed.

"What's Darla done?" Eddleman asked.

"What do you mean?" asked Matt pointedly.

"You're in her room. You must suspect her of something."

"Do *you* suspect her of anything, Mr. Eddleman?"

"No, no," he replied, waving his arms, his fingers

catching on one of Darla's thigh-high stockings. Embarrassed, he batted it away as if it were a spider web. "We're just friends. She didn't fool me, if that's what you mean."

"Fool you, Mr. Eddleman?" said Matt with a strategically raised eyebrow. "How would Ms. Hart 'fool' you?"

For a guy who historically distrusted legal authorities in every corner of the globe, Matteo was surprisingly good at imitating one. In fact, his Joe Friday delivery was so convincing I had to bite my tongue to keep from bursting with laughter.

"She's not who she said she was, *that* much I knew," Mr. Eddleman continued. "But I didn't think she was a criminal. And certainly not a drug smuggler . . . or whatever it is you're after her for doing."

"Mr. Eddleman," I said, having gathered enough nerve to act the part of Ms. Vanderweave. "Just what is your relationship with Ms. Hart?"

There, I thought, that sounded authoritative.

Matteo shot me a look—I think he was amused at my getting into the act. I ignored him, and did my best to keep a straight face.

Darla Hart may not have pushed her stepdaughter down a flight of stairs, but she had pushed her into nude dancing at one time, and she might have been trying to enlist the girl in some sort of blackmail scheme. Matt and I really did need to resolve any outstanding questions about the woman—including the question of her alibi.

"Well," Eddleman said, his eyes on the floor. "You know how it is . . ." His voice trailed off.

"We *know* you're a married man, Mr. Eddleman."

"Oh, please . . . please don't tell my wife about this." He looked panicked. "Thirty-one years I've been married. I do care for my wife, and I'd never think of leaving her."

"Then why were you seeing Darla Hart?" I pressed.

Eddleman sighed and his shoulders sagged.

"We met in one of those sexy Internet chat rooms," he said. "She flirted with me. I flirted with her. We exchanged a few e-mails, and after a while . . ."

His voice trailed off again and he shrugged as if what came next was inevitable.

"When did you begin sleeping with Darla?" asked Matt.

"Just a few days ago, after she came into town," Eddleman replied. "We had a date and hit it off."

"You say you love your wife, Mr. Eddleman," said Matt. "Didn't you consider blackmail?"

Eddleman sighed again. "I'm a very wealthy man, Agent Savage."

"All the more reason to fear blackmail," I pointed out.

"I have money to spare. You see what I mean?"

"No," I said.

"Darla . . . Women like Darla . . . They think they're clever. Sharp operators, you know. They meet a man like me and see dollar signs. Darla never talked about money, but I knew she would get around to it. By that time I figured we'd be sick of one another or the romance would go sour. Then I *would* part with a little money. Enough so that she would go away, no hard feelings."

"Sounds like you've done this before," Matt said.

Eddleman nodded. "Yes, I have. And do you want to know why?"

Matt shifted, didn't ask. For the first time, he looked uneasy. Well, Matt was a man. He probably already figured he knew the answer. But *I* sure wanted to know Eddleman's answer.

"Why, Mr. Eddleman?" I asked pointedly.

Through the thick lenses, his eyes were watery blue, almost as washed out as his skin. Even sitting up, the little man's shoulders were slightly hunched, his chest sunken. Mr. Arthur Jay Eddleman had clearly spent too many long, unhealthy hours indoors, poring over numbers and ledgers.

Suddenly I did know why. He didn't have to say it. But I'd already asked—

"I got married young, Ms. Vanderweave," he said. "Young and poor may sound romantic, but it is not. I spent my twenties working in the daytime and going to night school. In my thirties and forties, I worked fifty, sixty, seventy hours a week to provide a good living for my wife and family. In my fifties I started my own firm." He paused, his eyes seemed far away. "That was when the real work began, let me tell you. Eighteen years of it."

Arthur Jay Eddleman shook his head. "Now I'm older and richer, but frankly I was feeling too old to enjoy my riches. My wife has her friends and shopping and in these last few years she has been sickly. My kids have their own lives, they don't need me hanging around.

"So I decided to meet women . . . Sometimes we hit it off. Sometimes we don't. I just want a little romance, a little fun, before the lights go out for good."

We sat in silence for a moment. Matt seemed to have run out of questions. Finally I spoke.

"Did Ms. Hart ever mention a stepdaughter named Anabelle?"

"No, never," Eddleman said. "Darla said she had friends in New York City, but I didn't meet any of them."

"One more thing we'd like to confirm," Matt said, rising. "And then I think we're finished."

"Sure," Eddleman said. "Anything to help prevent drug peddling or smuggling or . . . whatever you're doing."

"Were you and Ms. Hart together this past Wednesday night?"

Eddleman didn't even hesitate. "The whole night," he replied. "My wife went to Scarsdale to visit our daughter. I met Darla at eight o'clock, Wednesday evening, right here at the hotel. We had dinner at the Rainbow Room, then walked around the city. We got back around mid-night, and I left at seven or seven-thirty Thursday morn-ing—my wife was due back at noon."

Matt and I exchanged glances. Darla's alibi was solid, all right. I nodded.

"Thank you, Mr. Eddleman," Matt said, taking him by the elbow and leading him to the door.

"Should I stay away from her?" Mr. Eddleman said, pausing on the threshold. "Darla, I mean."

"That would be wise," Matt replied. "But if you do see her again, don't mention this encounter. It may jeopard-ize our investigation, and that's a crime."

So's impersonating a federal official, Matt, I thought.

"Thank you for your cooperation," Matt said, pushing the door.

"Nice meeting you, Ms. Vanderweave," Eddleman said with a creepy smile that told me the guy wasn't about to quit with Darla. Yuck, I thought. And with his wife still at dinner right downstairs.

He was still waving at me, his eyes on my cleavage, when Matt closed the door.

"We've got to get out of here," Matt said. "Darla could come back any minute."

"Even worse," I replied, my stomach rumbling. "We could miss the main course."

Twenty-Four

〜〜〜〜〜〜〜〜〜〜〜〜〜〜〜〜〜〜〜

GEORGE Gee and his Make-Believe Ballroom Orchestra had just begun bouncing big band swing off the four-story ceiling, coaxing a slow parade of couples toward the dance floor, when Matt and I returned to the charity dinner.

"The band's good," said Matt over the jaunty jump of woodwinds and barking brass.

"Very," I said. "That's George Gee and his band. They're the darlings of the Rainbow Room these days."

The Rainbow Room was one of the most elegant dinner-dance clubs in New York—high atop Rockefeller Center, it was about the only place left where dancing cheek-to-cheek in elegant evening clothes was even remotely possible.

"Wanna take a spin with me?" Matt asked.

I gave him the *puh-leeze get real* look. "I'm going for the Engstrums," I said, double-checking the seating chart in the silent auction program.

"What are you going to do?"

"Stir up the nest," I said. "See what flies out."

"Good. I'd like a whack at Junior, myself."

I noticed Matt's fists clenching and made a split-second decision.

"No," I said. "Let me do this, Matt. I've got an act in mind. It will work better solo. Get a drink at the bar and wait for me there."

"Really? You think you can pull something off alone?"

"Sure," I said, even though I wasn't. On the other hand, the Vanderweave impersonation went pretty well, and my doing it alone was a much better bet than bringing Matt along wearing his fury on his sleeve.

"Well, okay, honey, if you're sure. You knock 'em dead for me. Especially that little shithead."

The "honey" caught me off guard, but I let it pass. Matt and I were working well together tonight, I thought to myself as I wove around the tray-toting waiters and crowded tables in the vast ballroom. We were even having a little fun with each other, but that didn't mean we were a couple again. Matt had to know that, I assured myself, so there was no need to set him straight.

The Engstrums were seated at table fifty-eight, about mid-room and not far from the dance floor. I recognized Richard, Senior, from photographs in the Web site articles Darla had bookmarked on her laptop.

A typical Swedish blond, the man wasn't exactly an albino but close. A white rabbit would be a fair comparison.

His wife, "Fiona," according to the articles, was a brunette of the Jackie O. variety. A willowy WASP in the way all socialite wives are willowy WASPs (even when they're Greek or Jewish or Nordic and not even technically the garden-variety Anglo-Saxon Protestants). I don't know why they all have the same looks and mannerisms. Maybe it's the extreme hygiene and slight dehydration from hours spent at spas and health clubs that cause the perpetually pinched, unamused look, the long, strained neck, the tight lips and drawn skin.

In face and form, Richard, Junior, appeared to take after his mother with a svelte stature, refined features, and dark hair. Odds were good he was part of the type I'd encountered many times before among the wealthy of this burgh. The "born of money and indifference" earmarks were there: floppy haircut, careless posture, even the "sensitive, intelligent boy" look about the eyes. Odds were he'd play up the latter in the presence of check-writing Mother and Daddy, but would drop it fast around his male college friends, who would share his penchant for mocking everyone and everything but their own pursuits of pleasure, usually drinking, drugging, and copulating.

Beside him sat a gravely thin young brunette with sunken cheeks and an expression of above-it-all boredom. Her little black sleeveless dress, the conforming little socialite number sold as a WASP "classic" by every high-end boutique in the city, seemed to be the carbon copy of his mother's. The two even wore similar strings of pearls at the neck.

Since I was certain that Anabelle had been seeing Richard, Junior, over the summer—and was now pregnant with his child—I had assumed upon approaching the table that the bored young woman sitting beside Junior here was a sister or cousin of his.

Time to find out, I thought.

Gathering my courage and suppressing some but far from all of my nerves, I glided up to the table with as haughty a mask as I'd ever pulled off. "Excuse me," I said, looking down my nose as far as I dared without appearing ridiculous, "but are you Mr. and Mrs. Engstrum?"

"Yes," said Mrs. Engstrum. "And *who* might *you* be?"

The tone was not polite and not meant to be. It was a

tone for intimidating and squashing, for warning a possible inferior to keep her distance. I'd come up against it countless times before and so barely batted an eyelash.

"I go by C.C., and I'm helping out the *Town and Country* photographer tonight," I said with an intentionally plastic smile. "Taking a few notes on select guests so we can follow up with a photograph. Would you mind speaking with me?"

Richard, Senior, looked right through me about halfway into my spiel. "I'm getting a drink," he said to his wife and brushed past without so much as a "Pardon me."

The rudeness didn't surprise me. Richard, Senior, was the sort who saved his efforts and manners for people that "mattered," and I was not pretending to be from the *Wall Street Journal* or *Financial Times.* My periodical front was the bible for the modern American social register, which meant Mrs. Engstrum was the one I had to buffalo—and the one I *meant* to buffalo.

I knew very well the best leverage I could apply in this situation was one mother to another. For that, I'd need to reel in Mrs. Engstrum.

"Town and Country, you say?" she asked, pausing at length to eye my Valentino gown with the judgment of the hypercritical. One can only assume I'd passed her evaluation process at the subatomic level when she finally said, "Yes, I'm sure we can spare a few minutes. Why don't you sit down?"

The response was designed to make me feel ever so grateful for her time, as if having a husband with a NAS-DAQ symbol were akin to inheriting the English throne.

Get a grip, sweetie, I was dying to say. Your husband's $95-a-share IPO was worth about two bucks the last time I looked. Not a spectacular calling card in the e-rolodexes of the little silver Palm Pilots on that ballroom dance floor.

But I didn't say that, of course. What I *did* say was "Thank you so much!"

And I sat.

The East Indian couple at the far end of the table rose just as I sank down, leaving a total of six empty chairs at this table for ten.

Presumably the Engstrums had so enthralled their fellow dinner partners with sparkling wit and dynamic conversation that their six dinner companions had run for the bar or the dance floor the very first chance they got.

I pulled my small notebook and pen out of my purse.

"Now, Mrs. Engstrum, let's start with you. I know your first name is Fiona—would you mind confirming the spelling?"

After the pretense of getting the family names correct for the "photo captions," I turned to the young woman sitting beside Junior.

"And you are?"

"Sydney Walden-Sargent."

"And your age, miss?"

"Nineteen."

"She's a sophomore at Vassar," said Mrs. Engstrum. "And you can print that she is indeed related to the celebrated Sargent family."

"Oh, yes, of course," I said, scribbling away.

The Sargent family, per se, hadn't achieved anything in any field that could be considered consequential. But they were famous nonetheless. The reason: Their legendary cousins, who had been winning national political offices and influencing government policies for decades. Thanks to their famous cousins, the Sargents had gained the clout to secure everything from executive positions at major corporations, and ambassadorships, to seats on prestigious New York museum and performing arts boards.

"They're engaged," said Mrs. Engstrum. "You can print that, too."

"Engaged, you say? How nice. Congratulations." I turned to Anabelle's beau. "Young Mr. Engstrum, you must be very happy. When did you first ask Miss Walden-Sargent to be your wife?"

The glazed eyes of Richard, Junior, attempted to refocus. Clearly, making any effort for this conversation was not high on his agenda (a chip off the old block). "What?" he said.

"I asked how long you've been engaged," I told him.

"Oh, how long," he repeated, glancing at Syndey. "Awhile, right? Last February."

"Valentine's Day! It was Valentine's Day," said Sydney Walden-Sargent, leaning toward me to imply I should make it sound good in the caption. "It was very romantic."

Junior smiled weakly and shrugged. "Yeah, that's right."

That's right?! I wanted to scream. *No, you little shit-head, that's wrong.* If you were engaged to little Miss Vassar here, then why the hell were you sleeping with Anabelle Hart half the summer? I felt my fingers squeezing the life out of my felt-tipped Scripto.

"Just a few more questions," I said tightly but was interrupted by the appearance of one of the Waldorf-Astoria's black-jacketed waiters.

"Coffee, decaf, or tea?"

They were about to serve dessert, I realized. Matt and I had missed the entire dinner. I hoped Madame wouldn't be hurt that we'd disappeared on her and her guests, but we were doing this for a good cause—her cause, saving the Blend.

"Nothing for me," I said to the waiter, hoping I could make it back to table five in time for coffee at least.

"Tea," said Mrs. Engstrum. "For all of us. Bring a pot, please."

"Tea?" I asked. "You prefer tea, do you?"

"We got into the habit when Richard was working in London. It's all we've been drinking now for over a decade."

"Isn't that interesting. I mean, in this age of specialty coffees. You, too, Mr. Engstrum?" I asked Junior. "You're a tea drinker, too? No espresso or cappuccino for you?"

"Ugh, no." He made an incensed sensitive-boy face. "Euro-trash mud. Wouldn't touch the stuff."

Now I really wanted to wring his neck. Not just for the insult to my business but because I hadn't forgotten that wet wad of tea leaves I'd discovered dropped into the double layers of garbage bags after the inside layer had been twisted closed for the evening. A cup of tea was the very last thing Anabelle had prepared and discarded before her fall. And since Anabelle was *not* a tea drinker, that meant her attacker was.

Time to play rough, I decided.

"Miss Walden-Sargent," I said, turning toward her, "were you by any chance in the city this past summer?"

"No," she said. "As a matter of fact, I was studying in Grenoble then touring with my parents."

"How interesting. Then you aren't a dancer?"

"A dancer? What do you mean?"

Junior's look of indifference was suddenly wiped clean. He sat up in his chair, his eyes wide.

"I mean, miss, that Mr. Engstrum here was seen frequenting the Lower East Side clubs this past summer with a young dancer, so I thought maybe there was some mistake about the date of your engagement—"

"Madam," barked Mrs. Engstrum, "I don't know who may have repeated such a tale to you, but you're seriously mistaken. You know, I have *friends* in the executive office of *Town and Country,* and I wasn't under the impression they employed checkout counter tabloid reporters. This interview is over, and after I've made a phone call or two, I'm sure your career will be, as well."

"Well, I see my time is up," I said, rising.

Mrs. Engstrum glared at me as if I was about to leak national security secrets to our mortal enemies. "Your time is up all right. And you'll be facing a lawsuit if you print a word of that lie."

"Interesting that you've called it a lie," I said, my eyes shifting to Richard, Junior. "But your son has not."

Before she could issue another threat or force her son into supporting their little cover-up, I turned and departed, heading straight for the exit.

As I'd hoped, Mrs. Engstrum caught my arm just as I was pushing through one of the many sets of double doors along the back wall of the ballroom.

"Oh, no you don't," she snapped, pulling hard enough to bruise.

"Ow! Fiona, ease up, there."

"How dare you threaten us with your lies," she hissed, yanking me toward a deserted corner of the hallway. "How dare you—"

"How dare I!" I rounded on her. "How dare your son, madam. How dare your son sleep with Anabelle Hart, get her pregnant, and then try to kill her this past Wednesday night and make it look like an accident."

The woman's face went completely ashen.

Bingo, Bingo, Bingo.

Junior had done it all right, and she knew it. I'd hit a bull's-eye.

"Who are you?" Her voice was barely there.

"Clare Cosi. I'm part owner and full-time manager of the Village Blend, the site of your son's depraved assault on Anabelle."

"Richard didn't hurt Anabelle. You're wrong. He made

a mistake sleeping with that girl, a stupid, stupid mistake, but he didn't do anything to hurt her, I swear—"

The woman looked absolutely stricken, and I faltered. The way the words came out—they felt so earnest and sincere. Was she telling me the truth? Or was her sincerity just a mother's gullible belief in her own son's innocence? Had Junior lied to her so well that she believed him? I didn't know, but I had to keep going now—it was the only way to know for sure.

"Richard *did* hurt Anabelle, Mrs. Engstrum. I found the evidence after the Crime Scene Unit left. I haven't brought it to the police yet, but I plan to—"

This was a lie, of course. A handful of tea leaves in a garbage bag did not prove a damned thing, but Mrs. Engstrum wouldn't know that and neither would Richard.

"I just wanted you to have a chance to help your son," I said, continuing the bluff. "I'm a mother, too, and one mother to another, I'm pleading with you to tell your son what I told you—talk some sense into him. If you convince him to give himself up by noon tomorrow, then I'll destroy the evidence. The authorities will go much easier on him if he turns himself in and you know it."

Fiona Engstrum looked stricken, stunned, pale as a ghost. Her eyes dampened with unshed tears.

"You're wrong," she rasped. "You're wrong. I called Richard Thursday morning. He was in his fraternity at Dartmouth. He was there the whole night, and I'm sure he can find witnesses to that fact . . . I'm sure he can . . ."

Something inside me twisted. How could any mother face hearing this about her child? And what if I was wrong? What if Richard didn't do a damn thing?

I couldn't even imagine what I'd do if someone accused my own child of such a thing. But then Joy would never in a million years do what Richard Engstrum, Junior, had done. Even if he hadn't caused Anabelle's accident, he'd clearly abandoned her. Maybe a night of tossing and turning was something he deserved even if he wasn't guilty. Anabelle didn't have that luxury. She was flat on her back in St. Vincent's ICU.

My resolve hardened.

"Remember. Noon tomorrow," I said coldly and walked away.

I could feel the woman's eyes burning a hole in the back of my Valentino. It took all my self-control not to steal a look at her as I strode back toward the ballroom doors, but to my credit I made it to the bar, where Matteo stood, without once turning around.

Twenty-Five

～～～～～～～～～～～～～～～～～～～～

"I need a drink," I announced to my ex-husband, my knees suddenly weak. "Kahlua, I guess."

The sweet, smooth, and syrupy Mexican liqueur was not that strong, but it had a flavor that comforted me—coffee.

"Here, try this," Matt said. "It has Kahlua in it."

I accepted the tall, frosty glass of nutty-brown, creamy liquid and took a big gulp. The concoction was smooth and delicious. It tasted like toasted almonds, coffee, and cream all at once. Then my eyes began to widen as the alcohol punch hit me.

"Ohmygod," I gasped. "What *is* that?"

"It's called a Screaming Orgasm."

I frowned at Matt. "I'm not in the mood."

"No, really," he insisted. "That's what it's called. Kahlua, amaretto, vodka, ice, and cream."

By the time he'd recited the ingredients, the vodka had kicked in and I didn't care what the hell the drink was called. I just wanted more of the same.

"We hit another wall," I announced dismally. I swirled the glass in my hand and leaned against the bar.

"I tried the mother-to-mother thing, then I strong-armed the woman." I sighed and rubbed my arm where Mrs. Engstrum had grabbed it. *That's gonna leave a mark.*

"She came back at me like a cornered panther protecting her cub. And then she got pretty emotional. She claims her cub was at his Dartmouth fraternity with witnesses the night Anabelle was hurt."

Matteo arched his eyebrow. "Too bad I missed the cat fight."

"You know what," I said miserably. "Maybe Anabelle had an accident, after all. Maybe she just tripped over her dainty little feet and plunged down those steps all by her clumsy self—"

I took another gulp of Orgasm and brother did I want to scream.

"Maybe we're ruined," I said, "because we have no insurance and Darla Hart is about to sic the best ambulance-chasing lawyer in New York City on us."

My voice must have been embarrassingly loud because at several nearby tables, heads turned. Matt diplomatically took the Screaming Orgasm out of my hand.

"What about your instincts?" Matt said softly. "What about your gut feelings?"

"My guts have been wrong before," I replied. "I married you, didn't I."

Matt didn't even blink. But he didn't deserve the remark.

Not tonight anyway.

"I'm sorry," I told him. "I shouldn't have said that. After all, we wouldn't have Joy if we hadn't . . . anyway . . . I'm sorry I'm just so damned upset. Madame bequeaths me part of her legacy, the Village Blend, and I screw it up in record time."

"You didn't screw it up," Matt said. "Flaste did. My mother did. I did. You were in New Jersey, raising our daughter, and I was off buying coffee in every country in the world except the one my wife and daughter were living in."

My fist struck the bar. Not hard, but a few people noticed.

"I'm sure Anabelle was a victim of foul play," I said. "It *can't* be an accident."

Matteo smiled. "That's the spirit."

I put my elbows on the bar and rested my chin on my hands. "But we're back to square one." I sighed. "Mrs. Engstrum is so certain of her son's innocence that she threatened me with a lawsuit if I told anyone of my suspicions. And it's quite possible Richard, The Junior Dick, is not guilty of anything more than being a complete shithead cad."

"Don't give up yet," Matt said, resting his hand on my bare shoulder. "You've only been an amateur sleuth for a couple of days. I'll bet Miss Marple took more time than that to learn her trade."

"You're right," I said with another sigh. "Why stop now when I've got only two people threatening to sue us."

"You know, Clare, Dartmouth isn't that far from New York."

"What do you mean? It's way up in New England, isn't it?"

"New Hampshire. The drive is under six hours."

"That's enough time to drive all night and still have people see him at the dorm in the morning, isn't it?"

"Yes, it is."

"So he might have done it after all?"

"The Dick's not clean by a long shot."

"And you know," I said, "Anabelle *could* wake up tomorrow and remember everything."

Matteo tapped the bar. "Knock on wood."

"Let's get back to our table," I said, pushing away from the bar. "Your mother is probably wondering what the heck happened to us."

To my relief, I managed to walk a straight line across the huge room. But it wasn't easy. A lot of guests had risen from their tables, and I had to rely on Captain Matt to take my hand and navigate us through the sea of milling formal wear.

By this time, sequined couture and vintage black ties were packing the dance floor and conductor George Gee (probably the only Chinese-American big band leader in North American) was directing his seventeen-piece swing orchestra to pay tribute to Glenn Miller by intermittently pausing their side-to-side waving of trombones, trumpets, and clarinets to shout, "Pennsylvania Six Five Thousand!"

"Good job, Mother," Matt told Madame when we arrived back at table five. "You've really got the place hopping."

"Well, now!" Madame exclaimed as he planted a kiss on her cheek. "Look who came back from their short trip upstairs. Matt and Clare, back so soon?"

"What'd we miss?" asked Matt.

"Oh, just four courses," said Madame with a wave of her hand. "But coffee and dessert are on their way."

"Sorry it took so long," said Matt, waving his Palm Pilot. "I, uh, had some trouble finding my little tool."

"Oh, I'm sure you did!" cried Madame with glee. "But I'll just bet Clare was a big help in that department!" A bawdy wink set the entire table chuckling.

"Matt really did need it," I said, not knowing what else to say. I mean, I couldn't very well shout, *Uh, people! Contrary to how this appears, Matt and I were* not *tossing in the sheets—we were tossing a suspect's room.*

"What was so important on that Palm Pilot, then?" asked Madame.

"I, uh, had to confirm the size of an order with one of my growers—" said Matt.

"Oh, really?" asked Eduardo Lebreux, suddenly interested. "Who?"

"Peruvian."

"What plantation?"

Matt smiled briefly. "Sorry, friend, trade secret."

"Matt's been the Blend's coffee buyer for two decades," Madame proudly announced to the table of ten. "Brokers for futures, as well. Learned the business from his father—who learned it from his. Of course, they always needed the steady hand of a dedicated woman to keep the place running like clockwork," she added with a pointed look at her son.

"Interesting. And how does one 'broker' for coffee futures?" asked Deputy Commissioner Marjorie Greenberg.

"Buy low and sell high," said Matt with a charming smile. "Actually coffee's a world commodity second only to oil."

"It's also the world's most popular beverage," I added by rote. "Four hundred billion cups a year."

"Yes," said Matt, "and we're attempting to sell every last one through the Village Blend."

The table of ten laughed.

"Well, I for one think the Village Blend is more than just a place to drink coffee," Dr. McTavish announced to the rest of the table. "It's practically an institution."

"We love the place," agreed McTavish's African-American colleague, Dr. Frankel. His corporate lawyer wife, Harriet, nodded enthusiastically in agreement.

"So do we," said Marjorie Greenberg. Her psychologist husband seconded, "It's a legend, all right."

"My out-of-town friends love it, too," said Harriet Frankel. "And my clients. All of them have heard of it over the years. All those wonderful old knickknacks and mismatched furniture on the second floor. It's so . . . so *bohemian*. It's wonderful!"

"I certainly hope it doesn't go the way of the other Village institutions," said Deputy Commissioner Marjorie. "Like the Pageant Book Shop and St. Mark's Theater."

"That theater's now a Gap store, isn't it?" asked Lawyer Harriet.

"The Village Blend will stand long after I'm gone," said Madame firmly. "I'm seeing to that." She threw me and Matt a pointed look.

"And reputation is the thing in this country, is it not?" said Eduardo.

"What thing?" I asked.

"I mean to your American buying public. You buy and sell things here under names—brands, no? And the most valuable of these brand names are the ones that have been around for many decades."

"Oh, right," said the psychologist. "You mean like Campbell's Soup and Ivory Soap?"

"Yes, yes," said Eduardo. "Now look at that Stewart woman's problems—"

"Oh, yes, Martha Stewart," said Harriet. "Bad bit of luck, getting caught in an insider trader scandal like that."

"She was seen as . . . how you say . . . tainted," said Eduardo, "so her company's stock falls."

"What's your point?" I asked.

"My point is that she was a *new* brand, not an old and trusted one in this country. Not yet. Not like Ivory Soap or Campbell's Soup, or the Village Blend. You see?"

"No," I said.

"Oh, I do," said Madame with a little laugh. "Eduardo has been after me to sell him the Blend. He had his heart set on making it a franchise."

"What?" I asked. "Like McDonald's?"

"Like Starbucks," he said sharply. Then seemed to

catch himself and soften the harsh tone with a forced chuckle.

"There will only ever be *one* Village Blend," said Madame. "As long as I own the place—and my intentions are respected by those who own it in the future. And I've made sure that it will be Matt and Clare here."

"Oh, fabulous!" "How wonderful!" "Here's to the on-going legacy!" cried voices around the table.

Matt and I glanced at each other. Everyone seemed genuinely happy at this news. Except Eduardo, whose smile was as plastic as they come.

Well, I thought realistically, he's lost the Blend for good. Why should he be happy for us?

Dessert and coffee were served about then. Madame had ordered coffee for both Matt and me since we'd been away from the table when the orders were taken.

I myself, having missed dinner, was overjoyed to see the steaming cup of coffee sitting next to a slice of flour-less chocolate cake garnished with mint leaves and rasp-berries. I practically inhaled it. Matt, on the other hand, simply frowned and grunted.

"What's the problem?" I asked.

"I'm desperate for a hit of caffeine," he said, "but I can't abide the coffee at these things. Dishwater and cream."

"Not tonight," I said. "The Village Blend provided the beans a few days ago, isn't that right, Madame?"

"It is," she said. "Clare roasted the beans over the weekend and shipped the bags up Monday."

"That's a lot of extra work, Clare," said Matt, sniffing the cup and taking a cautionary sip. "Not bad. I hope you charged the Waldorf a pretty penny."

"It's a charity benefit, Matt. I *discounted* the rate."

Matt let out a frustrated sigh at this news.

Eduardo Lebreux, on the other hand, let out a hearty laugh.

"Something funny?" I asked.

"Yes," said Eduardo. "The small business owner has to play whatever angles he can. The big pockets will take the tax write-offs anyway. You should have listened to your husband."

"Matt is not—" I stopped short of adding *my husband.*

(I did plan to make clear to Madame that Matt and I would never again be man and wife—no matter how many times she introduced us the other way—but I wouldn't do that to her in public. I had no interest in embarrassing her here so . . .)

Instead, I said, "Matt is not—*correct,*" and added, "There's no need to take a profit at the expense of a fundraiser for a good cause."

"Even so," said Eduardo, "this is America. Whether the coffee tastes good or not is beside the point."

"Excuse me," said Matt. "But that's my *entire* point."

"Maybe for you," said Eduardo, "but you are not common. Most of the people here would drink down whatever came to them at the table, even if it tasted like, as you say, dishwater. They would drink it down and think it was good because it was being served to them in a Waldorf-Astoria cup, you see?"

"No," I said, getting slowly annoyed.

"Most people in America decide what they like by the brand name," said Eduardo. "It is the *package* they buy, not the contents. You see?"

"No," I said. "We Americans might buy something once or twice because of an advertisement or marketing campaign or even brand loyalty, but if the quality goes bad on us, we're gone. You'll lose us forever. Haven't you ever heard of the expression 'Where's the beef?' "

"No."

"Trust me," I said. "It's red-white-and-blue. And there's nothing as American as the pragmatic expectation of getting what you pay for. Perhaps it's the *Europeans* with whom you're confusing us—the Old World idea of believing aristocrats or royalty at face value."

"We shall have to agree to disagree," said Eduardo with an unqualified sneer.

"Yes, we shall," I said then took a long, satisfying quaff from my steaming cup.

It was Friday night, one of the busiest for the Village Blend, and in another hour Tucker would be expecting barista backup from me.

For a moment, I closed my eyes and simply savored the rich, nutty aroma of the house blend. In no time, the earthy warmth seeped into my every molecule, recharging my weary bones with a splendid jolt of renewed energy.

Thank goodness, I thought. With miles to go before I slept, I was going to need it.

Twenty-six

~~~~~~~~~~~~~~~~~~~~~~~~~~

"Franchise my ass," I told Matteo as we climbed up the Blend's back staircase. We were heading for the duplex apartment to change out of our evening clothes. I was still stewing over the insulting comments of Eduardo Lebreux at dinner.

"Hmmm. Now there's an interesting idea—"

"What?"

"Your ass. You have a nice one. I just don't think franchising it would be remotely legal."

"Matt! I'm serious!"

"So am I."

The Blend was hopping tonight as our taxi pulled up out front, but Tucker and his two part-timers had it under control. Tucker even told me I didn't need to come down until closing, and that was fine with me. An hour or so off was just what the doctor ordered.

Matt pulled out his key and unlocked the apartment's front door. Java greeted me with an ear-piercing *mrrrooooow*.

"What was that? A jaguar?"

"That means, I'm hungry," I translated for Matt.

"Big sound from a little cat."

"She's got a mind of her own," I said.

"Just like her owner," Matt said.

"Why, thank you." I scratched her ears and poured her some chow. Then I filled the bottom half of my three-cup stovetop espresso pot with water, quickly ground a dark-roasted Arabica blend, packed the grinds into the basket, dropped the packed basket on top of the water, screwed the empty top onto the water-filled bottom, and put the reconnected little silver pot onto the burner.

"I just can't believe Lebreux would even *think* of that plan," I said, continuing my rant.

"Franchising the Village Blend? Why not?" said Matt, pulling loose his black tie and undoing the top buttons of his white dress shirt. "C'mon, it's not a bad idea."

"I can't believe you said that!" I cried, pulling two cream-colored demitasse cups from the cupboard. "The man wanted to take the Village Blend to new lows. Use the Blend name to package up cheap products at premium prices. That was more than obvious from his stated philosophy. Sounds an awful lot like that Kona scandal to me. Need I remind you of those details?"

"No," said Matt dryly, "but I'm sure you will."

As he'd already heard his mother repeat countless times, Matt knew very well the tale of how a ring of coffee-broking con artists had been caught transshipping inferior beans through Hawaii, then rebagging and re-selling them as the one-of-a-kind Hawaiian-grown Kona.

"In Eduardo's view," I said, "that Kona con would have been a keen little trick to play on the American public. Maybe I should have reminded him that the Kona scheme also landed the perpetrators in federal prison."

"Calm down, Clare. I'm not Lebreux. If I wanted to franchise this place, I'd do it the *right* way."

"I don't want to hear the word *franchise* out of your mouth ever again, do you understand?"

"I'll make you a deal," Matt said, shedding his jacket and cufflinks and rolling up his sleeves. "You tell me what I want to know, and I'll nix the word from my vocabulary."

"What do you want to know?"

"Don't laugh—"

"What?"

"The cup. You saw something in that cup."

"What cup?"

"That kid Mario Forte's espresso cup. After dinner, when I brought it down to you in the Blend's basement. You saw *something*. I could see it in your face."

"Oh, for Pete's sake—"

I couldn't believe Matt was still thinking about that twenty-four hours later!

"Come on," he said. "Tell me."

"Matt, conditions weren't even right for an accurate reading! The coffee that was in that cup didn't produce enough residue," I lied. "And I was really distracted at the time you showed it to me. I barely glanced at it."

Okay, so I didn't want to tell Matt the truth. In the split second I gazed into that cup, I did indeed get a clear and certain picture in my mind of Mario's character, personality, and path in life—

The image I saw in the residue was called The Hammer, the sign of a forceful, strong, and independent spirit, a leader who turns dreams into achievements. That was very good. Unfortunately, for Mario, his "Hammer" was surrounded by dried grounds in the shape of barbs or licks of fire. That meant that his life would be fraught with peril—and much of it would be of his own making.

Those with the Hammer sign seldom choose an easy

path in life, and that hammer would have to pound a lot of nails before any true happiness would be possible.

Seeing that in the grounds actually made me sad, because I knew if Joy was serious about Mario, then she had a long, hard road ahead of her.

Why did I know this? Because the first time I read my ex-husband Matteo's grounds, I saw the exact same thing. So I gave my ex-husband the only answer I could.

"There was nothing there," I told him. "I didn't see a thing."

Matt stared at me for a moment. He didn't want to believe me. But I wasn't giving him any choice.

"Guess the word *franchise* is still in my vocab, then," he said, crossing his arms and raising an eyebrow.

"I can live with that," I said.

"And me?" he asked. "Can you live with me?"

"We'll see," I said.

"You were stunning tonight, you know," he said, moving toward me.

"Stop it."

"No really. You were really brave. And you looked stunning, too, by the way, but you already knew that."

The espresso water was boiling and the moment had come for the water to be forced up through the grounds and into the top of the pot. This was my favorite moment, when the entire kitchen was about to become saturated with an intoxicating aroma.

Matt moved in close and his liquid brown eyes seemed to drink me in. I had returned the expensive rosebud-jeweled necklace to Madame in her suite, but I was still wearing the off-the-shoulder Valentino gown. My neck and shoulders felt very exposed, very vulnerable, and his hands slowly lifted to touch that part of me.

His fingers were strong and rough but surprisingly gentle as he slowly and sweetly massaged my tense muscles. The slightly coarse skin of his fingers tickled . . . it had been a long time since he'd touched me like this, his dark gaze holding fast.

"I've missed you," he whispered, then his head dipped down and his lips brushed mine.

I closed my eyes, wanting him, not wanting him . . . he pulled me into his arms. The earthy mix of steaming espresso and the sweet warmth of male cologne sent my head spinning. He brought his hand to the back of my head, opened his mouth, insisted we deepen the kiss.

Oh, yes . . . the man could kiss. There was never any debate about that. Tender and aggressive at the very same time. Relaxing yet inflaming.

I let go, wrapped my arms around his broad shoulders, held on, and kissed back. He tasted as good as I remembered, the chocolate and Kaluha still lingering on his tongue.

The aroma of coffee completely enveloped us now as the heated water shot up through the grounds and settled in the top of the pot as finished espresso.

"It's ready," I murmured, pulling away.

"Let it boil," said Matt, capturing my lips again.

Given my happy position in Matt's arms, not to mention my level of almost-forgotten arousal, I didn't have it in me to protest. Sure, my logical, pragmatic self knew this was really, really stupid. But I wasn't listening to that self at this moment.

"Let's go upstairs," whispered Matt.

I nodded.

He reached over and turned off the burner, took my hand, and led me through the living room. Maybe, if the phone hadn't rung, things would have turned out differently that evening. But the phone did ring.

"Let it go," said Matt.

"It could be Joy," I said, and he nodded, picking it up himself.

"Hello?" he said. He listened for a minute, then his face fell. His eyes met mine. "It's Dr. Foo," he said. "Anabelle didn't make it, Clare. She just died."

Twenty-seven

〜◎〜◎〜◎〜◎〜◎〜◎〜◎〜◎〜◎〜◎〜

"Good night, Tucker," I said an hour later. "Go home and get some sleep. The Sunday morning shift is a busy one."

"No way, Sugar," Tucker replied. "You went to the ball, now it's this Cinderella's turn to par-tee."

With a wave, Tucker disappeared into the night.

I locked the front door and made myself one last espresso shot. I was so tired, I actually left the grounds in the portafilter, telling myself I'd clean it properly *and* take the last bag of garbage out in the morning. This was a real breach for me, but hey, I was the boss and it had been one rough night.

I stirred a bit of sugar into the demitasse cup, drank it down, then headed up the stairs to the small office on the second floor, the day's receipts tucked under my arm.

I switched on the halogen lamp above my desk, then stepped up to the small black safe set in the stone wall. The safe had a brass dial, handle, and trim and had served as the sole vault for the Blend's valuables for over one hundred years.

On the right side of the safe hung a sepia-tinted photograph of a man with dark, intense eyes and a rakish mustache—a turn-of-the-century portrait of the Allegro family patriarch, Antonio Vespasian Allegro.

On the left side of the safe hung a glass display case that held a worn, stained, century-old ledger book that was said to contain the secret Allegro family coffee recipes—painstakingly recorded by the hand of Antonio Vespasian and entrusted to succeeding generations of Allegros.

I paused, staring intently at the photograph of Matteo's great grandfather. I recognized the strong chin, the hint of arrogance, and the undeniable intelligence in the man's eyes—they belonged to Matteo, too.

In many ways, marrying into the Allegro family was akin to entering a secret society, like the Freemasons, the Illuminati—or the Mafia. Secrets, secrets, and more secrets . . . about the family business, the specialty beans, the roasting process, the one-of-a-kind blends.

Short of taking a blood-oath of *omerta*, I was beginning to suspect I was in for life. Madame was certainly doing her best to make it so. And judging from his actions tonight, so was Matteo.

Shaking off these thoughts, I opened the safe, stuffed the day's receipts into it, closed it again, and spun the tumbler. I was exhausted and ready for bed—*alone.* I'd made that conviction clear to Matt after I'd finished crying about Anabelle . . .

The news of her death shocked me to my senses, and though Matt had been upset, too, he saw no reason why we couldn't find comfort in each other's arms, between a clean set of sheets.

I gently reminded him of our divorce. And the reasons for our divorce.

This led to his accusing me of being scared to give him another chance, which I didn't dispute.

The fact that I didn't dispute it set him to stewing, but I got the impression he hadn't given up quite yet. He still had a few days to work on me after all, before he'd be flying off to South America, or Africa, or Asia, or god knows where his next plantation appointment was.

I tearfully made the point that his coffee brokering might be the best thing for him to concentrate on right now since the Blend could very well be lost forever.

Anabelle was dead. That was awful enough in itself. But there were undeniable repercussions—

She'd never be able to tell us who, if anyone, had pushed her down the stairs. There would be an autopsy, but Dr. Foo didn't think it would prove anything. The hospital had already done a thorough exam, blood tests, everything. Beyond bruises that could be attributed to her fall, what more could be learned?

No, Anabelle's stepmother would be swooping in with a vulture of a lawyer in no time. We were ripe for the picking, that was certain.

I sighed. Regardless of this legendary coffeehouse's future, the Blend was still my responsibility tonight, and I had one more thing to check on before I could finally crawl into bed and cry some more.

Earlier I had asked Tucker to clear some space near the roasters if he found the time. Matteo's first shipment of Peruvian coffee was due to arrive early tomorrow morning. (That little announcement at dinner about greenlighting the shipment with his Palm Pilot was just a ploy; he'd greenlighted the order weeks ago.) Now bags and bags of raw beans would have to be stored in the cellar until they were roasted.

Unfortunately, I forgot to ask Tucker if he'd got the job done. Now I would have to go down into that dark, scary basement and check for myself.

I closed the office, crossed the length of the Blend's darkened second floor, weaving through the bohemian clutter of mismatched sofas, chairs, and lamps, and descended the stairs to the first floor.

On the landing above the basement steps, I hit the light switch. Down in the cellar, there was a bright flash, then a loud pop—damn, the stairway's bulb had blown.

A whole bank of fluorescent lights had been installed to illuminate the basement roasting area, but the switch that controlled them was down there in the darkness.

I almost threw up my hands right then, but I suddenly got worried there might be a short circuit or something. I didn't want to top off this perfect week by burning the whole place down, so I grabbed a flashlight and a new bulb from the pantry area just off the landing.

With one hand on the wooden rail, I carefully walked down the stairs, acutely aware that Anabelle had taken her fatal plunge right here. My footsteps echoed in the stairwell as I moved, and I breathed a whole lot easier once my foot touched the concrete basement floor.

The area was pitch black, but the light socket was just at the bottom of the steps. As I fumbled to find it with the flashlight, I heard a sound. The hardwood creaked above my head. It creaked again. *Footsteps.*

Someone was walking across the floor inside the Blend.

Matt? I thought. But that was highly unlikely. Although he'd offered to help me close tonight, I made it clear I wanted some space from him to think. He'd announced that he, therefore, had no choice but to sulk.

I froze, hearing the steps again. They were very tentative, which told me it most certainly *wasn't* Matt. If my headstrong ex-husband was anything, it was *not* tentative.

Who could it be then?

I held my breath, trying to remember if I'd locked the

shop's front and back doors. I had. I was sure of it. But I hadn't set the burglar alarm.

I tried not to panic. I knew I was trapped. There was no telephone down here, no way to call the police and the only other way out was the trapdoor to the sidewalk, which was bolted from the outside as well as the inside. If there was an intruder up there, the only thing I could do was stay down here until he was gone and hope he didn't find me.

Heart loudly beating, I listened to the person finish stepping across the room. A minute later, the footsteps sounded on the staircase.

Ohmygod, ohmygod, he's coming for me!

I found a hiding place behind the roaster, turned off the flashlight, crouched into a ball, and listened.

The steps continued on the stairs, but the sound grew softer, not louder. The intruder was heading *up* the stairs. Not down. He was heading to the office.

The safe! We were being robbed!

I strained my ears, but could hear no more.

I couldn't just hide here, I decided. I had to try to get to a first-floor phone at least. I climbed the stairs. Near the top, I heard the sound of glass shattering inside my office, and without thinking, I screamed at the top of my lungs.

My Java-like jaguar yowl echoed off the windows. Whoever the hell was in my office had heard it because I heard the crash of my halogen lamp come next.

Within seconds I saw a black leather–clad figure charging down the stairs with a book under his arm.

A book!

I remembered the shattering glass, and I knew. *Oh, god.* The glass case beside the safe! This intruder hadn't come for money, he'd come to steal the Allegros' legendary book. *Bastard, bastard, bastard!*

As he flew toward me, I saw he was a younger man with a short blond crewcut. I didn't recognize him, but I saw a flash of eyes—bright blue. He extended his arm like a football player, and the force of it plowed into me hard.

"Hey!" I howled.

I was a split-second from tumbling down the basement steps when I grabbed at the wooden handrail. Miracle of miracles, my fingers closed on it in time.

Good god! I thought. *This is what happened to Anabelle! He didn't get the book two nights ago. She must have surprised him, and he fled!*

I dragged myself up in time to see the stranger running toward the front entrance. He leaned quickly toward the front window, and he still had the book under his arm. Now he was fumbling at the door. What the hell was he doing?

"Matt! Matt!" I screamed as loud as I could.

Luckily, Matt must have heard the crashing, and he was by my side almost as soon as I started yelling.

"Clare!" Matt cried, flying down the stairs and flipping on the bank of first-floor lights. "What the hell—"

"Burglar!" I screamed, pointing toward the front door.

The flash of bright lights had already spooked the intruder. He had given up his struggle at the door, pulled it open, and ran off.

I raced to the front door. "He had a key!" I cried, seeing it in the keyhole. I pulled it out and held it up. "That's why he'd been fumbling. He'd left it in the door for a quick getaway but couldn't get it out quick enough."

"I'll call the police—"

"No time!" I said. "We can't risk him getting away . . . He has the coffee book."

"Do you think you can recognize him?" he asked.

I nodded.

"Let's go," said Matt. "Looks like he ran up Hudson."

We locked the door behind us and raced off.

Twenty-eight

The chilly autumn air felt damp. Neither of us had jackets, but at least we were both wearing sweaters as we hurried through the light gray mist rolling in from the nearby river. It was past midnight, and a typical Friday for the Village. Raucous crowds of men and women were still reveling on the narrow cobblestone streets, leaving movie theaters and gathering around the area's clubs, bars, cabarets, and late-night eateries tucked among the darkened shops, art galleries, and apartments that occupied the Federal-style red brick townhouses.

"There he goes," I said. We were closing in fast on the intruder. As he crossed Grove, my eyes locked on to his blond crew-cut and shiny leather jacket. He was still clutching the book under one arm and he had something else, something bulky, under his coat.

"Look, Matt, I think he stole the Blend plaque, too!"

I rushed forward, impatient to confront the guy, but Matt's large hand clamped on my small shoulder.

"What are you doing?" I demanded.

"Don't get too close, not yet," said Matt. "And let me see that key."

I handed Matt the key. He examined it as we walked, using the light from the streetlamps.

"This duplicate was made at Pete's Paint and Hardware over on Perry Street," Matt said. "Here's their logo. The Blend has an account with Pete's."

"So—"

"So, this duplicate key was made by someone who used to work at the Blend," said Matt. "And you know who comes to mind immediately?"

"Flaste," I said. "Moffat Flaste."

"And he probably charged the Blend to copy the key, to boot," said Matt, disgusted.

"Yes, it *has* to be Flaste," I said. "The thief not only had a duplicate key, he knew exactly where to find the book in the manager's office. And Flaste tried and failed to steal the Village Blend's plaque before, didn't he?"

"Yes, he did," said Matt. "The truth is, I suspected him of something the moment I heard he'd intentionally let the Blend's insurance lapse."

"And don't forget he once worked for Eduardo Lebreux, who told us he wanted to franchise the Blend but couldn't get Madame to sell," I pointed out.

"You're right. Flaste was an off-the-charts bad manager," said Matt. "With Pierre dead, Lebreux must have paid off Flaste to run the business into the ground so Mother would sell—and when that didn't work, and Mother got you to manage it again, Flaste must have decided to get even with this burglary."

"It all fits, but still . . . what good is that book of coffee recipes without the Blend name?"

"Not much," said Matt. "And Lebreux would know that. That's why I doubt he's involved here. Flaste probably arranged the theft under the assumption that the book would be worth something to Lebreux."

"And how do we prove all this?" I asked.

"It won't be easy. We have to hope this burglar we're trailing is going to meet up with Moffat Flaste. If not, we'll have the guy arrested and hope he spills his guts. And if he admits he tried and failed to burglarize us the other night, killing Anabelle in the process, that means Flaste is behind what happened to poor Anabelle. And, Clare, if that's true, I'm going to break that fat man's—"

"Matt, calm down. First things first. Let's not lose Mr. Crewcut."

We continued to follow the burglar up Hudson. At Christopher Street, he turned right.

Now keeping him in sight grew difficult. Christopher Street was always hopping on the weekend, and tonight was no exception. Crowds of mostly men packed the sidewalks, spilling out of the lively pubs, most of which, on this small stretch, were gay bars.

Music flooded the street, everything from techno dance and disco to Judy Garland. As the intruder hurried through the crowd, two men walking arm and arm whistled at him—we were on Christopher Street all right.

Passing one of those all-night T-shirt, tobacco, and magazine shops that still thrive in the Village, the burglar ducked into a glass-fronted bar called Oscar's Wiles.

Through the window, I could see that the clientele was all male and mostly young. Men in tight pants, leather vests, and sweaters, all buffed and pecked and tanned. I thought of the single women I knew in New York and momentarily sighed.

We watched as the crewcut youth ordered a beer then hunkered down in his seat and peered at the door, as if he was waiting for someone. A customer swung the door wide, releasing a burst of throbbing disco beat, and Matt and I ducked back, away from the front of the place.

"What do we do now?" I asked.

"You're going to have to go in there," Matt replied.

"What?" I cried. "Why *me*?"

"Because if he is meeting Flaste," said Matt, "then Flaste will recognize me the moment he steps through the door!"

"But Flaste will recognize me, too," I argued. "And don't you think I would stick out like a sore thumb in a gay bar full of *men*?"

"You might have a point," Matt said. He took my elbow and led me back to the all-night store.

"Wait!" I cried, halting in front of a pay phone. "I'm going to call Quinn. He'll know what to do."

Matt rolled his eyes but didn't protest. "I'll be right back," he told me.

I dialed the precinct, but Quinn was unavailable. I told the desk sergeant who I was, and that I needed to meet Detective Quinn at Oscar's Wiles off Christopher Street just as soon as he could get there, and that it was an emergency. The sergeant sounded dubious, but he took down the information.

Then I called Quinn's cell phone number. I got his voice mail, so I left a message and prayed that Quinn would get it in time.

Just as I hung up, Matt exited the store with a big plastic I LOVE NY bag in his hand. Inside were two T-shirts, a FDNY baseball cap, a navy hooded sweatshirt with the word YANKEES emblazoned across the chest, and three bottles of water. Matt led me to a shadowy corner across from Oscar's Wiles.

"Can you see him?" Matt asked as he fished inside the plastic bag.

"He's still there and still alone."

Matt opened a bottle of water and poured some of the

contents into a T-shirt. Before I could stop him, he scoured my face with the sopping wet material. I howled.

"Hold still," Matt said. "I have to get this makeup off."

"Well, leave the skin in place," I shot back, shivering as a trickle of icy water ran down my neck.

"Put this on," Matt said, pushing the hooded sweatshirt into my hand. While I pulled it over my head, he studied me.

"Your jeans will do," he said.

"Gee, thanks," I muttered. I straightened the sweatshirt while Matt tucked my hair up inside the baseball cap. He tamped the hat down until the brim was touching my ears. Then he eyed me critically.

"You almost look like a boy, but we've got one big problem," Matt said, scratching his chin. "Well, actually *two* to be exact."

"Excuse me?"

"Your bust," Matt said. "You'll have to take off your bra."

I reached under my shirt, unbuckled my Victoria Secret underwire, then slipped my arms out of the sweatshirt and removed it.

"Nope," Matt said. "Still too big."

Before I could protest, he reached up under the hooded sweatshirt and grabbed the shirt I wore under it. He pulled the material tight over my chest, flattening my breasts. Then he tied the excess cloth behind my back.

"I can't breathe," I complained.

"Voilà," Matt said, taking my shoulders and turning me around. I gazed at my reflection in the window of a parked car. It was scary. I *did* look like a young man.

"This is creepy," I moaned.

"Go," Matt said, thrusting me forward. "Get as close as you can and watch what happens."

I crossed the street, trying to imitate a man's walk. I wasn't sure if I was pulling it off, but I must have been doing something right. As I entered Oscar's Wiles, a passerby whistled. I almost smiled back. He was kind of cute.

Because of the smoking ban in public places, Oscar's Wiles was thankfully free of tobacco smoke. Here the odor of burning leaf was replaced by the smells of beer, men's cologne, and leather—lots and lots of leather.

The style of the interior was vaguely Tudor, with white stucco walls trimmed with some dark wood. A large stone fireplace dominated one wall, but the hearth was cold. The tables and chairs were made of heavy dark wood that matched the trim on the walls. Hanging all around were framed lithographs of country squires and gentlemen posing in tight-fitting hunting attire, which I thought appropriate given the sport at hand.

I swaggered up to the bar.

"Gimme a brewski," I said with a testosterone sneer, tossing a bill on the counter. "An' keep da' change."

To my surprise, the bartender didn't give me a second look. I took the mug in my hand, blew off some foam, and made a show of gulping from it. But instead of drinking, I stole a peek at my prey through the amber liquid.

Suddenly a thick, hairy arm fell across my shoulders. It was so heavy I was almost pushed to my knees.

"You look lonely, boycheeks," a husky voice rasped in my ear. "Need a place to stay for the night?"

Oh, crap. It's Ron.

Ron Gersun, to be exact, the local butcher, and I didn't want him to recognize me. Ron had a shop in the meat-packing district and was famed for his prime rib. I was used to seeing him in a bloodstained apron and hair net. Tonight he was quite fetching in a leather vest and no shirt, his sweaty pecks, anchor tattoo (who knew?), and tangled chest hair visible for all to see.

Well, well, Ron, I could just hear Tucker saying. *It ap-*

pears you don't do all *of your meatpacking in the butcher shop!*

"Uh, no offense, pal, but not tonight," I huffed in a voice so gruff it tickled my throat. Then I ducked under Ron Gersun's beefy arm and slipped away.

I made my way across the bar and grabbed a seat closer to the crewcut burglar. He didn't even glance in my direction, just kept staring at the front door. Outside the tall windows, I could see no sign of Matt. I figured he was still lurking nearby. Otherwise I'd kill him.

The door opened and a short, round figure waddled in. From across the room I recognized the man—

Moffat Flaste.

The man's beady pig-like eyes scanned the room. He seemed nervous, and there was a patina of sweat on his fleshy cheeks and over his upper lip. He scanned the bar until he saw the burglar. Their eyes met and the youth nodded.

Flaste seemed to get even more tense. He didn't approach the youth right away. Instead he ordered a drink and lingered at the bar, taking a few sips. Finally the youth got impatient and motioned him over.

Flaste walked right past me, sat down across from the crewcut, and began to talk to him. But I couldn't hear a damn thing!

They were sitting no more than seven feet from me, but the music was so loud I couldn't hear a word. I had to get closer.

I rose and lifted my glass, taking a sip of the bitter brew as I moved toward their table. Flaste and the youth were locked in conversation. Finally the young man reached under his jacket and pulled something out. He placed the Allegro family recipe book on the table and slid it toward Flaste, who grabbed the book and tucked it under his own jacket.

What about the plaque? You took the plaque, too, you bastard. Where is it?

"We meet again," a voice said in my ear. I felt the tickle of a stubbly chin as, once again, a crushing arm fell across my shoulders. This time Ron Gersun pulled me close to his chest and shook me like a doll.

"Ain't it a small world," he said in a tone I am sure he thought was seductive. I tried to pull away, but Ron held me tight. He reached up and tickled my chin with a sausage-thick finger.

"Smooth as a baby's behind," he purred. I tried to duck under his arm again, but he'd figured out a way to counter that trick.

Great. After a parched decade of living like a nun, I'm finally awash in persistent male suitors, and I can't do a thing with them!

"Give us a kiss," Ron said. His lips smacked and I felt his stubbly chin scrape my neck.

Meanwhile, Flaste drew an envelope out of his pocket and pushed it across the table to the youth. The burglar pocketed the envelope and smiled. Flaste stood up. He was going to leave. I moved to follow.

"Where ya' goin'?" Ron asked, almost hurt. "Give me a chance."

Stretching his long arm, he reached out to pull me back. The movement caught the bill of my baseball cap and knocked it from my head. My wavy chestnut hair tumbled down to my shoulders.

"Hey! What's this?" Ron backed up in confusion. "Wait a second. I know you! You're the *coffee* lady!"

The entire room full of men turned my way, including Flaste and the crewcut. The flash of recognition crossed their faces.

Crap!

Flaste let out a squeal and bolted for the exit. The blond crewcut was faster and got there ahead of him. But as he yanked the front door open, a tall, broad-shouldered figure draped in a beige trenchcoat appeared on the threshold and blocked the burglar's escape.

Detective Quinn!

And right behind him came Matteo. Fists clenched, eyes flashing, he was spoiling for a fight.

The burglar pushed at Quinn, but he would have had better luck trying to move the Empire State Building. Quinn slammed the youth against the nearest table, doubled him over, pulled his arms behind his back, and cuffed him in one continuous, seemingly effortless motion.

Flaste, however, was inching toward the door, clearly hoping to escape while Quinn's attention was elsewhere.

"Stop Flaste!" I cried. "He's got the book."

The fat man paled. Then Flaste squealed again and ran right at Matteo in an attempt to bowl him over. Big mistake. A loud, meaty thwack made every patron in the bar wince. Moffat Flaste exhaled loudly and doubled over. Matteo had sunk a right hook into the man's prodigious gut. Now Matt stood over him, fist raised for a second strike.

Quinn reached up and seized my ex-husband's arm.

"That's enough," the detective said.

As arm-wrestling matches go, this one could have been a tossup. But Matt backed down. He saw that Quinn was right. After one hard punch from Matt, Flaste had sunk helplessly to the floor. Still wheezing, he didn't even notice when the Allegro family recipe book spilled out of his jacket.

"You're under arrest for burglary and receiving stolen goods," Quinn announced. "You have the right to remain silent. Anything you say can and will be used against you in a court of law . . ."

Twenty-nine

"**Mystery** solved," I proudly told Quinn ten minutes later on the sidewalk outside Oscar's Wiles' front window.

"It would seem so," he said, looking down at me.

Two patrol units of uniformed NYPD officers had already rolled up to the dirty brick building, their sirens and flashing emergency lights drawing a fairly large crowd. It appeared we were the biggest show in this part of town at the moment. Hoots and hollers abounded among the half-inebriated onlookers, along with an out-of-tune rendition of the theme from *Cops*.

One pair of officers controlled the crowd while two more packed Flaste and Mr. Blond Crewcut into the back of one of the vehicles.

"Hey, there, Ms. Cosi!" called one of the crowd-control officers over the mess. It turned out to be Officer Langley, the lanky young Irish cop I'd introduced to Greek coffee the other day.

"Oh, hi!" I called back. "How are you?"

"That's *our* question for *you*!" said his darker, shorter partner, Demetrios, as he attempted to keep back the pair of drunks singing "Bad boys! Bad boys!"

"I'm fine," I said. "Not a scratch! Thank you both for your help!"

"Hey, all in a day's work," said Langley. "Right, Lieutenant?"

Quinn didn't smile. He seemed to be mildly allergic to that facial expression. But he appeared pleased enough nonetheless. He lifted his square chin toward me and said, "*Her* work. Not mine. You did a good job, Cla . . . uh, I mean . . . Ms. Cosi."

I appreciated the fact that he *almost* called me by my first name in public. It wasn't exactly the beginning of a beautiful friendship, but it was something.

"No luck," said Matteo, coming out of the bar.

"You're kidding," I said. "I can't believe it. I really thought I saw Mr. Crewcut carrying the Village Blend plaque. And if he did take it, then it's got to be in this bar."

Quinn told me to wait a moment. He walked over to the patrol car and ducked his head into the back seat that held Flaste and Crewcut. After a few minutes of talking to the men in cuffs, he came back.

"No help. Sorry," Quinn told me. "They're lawyering up."

"Excuse me? Lawyering who?" I asked. Quinn was about to explain what the heck that term meant when Matteo cut in—

"Anything they say can and will be held against them in a court of law, Clare. So they're not talking until they see a lawyer."

"That's right, Allegro," said Quinn. "You have some experience with that, do you?"

"Let's not get personal, Quinn—"

"Gentlemen!" I cried. "This doesn't solve the problem at hand. I would like to find the Village Blend plaque. Beyond monetary value, it is an historic antique that means the world to a woman who means the world to me. So what do we do?"

"If you're not absolutely sure he stole it, and he's clearly not admitting a thing," said Quinn, "then double-check back at your shop. Confirm that it is indeed missing. Once you do that, we'll take it from there."

"Okay," I said. "That's easy enough. I'll go back right now."

"I do need your statement, however, Ms. Cosi," Quinn said. "And Mr. Allegro's, too."

"Clare," said Matt, "why don't you go on back to the Blend and check on the plaque, and I'll go with Quinn and get the statements started."

"Matt, there's no reason I have to be the one to go back to the Blend. Why don't *you* go back, and *I'll* go with Quinn—"

"No," Matt instantly responded. "I mean . . . uh . . . we locked the front door but the lights were flipped on before we left, so customers might think we're still open—"

"But you can turn off the lights as well as me."

"—*and* I'm pretty sure I left the door to our duplex ajar," added Matt, "so your Java may have wandered down into the coffeehouse. And Java doesn't know me well enough to come when I call."

"Oh," I said. "Yes . . . I better go back right away then. She might run and hide from you. And Java's had enough stress adapting to the duplex already—who knows how she'll react once she figures out there are two more floors plus a basement to sniff out and mark."

"Mark?" asked Matt. "You don't mean—"

"Java's a girl. She won't spray. But she may feel the

need to rub up against every stick of furniture in the place."

"Then you better get going." Matt was speaking to me, but leveling a strange sort of warning gaze at Quinn.

Why did I get the impression my ex-husband didn't want to be the one to go back to the Blend because that would leave me alone in the hands of Quinn for twenty minutes? Oh, well, *que sera sera*.

Langley and Demetrios gave me a ride back to the Blend in their patrol car. I waved good-bye as they drove off and used my key to get back inside (the duplicated key was evidence and Quinn had wanted it).

Not taking any chances, I relocked the door immediately—and exhaled, feeling safe at last.

Unfortunately, with one glance in the front window, I saw the bad news. As I'd suspected, the store's only window signage, the famous Village Blend plaque, which had announced FRESH ROASTED COFFEE SERVED DAILY to its customers for over one hundred years, had been stolen.

"Well, Quinn," I muttered. "Guess we've got ourselves another mystery."

I knew Quinn wanted me at the precinct for a statement, so I began to walk swiftly toward the staircase. Hopefully Java hadn't wandered far from the duplex apartment. My guess was she'd descended to the second floor's cozy setup of sofas and chairs and was sniffing up a storm.

"Java!" I called. "Java Jive!"

She always came when I called. So instead of wandering the four floors of the entire building, I decided to stay put and keep calling her. Absently, I noticed the empty demitasse cup on the counter. I automatically took it to the sink.

"Java!" I called again. Now that I was behind the

counter, I remembered there were used espresso grounds in the portafilter. I had just knocked the wet grounds into the garbage can below the counter when I heard a male voice say, "Good evening, Ms. Cosi."

My heart nearly stopped. The coffeehouse had been locked up tight. No one was supposed to be here.

A light blond, pale-skinned man emerged from the pantry area. He was wearing a finely tailored overcoat, and his features looked familiar, but for a moment I couldn't place him. I was too busy freaking out about the fact that he'd been waiting silently back there. A white rabbit in the gray shadows.

"Who are—"

My voice choked when I saw he had something in his hand, and he was pointing it at me: *A gun. A gun. A gun. My god! My god! My god!*

Still behind the counter, I glanced down. There was nothing to defend myself with—no knife, no pick, not even a glass I could throw. I was simply staring at grimy black coffee grounds. The stranger couldn't see my hands, so I grabbed a fistful. I wasn't sure what I'd do with it, but my gut told me to grab something, anything.

"Step away from the counter and do as I say."

"Who are you?" I asked, as I dropped my hands to my sides and stepped out toward the main room, where the stranger was standing.

"Oh, Ms. Cosi," he said, "I'm insulted. Don't you remember meeting me this evening?"

I stared a moment then blinked, stunned by the recognition. The man was right. I did know him. He was Richard Engstrum, Senior. I'd met him at the Waldorf charity ball.

I swiftly put together the reason he was here. Obviously, his wife had told him about my threat to go to the police tomorrow with evidence against his son. He must have come to protect his son, I decided. So all I needed to do was set him straight!

"Mr. Engstrum, listen to me—" I was about to tell him we'd caught the guilty parties tonight. I was even going to apologize for accusing his son of wrongdoing, but he interrupted me.

"No, Ms. Cosi. I'm the one with the gun. So *you're* going to listen to me. I want you to know it was Anabelle who chose to have the first 'accident.' I simply made sure she had a second one. The fact is, I did try to talk her out of the blackmail. But she wouldn't listen. So you see, since she left me with no choices, I left her with none."

I suddenly felt sick to my stomach. Engstrum wasn't here innocently chasing down some ploy of mine. That was now abundantly clear. He had just confessed to murder.

"It was you?" I asked in a weak voice. "You wanted her to lose the baby?"

"Yes," said Engstrum.

"But she lost her life."

"Yes, I just heard about that. And that's why you're going to lose yours, too, unless you give me the evidence you say you have against my son."

Don't lose it, Clare, I told myself. *Don't freak out. Keep it together. Think!*

"It's with the police!" I cried abruptly. "And they're coming here any second!"

"No they're not. You're bluffing. I run a high-stakes business, Ms. Cosi. I know when people try to bluff me, and you're bluffing now. I saw you wave good-bye to that police car a few minutes ago."

Engstrum cocked the gun. It was small, but it looked big enough to kill. His hard, emotionless eyes gave me the impression he'd pulled the trigger on people already—maybe not *gun* triggers, but there were all kinds of other triggers that when squeezed hurt and ruined people.

I'd seen his type before. The type who could look at a human being and then assign a worth based solely on a coldly calculated business strategy or perceived use in obtaining one or another kind of self-gratification. People were no longer people, just pawns, just numbers. Madame Blanche Dreyfus Allegro Dubois had seen his type before, too. Back in World War II they'd worn swastikas.

"Really, Ms. Cosi. Do you want to die like this?"

"No! Please!"

"Where is the evidence?"

I thought fast. If I could lure him toward the stairs . . . and employ some sort of distraction . . .

"It's in a locked container," I lied at last. "In the enclosed alley. Right out back."

"Let's go get it. *Together.*"

He waved the gun, indicating that I should lead, walking in front of him. I felt my mouth go dry, my legs go weak. Adrenaline flowed through me like a hundred cups of coffee.

"Don't you have any conscience?" I asked, trying to mentally push him off balance. "Even if you don't care about Anabelle. How could you kill your own grandchild?"

"*Child.* Not grandchild."

"What?!"

"I have no remorse, Ms. Cosi, because Anabelle Hart had it coming. She brought it on herself."

"What!"

"You can't sell yourself as one thing and then turn around and expect to be bought as another."

"I don't understand."

"She was a nude dancer when I first saw her. Sure, I flattered her with some jewelry and some nights at the Plaza, but that didn't mean I bought her as anything more than a little tramp, even after she quit the nude dancing. She thought she'd found her sugar daddy to fund her little artistic delusion. Getting pregnant was a stupid calculation on her part. I don't dance to the tunes of tramps, they dance to mine."

"But your son? She was seeing you son. I don't understand—"

"When I told her to get lost, she went after my son to spite me. She suckered him into a relationship to get me to pay up. But her only leverage was that pregnancy—so I got rid of it."

"*And* her. She *died* of her injuries!"

"That's too bad, but like I said, she had it coming. She brought it on herself."

My head was reeling, my mind racing. I suddenly remembered two things that Esther Best had said—that Anabelle had been arguing with her stepmother about money for a few months now . . . and that she'd talked to "Richard" before going to work the night she was assaulted.

All along, I had thought Richard was Richard, Junior. But it was the father. It was Richard, Senior, whom Anabelle was trying to blackmail—clearly with the help of her stepmother, who had bookmarked all those Engstum System Web sites on her laptop.

"How much did she ask for?"

"One million."

"Oh, god . . ."

Engstrum was worth well over fifty times that. Suddenly, Arthur Jay Eddleman popped into my mind.

"Why didn't you just give her some money and tell her to go away?" I said. "She was pregnant with your child after all—"

"First rule of business, Ms. Cosi, *never* pay more for a service than it's worth. I had no intention of ever parting with one red cent. Now let's get that evidence. Do *not* move unless I tell you. Otherwise I will shoot you."

"Okay, okay, please don't shoot."

We'd come to the back door. It was chained and bolted.

"Unchain the door," he said. *"Slowly."*

I did.

"Now unbolt it."

I did.

"Now slowly open the door."

I was about to pull open the door when, at last, I got the distraction I was waiting for—

Mrrrrroooooooooowwww!

Java's jaguar-like "I'm hungry!" screeched into the tense silence of the stairwell. As Engstrum turned his head toward the noise, I spun, hurling my fist full of grounds. They hit his face, further startling him.

Remembering Dr. Foo's chats about Wing Chung Gung Fu—and how small stature could be used to advantage—I immediately ducked low under Engstrum's arms and kicked out, striking hard at his knee.

"*Aaaah!* Fucking bitch!" he cried. The gun went off but missed.

The back door was on the landing just above the narrow staircase to the basement and the strike sent him off balance. I struck at his knee again and down he went, tumbling head over heels all the way to the cold basement floor.

I didn't know if or how badly the man was hurt so I raced for the front entrance, knowing I'd find help faster on Hudson than through the back alley. I was digging in my pocket for the key when I saw two familiar faces at the door.

Langley and Demetrios!!

They waved. Later, I would learn they'd been sent back over by Quinn to take me to the precinct for my statement. But that moment I didn't care why they were there, I was just overjoyed to see their smiling faces, which dropped to grim alarm when I unlocked the door, tore it open, and screamed bloody murder.

Drawing their guns, they were at the back landing in seconds.

But there was no need to fire. Or even to pull out cuffs.

Richard Engstum, Senior, was sprawled at the bottom of the Blend staircase, unconscious. A wad of wet coffee grounds and a couple of well-placed kicks had reduced the fortified captain of e-business investments to a ragdoll of flesh and bone.

Now he was broken, bruised, and battered . . .

Just like Anabelle.

THIRTY

～～～～～～～～～～～～～～～～～～～

"Don't you know that old saying, Clare?"

"What?" I asked Madame.

"You know you're ready to die when you can no longer make a fist."

Madame presented her open hand to me. Slowly but surely, she clenched each finger until she'd made a rock-solid ball.

"There, you see, dear. Nothing to worry yourself about. I'm feeling just fine."

It was one week later. The police and media had come and gone, and things were slowly getting back to normal at the Blend. Madame stopped by for a visit—no longer in mourning black, thank goodness, but in a cherry red pantsuit.

With all the publicity, Matt and I finally told her all about what had transpired. She didn't understand why we'd kept it from her. That was when Matt and I agreed to come clean with what we knew about her condition.

With a French-pressed pot of Kona, Matt and I took her up to the second floor to finally discuss it.

Madame refused to admit a thing to us about her cancer, and I was growing alarmed. She seemed to be in outright denial.

"Madame, Matt and I love you," I said. "Don't you want us to know?"

"*Know.* Know what?"

"There's no use pretending," I told her at last. "I saw you at St. Vincent's with Dr. McTavish."

Madame's face actually paled.

"There, you see? We know," said Matt. "So there's no need for your pretense any longer."

"I'm sorry I didn't tell you," she said. "But I didn't know where it was going. Now I do."

"And?" I asked, afraid to hear the worst.

"And . . . We're dating. I admit it," said Madame.

"You're dating your oncologist?" I said.

"*My* oncologist? Well, I suppose he's mine. That's the way we put it on Valentine's Day, don't we? Although that's quite a few months away yet."

"Wait a second," said Matt. "Mother, do you have cancer or not?"

"Cancer? No, for heaven's sake, I just had a spectacular physical. My doctor tells me I'll live another twenty years. Maybe more. Why ever would you think I had cancer?"

"Because you were seeing an oncologist!" I cried.

"My dear, I was—and am—seeing a *man* with as much sex appeal as Sean Connery. The fact that he's an oncologist is beside the point—"

"B-but you were sitting in a *wheelchair*," I said. "Last week. On the cancer treatment floor—"

"Oh, my goodness! You must have seen me the day I'd finished passing out silent auction booklets at the hospital. I was wearing new shoes that day, and my feet hurt, so as a joke, Gary wheeled me around to deliver the last few booklets."

"Ohmygod, and all this time we thought—"

"What? That I was dying of cancer?"

"Yes!" Matt and I said together.

Madame laughed. "That's so ludicrous."

"I don't know," I said, becoming slowly irritated. "Why else would you have gotten each of us to sign those contracts—without *once* mentioning the fact that you were making us de facto partners."

"Why else indeed?" said Madame.

"This opens another whole line of discussion," I said. "And since you're *not*, in fact, dying of cancer, I'd like to point out that—"

Madame looked at her watch.

"—Matt and I cannot share the duplex apartment," I continued. "It's crazy."

"You know, I just remembered something!" Madame announced, rising. "I'm running late! Gary is picking me up for an early dinner then we're going to the new Albee play. We'll have to discuss this another time!"

And with that pronouncement, Madame swept out of the Blend, leaving me and Matt to, as she put it, "work it out" between us.

Of course. As usual.

We're still working it out, that's all I'll say for now. As for Flaste and Crewcut (who turned out to be a delinquent with an outstanding warrant named Billy Schiffer), here's the scoop—

Flaste admitted Eduardo Lebreux had hired him to ruin the Blend. But when the plan failed, that was the end of Lebreux's involvement. As we suspected, Flaste hatched the little burglary plan all by himself, hoping to make a tidy profit selling the secret Allegro book of recipes to Lebreux.

Since Lebreux's involvement was underhanded but

not illegal, we couldn't do much more to him than chew him out verbally—which Matteo did admirably—ruin his reputation in the business, and shun him socially, which Madame is seeing to with her characteristic marble-fisted determination.

As for Flaste and Schiffer, they're drinking jailhouse coffee now, which is probably punishment enough, even without their sentences.

And what ever happened to the Village Blend plaque?

Well, my old friend the butcher, Ron Gersun, walked in with it the day after the burglary.

"Ron!" I cried, seeing the plaque tucked under his beefy arm. "Where did you find it?"

"It was there . . . you know. . . . in Oscar's Wiles."

"Where? Matt said he looked *all over* that bar."

Ron's expression turned sheepish. "It was in the men's room."

I pictured my ex-husband in his search high and low, but then coming up against the men's room door and stopping short. Matteo Allegro would fearlessly trek any-where in the world—Central America, Africa, Asia. Any-where but a Christopher Street men's room. What a chicken.

"I guess Schiffer must have stashed it in there when I was around the corner stuffing my hair into a baseball cap," I told Ron.

"You know, you looked kind of cute," he said. Then he scratched the back of his head. "I mean as a guy."

"Oh, thanks," I said. "I think."

I wanted to tell him that he looked pretty good, too, in his leather vest with his tangled chest hair and anchor tat-too, but I thought it best to derail that train of thought fast. My god, this was one weird world we lived in. Maybe Eduardo Lebreux was right after all—sometimes it all came down to the packaging.

"Well, see ya around, there, Coffee Lady."

"Have a cup?" I offered. "On the house?"

"Yeah, sure. Thanks."

"Latte?"

"Hell no! Lattes are for girly men. Make mine a *doppio* espresso!"

"One double espresso coming up!" I said, praying all the while that Ron Gersun never *ever* discussed his coffee bar preferences with Detective Quinn.

Quinn himself is a regular now. Double tall lattes are still his favorite.

I keep pressing the detective to let me help him solve another crime, but after I almost got myself shot, he warned me to stick with coffee from now on and leave murder to the professionals.

Which brings me to the case at hand—

Unlike Anabelle Hart, Richard Engstrum, Senior, survived his fall down the Blend steps. He was hospitalized for a few weeks, but that didn't deter the District Attorney's Office from charging him with murder, attempted murder, aggravated assault, and a host of lesser charges including unlawful entry. (It turned out Engstrum had taken the front door key right off Anabelle's ballet-charm key ring the night he assaulted her. When Quinn and I found the key ring in her purse the next day, it appeared untouched, so we never checked each and every Blend key to see if one was missing.)

"The Manhattan DA is piling it on Engstrum," was how Quinn characterized the many charges.

Engstrum's lawyers took one look at the photograph of the victim—pretty, young, talented, pregnant, and dead Anabelle Hart—and their client—a businessman with a bubble-like IPO that made him rich while taking his investors on a one-way ride to Suckersville—and urged Richard Engstrum to accept a plea bargain.

Given the fact that my testimony combined with the DNA testing on Anabelle's fetus would have sunk him in front of a jury, he did the wise thing and agreed. Though his sentence is still pending, Quinn tells me he will probably get twelve years of hard time for assault and criminally negligent homicide, and attempted murder. But that's not all he was in for . . .

Mrs. Darla Branch Hart got what she wanted, too, even if Mrs. Engstrum did not. You see, Anabelle's stepmother filed a ten-million-dollar wrongful death suit against Richard Engstrum, Senior. This news even made the pages of *The New York Times*.

It was one of the few times a New Yorker with the Engstrums' Upper East Side address *didn't* want the *Times'* attention—I tell ya, publicity's a real bitch when it's the wrong kind.

The Village Blend was mentioned in the papers, too. The *New York Post* headline said our coffee was "to die for."

"Aw shucks," I told the reporter, "it's all in the grounds."

But even with my tasseography, I didn't see *this* one coming. I mean, I remember Anabelle telling me she'd learned how to handle garbage. As a nude dancer, I have no doubt she thought she could. One kind of garbage. The obvious kind. Just not the other.

As I've said before, packaging can be deceiving. Anabelle's mistake was not understanding that there was a kind of garbage that masks its odor with five-hundred-dollar-an-ounce toiletries. And the hard truth is, when you decide that you're clever enough to play with garbage—bad smelling or sweet smelling—you're fooling yourself if you think you can walk away without some of it rubbing its stink off on you.

I just wish Anabelle had stuck to the high road. She was a diligent worker. She had the seeds of good character. And she had come so close to achieving her dream. But sticking to the high road can be a difficult business, even for good people. The altitude alone can exhaust you.

Not long after these events, I opened the Blend one morning to find Dr. Foo waiting. We made our usual small talk, but he saw I was rather low. When he asked me why, I confided everything I'd learned about Anabelle. Not her death—he already knew about that—but her fall.

He said he was sorry, and he also said something about how he himself was still learning how to accept that sometimes, no matter how hard we try, we cannot help the people we care about. As a medical resident working in St. Vincent's intensive care unit, he'd had many challenges along those lines.

"How do you cope?" I asked.

"I don't know," he said. "I guess I find a way to grieve then try to let it go. Like the Buddhist saying, 'You must close the book.' "

"I guess there's something to that," I admitted. "I mean, life goes on, and the people who are still alive need you."

"Just as the people in your life need you," he said.

And so I grieved for Anabelle Hart, and I still remember her in my prayers, but I accept that it is now time to close *her* book.

To me, she will always be young and beautiful and graceful—and sadly—misguided and ruined and dead. I just hope she felt a measure of peace when the crime of her murder was solved, and that wherever she is now, she has perpetual music and an unending expanse of smooth and level floor.

RECIPES FROM
THE VILLAGE BLEND

The Village Blend's
Caffé Cannella

1. Place a very thin slice of orange at the bottom of a cup.

2. Pour a steaming hot, dark-roasted coffee (Italian or French roast) onto the orange slice.

3. Stir with a cinnamon stick, which remains in the cup to continue flavoring the beverage. Let steep for a minute.

4. Add a dollop of sweetened whipped cream and sprinkle cinnamon to taste. (Additional sugar is optional.)

The Village Blend's
Raspberry-Mocha Bocci

1½ ounces chocolate syrup
1½ ounces raspberry syrup
2 ounces freshly made espresso
7 ounces steamed milk
Sweetened whipped cream
Sweetened ground cocoa
Shaved chocolate curls
Raspberries

1. Pour the syrups into the bottom of a 12-ounce cup.

2. Add the espresso.

3. Fill with steamed milk.

4. Stir the liquid, lifting from the bottom to bring the syrups up.

5. Top with sweetened whipped cream, sweetened ground cocoa, and curls of shaved chocolate. Serve on a saucer with raspberries.

Clare's Cappuccino Walnut Cheesecake

(Or, what to do with your leftover espresso!)

1 cup finely chopped walnuts
1 cup granulated sugar
3 tablespoons butter, melted
32 ounces cream cheese, softened
2 tablespoons all-purpose flour
4 eggs
¼ cup sour cream
¼ teaspoon cinnamon
½ cup strongly brewed espresso (bean optional)
1 teaspoon instant coffee

TOPPING FOR CHEESECAKE

1 cup semi-sweet chocolate chips
⅓ cup heavy cream
¼ cup espresso
1 tablespoon cocoa powder
1 tablespoon cinnamon
Sugar to taste

PREPARATION

1. Preheat oven to 350 degrees.

2. Combine walnuts, 2 tablespoons of sugar, and the butter in a bowl and mix well. Pour mixture into 9-inch springform pan and press onto bottom. Set aside.

3. In a food processor combine cream cheese and the rest of the cup of sugar. Mix until light and fluffy and completely combined.

4. Add flour and eggs, one at a time.

5. Add sour cream and cinnamon.

6. Dissolve the instant coffee into the espresso, then add to cream cheese mixture.

7. Pour into the pan and bake for approximately 1 hour (some ovens may require ten to fifteen extra minutes). Shake gently to test. Cake will be firm when done. Top will be lightly browned. Cool completely.

TOPPING

1. Heat all ingredients and stir until melted.

2. Drizzle topping over the cooled cheesecake.

3. Chill cheesecake before serving.

Black Russian

A cocktail made with two parts vodka and one part coffee-flavored liqueur (such as Kahlua). Serve over ice. For a White Russian, add cream.

Screaming Orgasm
(also known as a Burnt Toasted Almond)

A cocktail made with one-half ounce Kahlua (a coffee-flavored liqueur!), one-half ounce amaretto, and one-half ounce vodka. Add 1 cup chilled heavy cream. Shake in a container with chipped ice. Serve in a tall, frosted glass.

(Note: For a richer dessert drink, substitute vanilla, mocha, or coffee ice cream for the cream; use a blender instead of shaking; and leave out the ice.)

Coffeehouse Mystery #2
Through the Grinder

New York City is full of dating mills, from singles bars to on-line matchmaking services, and Village Blend manager Clare Cosi is wary of sending her heart through those "shop-and-drop" grinders. However, at almost forty and divorced for many years, she's ready to sign up for what appears to be a somewhat harmless mixer. "Cappuccino Connection Night" is a social gathering held once a month at her coffeehouse. A Greenwich Village church group has organized these nondenominational evenings, billing them as a way for mature adults to meet the opposite sex over a nice, civilized cup of coffee. Unfortunately, both her ex-husband, Matt, and her detective friend, Lieutenant Quinn, finally agree on one thing— "All the men who show are sure to be losers." But Clare makes a connection with a man who is a self-made millionaire with a great personality, knightly manners, and chiseled good looks. He even loves a good espresso. Is he too good to be true? Maybe. Because Clare soon discovers that wherever this guy goes, the mysterious death of a woman follows. Coincidence? Or is this Mr. Right trying to get rid of a stream of Ms. Wrongs? And if he *is* practicing a deadly form of elimination . . . is Clare about to become his next girlfriend . . . or his next victim?

Clare Cosi, manager and head barista
of the landmark Village Blend coffeehouse,
can brew a beverage to die for.

THE COFFEEHOUSE MYSTERIES BY
CLEO COYLE

Includes recipes and coffee-making tips!

penguin.com

M851AS0313